SAD SWEET DREAMER

SAD SWEET DREAMER

N. WILSON ENOCH

iUNIVERSE, INC.
NEW YORK BLOOMINGTON

Sad Sweet Dreamer

iUniverse books may be ordered through booksellers or by contacting:

iUniverse
1663 Liberty Drive
Bloomington, IN 47403
www.iuniverse.com
1-800-Authors (1-800-288-4677)

ISBN: 978-1-4401-0907-2 (pbk)
ISBN: 978-1-4401-0908-9 (ebk)

Printed in the United States of America

iUniverse rev. date: 11/12/2008

For LeNorris Rayam,

friend, brother, and 'Storysinger', who's time among us

was way too short.

Author's Note

'Sad Sweet Dreamer' is a work of fiction. The events, characters, locations (with the exception of actual localities employed as setting within the narrative) and storylines within this manuscript are products of the author's imagination, and not intended to mirror any real events, or real persons, living or dead. Certain historical occurrences and real persons are mentioned in the narrative, but are employed to further the storyline, and do not change the fictional nature of the story.

Lastly, the name 'Hebert' is properly pronounced 'Ay-bear'.

Acknowledgments

United Cerebral Palsy, of the Washington D.C. region, for their helpful information concerning Cerebral Palsy

Nate Jenkins, of Bowie, MD, for providing helpful information about augmentive devises that assist people with Cerebral Palsy in their day to day lives, as well as for patiently answering every question I could think of.

Carol Hawker and Delores Thompson of United Methodist Family Services, Arlington, VA, for their friendship and efforts regarding the adoption of my children, Anna and Thomas; and also Martha Arntzan, long lost buddy and former colleague. The three of you are living proof that there is such a thing as a sane psychiatrist.

Sincere thanks to you all.

BOOK ONE

DENNIS AND MARYUM

1

On the night Dennis Williamson McClain was born, the heavens were set aflame with a million shards of bluish green light, heedlessly cascading across the eastern horizon. Local meteorologists had labeled the night show a meteor shower, unusual for its intensity and brightness perhaps, though nothing particularly special, or exceptional. But to Dennis' mother, the night lights were a sign; a glorious show of starlight occurring the night of her son's entrance into this world of woe.

Sophia Zetie McClain was only nineteen years old when she gave birth to Dennis. Her life, like the struggle she endured to bring him into the world, had been difficult. Cursed with her grandfather's illness, Sophia had put up with people telling her what she could and couldn't do all her life. What she could and couldn't have. No sugar, no alcohol, watch your starches, Insulin three times a day, etcetera and blah that she'd grown just too tired of listening to. Now was her time, and Sophia was determined to live it as she chose.

She didn't remember the name of Dennis's father, at least not officially. The boy had come and gone, taken what he'd wanted and got in the wind, thinking nothing of the one he'd be leaving behind. Sophia wanted no part of him, knowing that she was soon to be a mother, and wanting what was best for the child, even if that meant raising him alone, even though some weren't about to grant her that freedom.

Sophia had worn loose clothing, sweaters, and coats most of the time, and since no one on campus ever questioned her about her pregnancy, she figured with the passing of October and November, no one would be any wiser. Someone was. Someone dropped a dime.

Summoned unexpectedly to a bleak, gray office in Richmond, Virginia, not far from the campus of Virginia State University, where she studied English, Sophia found herself explaining the whys and wherefores of her situation to a seemingly impatient social worker.

"Miss McClain, we have to be practical about this." Mellissa Ahless, an investigator with Central Virginia Child Welfare Services, had spoken on that somber afternoon. "You are an Insulin dependent diabetic, and you aren't in the best of health. You're risking all manner of complications by continuing this pregnancy. At best, you stand a good chance of having your kidneys, or some other vital organs, conk out before too long. We need to think of your best interests."

"Miss Ahless, I am not having an abortion. I'm not so in love with my life that I can't risk it giving birth. Besides, I'm a little far along for that option, I think."

"I wasn't referring to abortion, Miss McClain." the older woman exhaled. "And it's Mrs. Ahless, though Mellissa will be fine. I wanted to suggest the possibility of finding a medical program where your progress would be monitored, after which....you'd be putting up the child for adoption."

"No. I'm not abandoning my child." Sophia glared at the woman, tall, dark, and menacing, like a sequoia tree that threatened to fall on her at any moment. The woman contrasted with Sophia, short, with a pale brown, almost yellow complexion, and stringy black hair that refused to grow beyond the nape of her neck. It also didn't help that Sophia's belly had begun to enter a room slightly before her nose did. David and Goliath seemed a fair enough analogy. Goliath continued on, a bit exasperated.

"Miss McClain,...."

"I'm not changing my mind, Mrs. Ahless. I came a long way, nearly a lifetime from my home situation to come to college here. Everything I did, I chose to do. You won't take that from me."

"I'm not trying to." the woman paused for a thoughtful, yet frustrated moment. "But you must know that your pregnancy is a special case, demanding special attention. If you insist on continuing as you are now without pre natal care, your prognosis isn't good."

"What are you suggesting, Mrs. Ahless?" Sophia questioned while pulling her loose fitting wool sweater tightly around her. It was late fall, soon to be winter, and Sophia wondered if this woman was ever going to turn a heater on.

"Miss McClain, I don't want to rob you of your impending motherhood." she eyed Sophia wearily, before uncrossing her arms and facing her as she leaned against her desk. "I have two daughters of my own, and I love them dearer than life itself. I don't doubt that you feel the same. But I also had good pre natal care. Healthy though I was, I wouldn't have risked not seeing a doctor during my pregnancies."

"Mrs. Ahless, I can't afford a doctor."

"We can find you one. That's the whole purpose of social services; to give aid to people who need it, but can't afford it. I'm not trying to interfere in your life, or run your business."

"Then you'll forgive me for thinking otherwise." Sophia renewed her defensive reserve. "Threats of legal action don't comfort me."

"Sophia, I'm very concerned about your emotional state. Your reluctance at contacting your family is troubling, at best."

"I never told anyone I was coming here." Sophia surrendered, weighing her grim freedom on the scales of here and now. "Trust me, if you knew my family, you'd understand why."

"I understand that you're an expectant mother suffering from diabetes, who resists the idea of getting some help. You won't tell me about your family or the baby's father. Put yourself in my place, Miss McClain; how would you deal with this situation?"

The question, like a stabbing pain that shattered a deep sleep way past midnight, was the opening of this story which changed drastically as each day passed into forever.

Seventy nine days later, Sophia experienced the final act of this greatest drama of her short life. A young hospital attendant with a smooth ebony complexion was rolling Sophia down the hallways of Medical College of Virginia Hospital in February of 1974, as she was on her way to one of the operating rooms. The boy was dispassionate as Sophia looked up and smiled at him. His tight eyes showed no expression, and she would have been disappointed were it not for Mellissa's firm grip on her hand.

"I'm glad you're here, Mellissa." Sophia spoke affectionately as she and her social worker proceeded along the long corridor. Mellissa, adorned in denim slacks and a brown wool pullover sweater, smiled while reaffirming the hand hold.

"Where else was I going to be? Your kidneys might have kicked out two days ago, but I'm not going anywhere." Mellissa replied, her thoughts focused on more than just Sophia's impending delivery. What few words passed between them-future plans, job training, low income housing-were heartfelt, but grimly colored by thoughts of what might lie ahead. Sophia was certain that she'd probably lose her scholarship after this. Mellissa was more concerned that Sophia might lose her life. Somehow, the older woman managed not to frown, or show how concerned she was about Sophia's condition. The show of meteors outside the windows of the hospital corridors gave her pause from the somber contemplations, and Sophia's childlike exuberance at the sight didn't hurt either.

"It's....beautiful." Sophia's eyes opened wide with wonder as she placed a hand on her stomach, caressing the one she'd read aloud to, sung songs to, and spoken with as if he were already born. "What a sight to greet one on the night of one's birth."

Sophia's joy reminded Mellissa of the beautiful simplicity she saw every day with her own young daughters, and she relented to the euphoria, smiling in spite of the knowledge of what her charge was about to go through.

3

"Okay, Sophia. Give me one more push. I see his head coming out."

Inside a sterile operating room, doctors and nurses attended Sophia as she bore down and grunted.

"Come on, Sophia. Just a little bit more. Push..."

She pushed and breathed, bore down as if her life depended on it. The worried eyes of the doctor suggested as much. Sophia gripped the sides of the Gurney she lay upon and in a primal howl that terrified everyone in the delivery room, she uttered the marching orders she'd unconsciously written for Dennis.

"AAAAAAAARGH!! Come on out, child!"

Almost immediately after that cry, Dennis came forth from Sophia's womb. A small child, dark and limp as a roll of licorice, Dennis came into the world and emitted a weak cry to signal his arrival.

"Miss McClain, congratulations! You're the mother of a beautiful baby boy." one of the nurses laid Dennis' still wet body on Sophia's chest, close to her beating heart, and she knew that her child was beautiful. His dark brown countenance belonged to his father, but Sophia looked into the amber eyes and she knew that Dennis' heart and soul didn't belong to the brigand that had deserted the both of them. Beautiful amber eyes that didn't hold a hint of the malevolence and deceit of the world into which he was born. He was beautiful, and Sophia closed her eyes to rest, just as the monitor watching her heartbeat suddenly alarmed, filling the operating room with a fearful scream.

"I got cardiac arrest!" a doctor declared, immediately placing a hand on Sophia's chest. He felt for the non existent heartbeat before turning his attention to the head nurse, who'd just removed the child from Sophia. "Get me some vital stats, now!"

"Blood pressure dropping! Respiration is shallow!"

"We're losing her, people! Get me twenty CCs of adrenalin, now!" the doctor ordered. A sense of doom spread throughout the operating room as the doctors and nurses furtively attended to their failing patient. The ominous premonition made its way out to the semi crowded waiting room where Mellissa sat, nervously tapping her fingers on the black plastic armrest of the chair she sat in. The head doctor had assured her that once Sophia's contractions began, there weren't going to be any problems. A quick glimpse at the gray stucco hallway beyond the waiting room's arched doorway told her otherwise.

She'd seen assorted medical personnel rushing towards the operating room, and heard the words 'Code Blue', uttered in frantic fashion. Mellissa almost prayed that the emergency concerned the guy in operating room two, who was having his gall bladder removed, even though she was certain that such wasn't so.

"Vital signs weakening." the nurse cried in the operating room, sweat pouring beneath her plastic cap as she moved aside for the arrival of the defibrillator. Quickly grasping both electric paddles in his hands and charging them up before descending on Sophia's limp form, the head doctor couldn't stop his gray locks from escaping below his medical cap as he shouted to the operating crew.

"Clear!" he declared, before applying the paddles to both sides of her chest. But Sophia didn't feel the jolt that savagely pummeled her, raising her jerkily off the operating table more than once. She remembered the noise, or so she thought, voices raised in concern and commotion below where she'd begun to ascend to. She didn't remain behind, looking up instead, at the light that beckoned above her.

The light, just like the ones she'd seen as the attendant rolled her down the hospital hallway, would arrive first. She could hear her grandmother's laughter again, much louder and lovelier than her fading memories had provided. The laughter gently dissolved into the smiling face of a star, which floated within range of her waiting hands. To hold and be held as the chaos below became faint and less important. The operating room roof had disappeared, merging into the evening darkness illuminated by the lights that had welcomed her offspring, who's beautiful face she'd seen long enough to know that he was there, and would be alright. Sophia thought of him for a long moment, a tear suddenly crossing the landscape of joy that had been planted on her face. But she walked on, the darkness becoming solid ground as the night lights gathered to become one in a welcome corner that Sophia eagerly entered into.

2

'February 19, 1974
MEMO: CENTRAL VIRGINIA CHILD WELFARE SERVICES
RE: Dennis Williamson McClain
TO: Executive Staff
FROM: Mellissa Ahless

On February 15 of this year, subject was born at Medical College of Virginia Hospital. Dennis' mother, Sophia Zetie McClain, died within a minute of his birth. Subject's father is unknown. Miss McClain did not name him, though he is likely one of her classmates at Virginia State University, in Petersburg. Further, all attempts at locating Miss McClain's family have been futile. She did not wish their involvement in this situation, and what information I could glean from her did not help in finding and notifying them.

Subject was named by his mother nearly a week before his birth.

Dennis was born with severe cerebral palsy, and the prognosis for future physical development is not good.

His mental facilities seem as highly developed as those of any normal newborn infant, and the APGAR test administered indicate that Dennis has the potential to develop a keen intellect in contrast to his disabled body.

Save the child being claimed by his father, or one of Miss McClain's relatives showing up to take custody of the child, CVCWS has no alternative but to place him in a foster or adoptive home that will adequately address his special needs.....'

Three times, Mellissa tried to write the memo, but profuse tears had kept her from completing it in a less than painfully personal fashion. She figured that the fourth time would be the charm, but once again, she couldn't get past her emotions about Sophia.

Mellissa's thoughts were too full of the happy moments she'd shared with Sophia in the short time she'd known her. Looking at the grey concrete blocks of her office, she was suddenly aware why she'd never really noticed the bland appearance of the walls before. Sophia had painted the place a million wonderful colors with her seemingly endless enthusiasm for the child Mellissa was certain the girl wouldn't live to see.

Picking up her now very cold cup of Chamomile tea, Mellissa saw in the liquid a reflection of the tear stained face she'd worn for nearly a week; her smile having departed the night of February 15, along with the last smile she remembered being on Sophia's face. Sorrowfully, Mellissa picked up her telephone receiver. There were calls to make.

"Good afternoon. I'm Mellissa Ahless from Central Virginia Child Welfare Services. I have....a newborn client with special needs whom I must place with an adoptive or foster family."

That call, the first of many to countless county and state offices, was laced with Mellissa's heartfelt prayer that, if nothing else, she could do right by the young girl who'd come to love and believe in her.

"Sophia, as much as I miss you, maybe it's better that you died." Mellissa sobbed. "God knows it's going to be rough for Dennis, but I'll help him as much as I can."

Thus she believed, though part of her knew she couldn't do even an ounce of what she really wanted, or what Dennis truly needed.

3

For Maryum Dupaul, things could have been much worse.

'I could have gotten killed in a car crash, or maybe been on board that doomed troop transport I got bumped from at the last minute during the Gulf War.' the thought flashed, and she passed it as quickly as the Ex-Lax her father used to swear by. Besides, she really didn't want to be dead, though she wasn't fond of being back at Langtree either, given the circumstances. Sitting in the lobby of the Psychology department of Connecticut's Langtree College, she'd already experienced Dr. McElroy's dispassionate acknowledgment of her earlier this morning, and his normally cherubic face became as colorless and gray as the soft curls that surrounded his head. Rather than look into her eyes, the pudgy little man stared straight at the wall before quickening his step, presumably to get away from her. She scratched the short cropped hair atop her deep ebony scalp before angrily exhaling.

'Fine. I'll see him in his office. Then his gray ass will have to look at me!'.

Not that she was eager for his company, but his smoke filled office might be preferable to the lobby's wallpaper, which had always reminded her of a dumb mixture of baby ducks and green lines. Still, Maryum knew that mouthing off about the room's decor would only make more difficult this appointment with the dean, which wasn't for academic counseling.

Surrendering her head to her waiting palms, Maryum somberly recalled happier moments in this hall. Moments like two months ago when she and Tracey Medrano were together.

"God, I wish you could have come down to Costa Rica with me for the holidays, Maryum. You'd have loved every minute of it."

Tracey Medrano was a peanut butter complexioned, full figured, six foot plus senior, whose long arms and legs possessed strong, but wonderfully feminine muscle. She and Maryum sat on a couch in the middle of the department lobby, not long after enduring another beginning of winter semester speech by Dr. McElroy, dean of the Psychology department. The man admonished all the students to not be surprised where the day or their academic lives would take them, but Maryum was more concerned with her upcoming classroom thesis work, and Tracey dreaded her impending internship, though her soiree south of the border had given her a respite from academic travail. Tracey's loose attire of sleeveless blue tee shirt beneath a blue denim jacket and wrap around, multicolored skirt, suggested that maybe the vacation wasn't totally over yet.

"I'm glad you had fun, though I'll never understand the nose ring." Maryum replied while gathering her textbooks from last semester in the crook of her arm. More conservatively dressed in black denim slacks and a maroon sweatshirt, Maryum contemplated selling her unneeded books at the campus bookstore later, though she was currently enjoying the sight of Tracey's euphoria. Most of the other students in the lobby seemed terribly nervous about the upcoming semester. Tracey was too blissful for that, and Maryum was getting a nice contact high watching her.

"I don't know why I waited so long, Mare." she affectionately addressed her shorter, darker friend. "Liviie saw me trying on one of hers in the mirror and told me to go for it."

"Really?!" Maryum waxed with amusement. "You sure this is just family love, or is there more to it?"

"Jesus." Tracey threw back her curly red head as the women sat on a couch in the middle of the lobby. "I guess I've talked about my cousin a lot since I came back, huh?!"

"Uh...yeah." Maryum grinned.

"It's weird, Mare, but for a while....I thought I was going to try ....making it with Liviie. I mean, I don't have a gay bone in my body....I think. But Costa Rica opened me up in ways I never thought of. Liviie and my other family members got all their meals right out of the rain forest. We went skinny dipping down at the beach, as well as at a lagoon near the house that they lived in. And I found out that Liviie loved girls, as well as boys. I nearly freaked the day she winked at me, but I was also kind of....excited."

"Oh oh. Do I need to put an armed guard in front of my room door?!" Maryum joked, just before noticing that one of her textbooks was already marked 'USED'.

"No. No, no." Tracey laughed. "Besides, Jeff and I have been together since way before he hitched up and flew in Desert Storm. Barring another war before his enlistment is up, our first appointment when he comes back from maneuvers will be with the justice of the peace."

"Good. Hopefully, I'll be finished with the D.D.E. program in time to witness the wedding, provided you guys invite me."

"I still think you're making a serious mistake, Mare. I've heard too many bad things about how Langtree handles that program."

"I suppose, but that's what I want to do with my life, Tracey. Developmentally disabled people didn't ask to come into the world and get mistreated. I think it's a damn shame how society loves to just warehouse those guys without trying to make the best of their potential. Besides, at least I'd have a good idea of what I'd be getting myself into."

"Think about it, kiddo." Tracey cautioned. "Everybody D.D. isn't Rodney. A lot of those folks only have a quarter of a brain instead of half."

"I don't believe...you said that." Maryum muttered with annoyance after staring at Tracey for a long moment; painfully wondering why she had to mention Rodney. Not that she didn't often think of her younger brother, who's untimely passing on the final day of his visit to Langree's campus during a late spring weekend last year had been devastating. The reality of his Downs Syndrome and possessing a weak heart that ultimately failed him the day before his twenty sixth birthday, only compounded the pain. "That was as cruel as they come, Tracey."

"That was truth, Mare. You're going to deal with folks who are in all stages of dysfunction. Your having to wipe Rodney's nose is minor in comparison to some of what you're about to deal with. I'm talking about folks who've never even gone to the bathroom by themselves. It won't be like you and Rodney. And I didn't say that to be cruel. I'm being for real. I hope you are too, and not dreaming."

"I'm not, Tracey. I just want to make a difference. Maybe I can't change the world, but I can make my corner of it a little brighter, okay?!"

So Maryum spoke, and Tracey obliged her, not wanting the discussion to evolve into a heated argument. Unexpectedly, Tracey was assigned to do her internship at D.D.E., alongside Maryum-who volunteered for the program in order to get credit towards her doctorate- and in a short number of days, the twosome were deeply involved in their brave new steps into professional life beyond academia.

The Developmentally Disabled Education program of Langtree College was located in a one story, red brick building three miles from the main campus. Situated close to a wooded area between several suburbs and apartment complexes, the facility had long served as a training ground for most of Langtree's students in the fields of education, sociology, and psychology. For the last few years, the D.D.E. program had also occupied the facility.

The D.D.E. program consisted of one administrator, two supervisors, five instructors, and two educational assistants, Maryum and Tracey being the beleaguered assistants this particular semester. Everyone was assigned the task of instructing and care taking for thirty five clients of various ages, disabilities, and levels of mental and physical function. Having all manner of tasks to carry out with the seven clients under her responsibility, Maryum quickly found out just how true Tracey's solemn warning had been.

Maryum's people; ranging from the tall, arrogant, wheelchair bound Deidre, who made sexual overtures to every man that visited the building; to Sean Marshall, short and bug eyed, who never spoke unless someone shouted loud enough in his ear, or let him hear music with stereo headphones, were an interesting collection that Maryum never found boring. And she was totally perplexed by George Russell, a strapping six footer who spoke only in staccato mumbles, and violently struck himself in the head while jumping up and down whenever he got upset. Worse, George tended not to flush after a bowel movement, preferring to reach into the toilet and play with the feces. Maryum checked on him one day when he'd spent a considerable period in the men's restroom, and found him chucking a turd between his hands as if it were a baseball. That day, she was totally exhausted by lunch time, and Tracey found her at her desk, face down on the desk top.

"Hey, wake up, Sis!" Tracey was in one of her 'Too Happy' moods as she approached Maryum. Her pink cotton blouse showed signs of just washed off catsup, but Tracey seemed oblivious to such distress while rolling her curly red hair into a ball atop her head. "We only got half an hour before we start classes again."

"Thanks for reminding me." Maryum wiped her eyes. "How about just peel my skin off and pour vinegar in my wounds next time?"

"Na. I'm partial to electro shock, myself. I hear it gives you a good buzz!"

"Great. I need something like that." Maryum laughed wearily, mildly inspired by Tracey's enthusiasm. "Either that, or a fresh shot of adrenalin."

"Hey, I could show you some of the postures and motions from Tai Chi that would help you get energetic. Even though you dropped out last fall, it's never too late to start learning again."

"More likely I'd want to use some of that Jui Jitsu Jeff taught you on a few of our coworkers." Maryum mused. "How about a game of checkers, instead?"

"Always! What's the booty?! Cash? Beer? Gasoline?!"

"Let's just play. We can get some brewskis later."

Grabbing a checker board from the nearby white plastic bookshelf holding books, writing pads, paints, and other materials used in the day to day operation of the program, Maryum couldn't deny her growing awareness of something else being way out of kilter. Tracey was enjoying her time in the D.D.E. program. Maryum, on the other hand, knew that the sooner the next four weeks passed, the happier she would be. She wasn't certain when the discontent of her situation had set in; whether during her first contentious weeks working with the other staff members, her acceptance of Tracy's dire warnings during the first day of the semester, or even the daily improvisation as regular routine-she and Tracey having to substitute bottle caps, coins, and marker tops for checker pieces as they currently did, being the latest-but Maryum had no doubt that the situation just wasn't working out for her, and that she only endured due to her friendship and working status with Tracey.

"Got you!" Maryum announced, having pulled a triple jump.

"No way, Mare! I still got pieces on the board."

"And I'll get them on my next move. Give it up, Tracey."

"Let's make it best three out of five." Tracey pleaded, catching twenty one year old Dennis McClain's entrance into the room from the corner of her eye. Maryum spotted the young man, long and dark, as he sat in his electric wheelchair, propelling himself towards the metal desk she and Tracy occupied. Tracey raised her head and smiled, though Maryum seemed to think that Dennis' primary attention had been cast at her. She couldn't be certain, since Dennis possessed very little physical coordination, but Maryum thought she detected a hint of interest, or sparkle, when Dennis' eyes and head rolled in her direction. Pushing the joystick on his wheelchair armrest, Dennis made his way over to the two women, and his eyes were wide with interest and curiosity.

"Hello, Dennis." Maryum smiled, rising above her lunchtime funk. "You want some of this action?"

Dennis eyed both women determinedly as he pulled out two straws he'd fashioned into a longer implement that Maryum stared at in surprise. Even more surprising, Dennis pulled up closer to the table and pushed one of Tracey's red checker pieces with the long straw, maneuvering it into a black piece close by.

"Jaaaa........jaaaump!" his head moved back as he struggled to express his thoughts. Maryum was dumbfounded, having not noticed that particular move on the board before.

"Thank you, Dennis!" Tracey eagerly moved her checker piece before finding another jump, and taking two more of Maryum's pieces as Dennis jerkily maneuvered his straws to show Tracey another move. This only goaded Maryum to vent defensively.

"Beginner's luck! I bet you can't take me without Tracey's help."

She immediately felt juvenile for having said that, but when she looked over at Dennis, he laughed and raised his long straw in a challenging fashion. Maryum remembered this demeanor from another time and place- like when neighborhood kids dared her to do a fast round of double Dutch jump rope during her childhood- and was nearly unnerved by Dennis' bravado.

"I think he wants to try you, Mare."

"Okay, Dennis. You're on." Maryum looked at her watch, seeing twenty minutes to go before classes began again, as well as dreading the prospect that she might actually get beat.

She did.

A day later, she spoke of it during a staff meeting.

"Maybe you'll think I'm exaggerating," Maryum spoke to her assembled colleagues in the beige colored activity room. "...but I suspect that Dennis McClain is a lot more intelligent than we initially thought."

She heard a snicker coming from Hebert Jeremiah, her least favorite coworker. He, six foot

five with long blond hair and a matching thin goatee, sat next to Sarah Goode, a tall redhead with

short bangs across her forehead and a concrete wall of make up on her face. Hebert whispered in

Sarah's ear while staring mischievously at Maryum, who ignored them both as she

spoke to the group. The center's director, Tina Monroe, full figured with boyishly short blond hair, adorned in a blue sweat shirt and faded blue denim pants, raised her head from the legal pad she'd been writing on to question Maryum.

"What prompted you to think this, Maryum?" Tina placed her fountain pen between her left ear and the hair at her temple.

"Well, the other day I noticed Dennis carefully examining a book in my office."

"Scuze me," Hebert flippantly piped up, raising his hand and stuffing his navy blue tee shirt in his khaki trousers while leaning back in his chair. "but just about all the clients here do that, and for sure they ain't a bunch of whiz kid."

"Hebert, Dennis wasn't doing the random, crazed, page flipping behavior that you're probably referring to, but was slowly examining the print before he went on to the next page." Maryum affirmed. "I'm sure some of the staff open books and just look at the pictures, Hebert, but that doesn't make them functionally illiterate, now does it?"

"Okay. Let's stay focused on our purpose for being here." Tina reasserted her authority. "Personal broadsides aren't necessary. Please continue, Maryum."

"Thank you, Tina. Were my suspicions based solely on my observing him flipping pages, I'd probably pass it off as happenstance. But Dennis has shown me a number of things. In particular, he came in on Tracey and I yesterday while we were playing checkers. He'd managed to fashion two straws together to help him move the pieces on the board. I challenged him to a game. He beat me twice.

"In a third game, Tracey and I double teamed him and he still beat us."

"Sounds like you and Tracey are lousy at checkers." Sarah blurted out, immediately drawing Tracey's silently disdainful glance, as well as muffled giggles from Hebert. Maryum spoke again, hoping to defuse the potential conflict, though she almost wished that Sarah was stupid enough to threaten Tracey physically, since she had absolutely no doubt about what would be the outcome.

"Seriously, I think that Dennis' situation merits a concentrated effort on our part to help him fulfill his full human potential."

"Tina," Hebert reentered the conversation. "I don't know who Miss Dupaul is talking about, but the Dennis McClain I'm thinking of is a twenty one year old dude who can't even make a sentence, ain't potty trained, can't feed himself, and slobbers oceans of drool every day. This guy is supposed to be some kind of brainchild?! C'mon?"

"Hebert, what I'm saying is that our approach to Dennis is based on the notion that because he lacks motor skills and control over his bodily functions, that he must be developmentally disabled as well. However, he may be far more intelligent than any of our other clients, and possibly as intelligent as some of us on this staff. We can't know that so long as we keep him cooped up in this program without searching for ways to determine his full range of capabilities."

There was a palpable silence in the room before Tina broke it with her spur of the moment assertion.

"All right, Maryum. We'll take that under advisement and start formulating new strategies in regards to what you've brought to our attention. Next on the agenda?"

That was when Jane Watkins, a mousey brunette with unkempt long curls raised her hand. Her small, perky breasts jiggled underneath her dark green tee shirt, and Maryum had barely submerged her anger at Tina's seeming dismissal of Dennis' needs, in time to wonder just why her child woman associate wasn't wearing a bra.

"Ahh...we got to make plans for this year's Easter egg hunt." she giggled, Sarah and Hebert grinning alongside her. Maryum, however, was furious that Dennis' needs were so immediately dismissed at this point. She also wasn't surprised. The question, she surmised, amongst most of the D.D.E. staff in regards to helping Dennis was probably not so much 'How?', but rather 'Why?!'. She resigned herself to the likelihood that Hebert, Sarah, and Jane wouldn't be motivated towards anything more than unimaginative care taking. She related such to Tracey later that evening, as the two of them retreated to Conchata's in search of sustenance and libation.

Formerly a corner store, Conchata's had been purchased by a group of local immigrants and turned into a café whose menu featured dishes from all over Latin America. The place was sparsely illuminated by candlelight and overhead lighting, and its adobe walls were covered with pictures, paintings, and artifacts denoting their respective South American origins. Maryum and Tracey sat in a booth near the wall facing the large front windows.

"Am I just being paranoid, Tracey, or am I really trying to talk common sense to brick walls? One psych major to another, tell me what's wrong with my approach?"

"Nothing, Maryum. Unfortunately, what's wrong is our situation. Hebert, Sarah, and Jane probably resent us because of our education. Tina," Tracey pensively sipped her mug of beer, and paused as though she hadn't meant to utter that name. "…probably resents us since she knows I'm going to graduate soon, and start working on my master's degree. You're going to finish your doctorate, and we're both going to move on to higher paying positions than she can currently hope to aim for. It hasn't dawned on her to maybe go back to school and finish her masters in social work, since she's too busy hating life and hoping to die."

The two of them rattled on as they drank beer, ate burritos, nachos, quesadillas, black beans, red beans and rice, and a host of other things that they consumed between the sixth and eighth hour p.m. Tracey also pulled out a business card from her purple shoulder bag, and showed it to Maryum.

"Starbright Institute for Disabled Adults?"

"Last fall, when my academic advisor was trying to get me an assignment for internship, this was one of the places he called. It's a program run out of New Haven in conjunction with Yale University and the University of New Haven. Unfortunately, I couldn't get there because they had enough interns for this semester. I hear it's a great place for disabled adults, particularly those who have exceptional intelligence."

"You mean Dennis?" Maryum still studied the card, holding it in the muted light of the restaurant's candles.

"Well for sure I don't mean Hebert, Sarah, and Jane." Tracey laughed while lifting the pitcher of beer to refill Maryum's mug. "They aren't disabled. Besides, I don't think they're bright enough to qualify. We might be able to get Tina in, though."

"The only place I'm interested in getting Tina, and everybody else in D.D.E., is in front of county social services board, so they can explain why they're doing such a piss poor job."

"They're not worth the bother, Maryum." Tracey turned serious. "At best, you can rise above. At worst, things threaten to get ugly. I mean, 'Real ' ugly."

"Tracey, I spent the first eight years of my life in North Philadelphia. I'm hardly panicked at the prospect of battle with any of that bunch."

"Maybe you should be." Tracey sobered again, slicing through her third burrito. "Apart from Tina's messing you up professionally, Hebert is a big, ugly son of a bitch. And I'm afraid that he might not deal with this in a rational fashion."

'Let him try!' Maryum thought, privately assuming that such was highly unlikely. She didn't think Hebert had the guts to physically threaten her, and the prospect of violence hadn't previously occurred to her. That would change the very next day.

Sometime after lunch at the D.D.E. center, Maryum happened upon Hebert snarling at Dennis in the main recreational room as some of the other clients beheld the unfolding melodrama. The air of the room was permeated by something more odiferous than merely the stink of Hebert's viciousness.

"Look man," Hebert's voice was sharp as he grasped the young man's shirt collar. "I'm tired of changing your damn diaper. You need to find a way to tell somebody when you got to go!"

"Excuse me, but what do you think you're doing?!" Maryum demanded as she entered the room.

"Hey, Miss Doo-Paul," he exaggerated annoyingly. "I think you better turn around and mind your own business."

"Excuse me, Mr. Hay-Bear, but grabbing Dennis' shirt collar and scowling like a madman doesn't work, okay?! You don't make a situation right by threatening people."

"Look, I don't give a shi......I don't care about what you think, and I ain't got time to argue with your college educated behind. You got a problem with the way I'm working, why don't you come here and clean him up?!"

"Fine! I will." Maryum tersely replied. "After which, I'm going to report you to Tina."

"Hey, fuckin' be my guest!" he uttered before storming out of the room, leaving behind Dennis, Maryum, and a few of the other clients who'd observed the scene only a little less bad smelling than Dennis' soiled clothing.

The rest of that day, indeed, the rest of that week, drew a solemn curtain over Maryum's experience in the program. True to her promise, she did go to Tina, though she relished having to do so less than she had changing Dennis' diaper. Somehow, taking him to the center's washroom had seemed a picnic in contrast to Tina's flustered, non committal, response to the complaint.

"Maryum, I will discuss this matter with him. Thank you for bringing it to my attention."

Maryum hadn't considered what Tina's response would be while putting on surgical gloves before undressing Dennis and lowering him with Tracey's help into the washroom's bathtub. The young man remained silent as Maryum ministered to him, perhaps grateful to not be enduring more scorn and angst from Hebert, or some other less compassionate staff member. Somewhere between the warm water, the antiseptic soap she used to wash Dennis with, the vulnerable look he gave her as she busily went about him with the soft body sponge, Maryum wondered how she lost sight of her immediate reason for having got in the D.D.E. program. Being confronted with Dennis' need reminded her that there should have been more to her thesis work than the second thoughts and anger that had plagued her for most of the last few weeks. Anger that had barely dissipated when Maryum later encountered Dennis just before the buses arrived to take all of the clients back to their homes, group homes, institutions, and other places where they dwelt, or were warehoused, during their time away from D.D.E. She'd finished freshening up in the staff rest room, briefly spoken to Tina, and was walking though the hallway in route to her classroom when she noticed Jane and Sarah quickly walking past her. Both women grew silent when they spotted Maryum in the hallway, scurrying away from her as if she were infected with the plague.

'So be it. The incident has become grist for the mill of the incompetent.' Maryum thought while walking into her classroom and unexpectedly seeing Dennis in the corner, observing her copy of 'The Autobiography of Malcolm X'.

"Hi, Dennis. Enjoying the book?" she was upbeat. Aware that she'd seen more of him than she was totally comfortable with this day, Maryum hoped that the embarrassment, the sheer humiliation, of having been cleaned up by her wasn't burdening Dennis' mind. "My dad got me reading that two summers ago. It's interesting."

He looked at her as she approached. Remembering Tracey's warnings of last month, Maryum tried not to read too much into Dennis' intense gaze, telling herself that it was only reflex that made him seem so thoughtful and introspective, but not fully believing that either. She pulled up a chair to sit beside him and Dennis made an effort to follow her movements. She wondered if this was a conscious action on his part, just before his attempt at speech removed all doubt.

"Sha....Shaaaa.....bazz!! Mal.....Ma...Malcolm."

Dennis' face took on an almost tortured contortion as he desperately sought to speak, and Maryum couldn't help noticing his fingers as they fluttered birdlike across the paper before settling on a line somewhere near the middle of the page. The line where Alex Haley related his first conversations about Malcolm's name change.

"Yes, Dennis. His full name was Malcolm X. Shabazz, or El Hadj Malik Shabazz. How much of this have you read already?"

She hoped not to betray the astonishment she was feeling at the moment, truly not knowing what was going to happen next as she waited, vainly perhaps, for him to try and say anything further. Oh, the intelligence, she pondered, that must be waiting behind those wide brown eyes.

"Dennis, I want to read this again someday. Will you help me?"

She so wanted to spend more time with Dennis to learn just how much he truly knew about the world around him. Today was a good starting place. Sadly, the day did have to end. Hebert saw to that.

"Dennis, your bus is here. Let's get moving." the gruff voice intruded into the room, and Maryum raised her head to see Hebert standing menacingly at the room door. She wondered why this dude couldn't have snuck out instead of honoring his bus duty responsibility today. That would have given her more time to speak with Dennis, to learn more about what he did and didn't know of the book he examined. She'd just wanted another moment to be near him, rather than surrendering him to this pained dismissal at the hands of one who'd become a staunch adversary. Dennis slowly maneuvered his joystick on the wheelchair, turning away from Maryum to go out the door, but in doing so, he dropped the book in her lap and brushed her cheek with his free hand.

She felt a wave of warmth arise within her, suddenly filling her mind and heart with all manner of longing and unexpected desire. Maryum felt her cheek as Dennis exited through the room door, scarcely believing what she felt, hardly understanding what might be going on, and wishing that she could have held his hand to the spot and learned even more than she already knew.

4

A week following her resignation from the D.D.E. program, Maryum was an unhappy passenger aboard a commuter flight from Connecticut, returning home to Philadelphia, Pennsylvania. The jarring recall of her last conversation with Dr. McElroy returned to her thoughts, bringing her more pain than the headache she'd developed from the high altitude popping of her eardrums.

"Ms. Dupaul, you've put this college in a very difficult position." the man stood menacingly adjacent to her as she sat on a couch in his too small office. He was only in his late forties, but his thinning gray hair and harried demeanor added at least a decade to his appearance. "The McClain's lawyer has stated that the only conditions they'll accept to forgo any litigation against Langtree is that we remove you from involvement in our clinical and educational programs."

"Fine. How about just kick me out so I can maybe transfer to Penn State, or Temple? They're closer to home. Otherwise, you're stuck with me until I get my PHD." she sullenly crossed her arms and stared at nothing in particular. Maryum observed Dr. McElroy nervously finger his gray white goatee, and wondered if his latest wrinkles and pronounced crows feet were the result of excess smoking, or the threat of impending legal action against the college.

"Ms. Dupaul, you're making this more difficult than it has to be." exasperated, he lit a cigarette. "We expel you-which we've no just cause for given your exceptional GPA-and the state social service board might think we're retaliating against you. They're already all over us about the current and past complaints about abuse and neglect at D.D.E."

"Frankly, Dr. McElroy, there has been a lot of abuse and neglect at D.D.E., and I really don't care what the state thinks about what you decide to do with me. But I'm not dropping out just to save you from the McClain's lawyer, so I guess you're up shit creek."

"We were also dumb enough to let a sex crazed, hard drinking, grad student loose in the program." he nearly spat out his cigarette, catching it with tense fingers a half second before his lips let go.

"Dr. McElroy, too many people are trying to cover their rear ends, and using me for toilet paper." clutching the couch cushions with tight fingers, Maryum delivered her next words with calm annoyance. "But then again, I'm not surprised that you can't see through this bullshit smokescreen. Or maybe you're just too panicked to bother looking."

"That still doesn't explain what you were doing in bed with that kid, Ms. Dupaul."

"That kid," Maryum eyed the man severely. "Is twenty one years old and has more brains in his pinkie than the whole D.D.E. staff combined. Dennis Williamson McClain is an adult, Dr. McElroy. An adult who deserved a whole lot better treatment than he was getting at D.D.E."

Maryum had said this before, in less difficult circumstances. She'd meant to discuss it with Tina again, privately, the Monday morning following her harrowing run in with Hebert. Unfortunately, Tina had been too busy trying to appease Hebert, who remained indignant over Maryum's interference. Moreover, the following Monday found Maryum in a mini conference with Tina, but the terms of their meeting only served to shatter any confidence Maryum had in the woman's ability, or competence, to run the program.

"Maryum," Tina's voice calmly, but firmly, crossed the desk that divided she and Maryum. "it was reported to me this morning by several of the staff here that you've been drinking on the job."

"Oh?" Maryum's response barely concealed her contempt. "I've got a pretty good idea who said this and I know why."

"Yes. I know that you and Hebert had words on Friday."

"We had more than just 'Words', Tina. He told me that I was too educated to be here. That I should have closed my mouth, turned my back, and just let him get away with abusing a client."

"I spoke to him about that." Tina placed her intertwined fingers on top of the desk defensively. "Yes, he was wrong."

"So why haven't you reported him to county social services?"

"Maryum, we don't need to confuse the issue, okay?"

"Tina, the issue is that I've been accused of something real serious by a guy who's retaliating against me because I reported him when he was messing up. I'd hoped that you'd be...."she was tempted to say 'Smart enough to see that!', but changed course mid stream. "....looking into his own abusive behavior instead of following up on some petty B.S. that he spread on me. I bet Jane and Sarah were his witnesses, right?!"

"Maryum, if this were just about what a few folks said, I could pass it off as B.S." Tina took a tense gulp out of her gray ceramic coffee mug. "But I'm also thinking about the group luncheon at Leonardo's last weekend, remember?"

"Yeah. So I had some deep dish pizza and drank a couple of mugs of beer. So did you, Sarah, Jane, Hebert, and Tracey, to name a few. So what?" Maryum noticed Tina eyeing her sharply while placing hr fingers prayerfully beneath her chin. "Okay, Tina. I also finished off the half carafe of Zinfandel that Jane was too smashed to drink anymore of. But then she was dumb enough to drink a couple of Margaritas beforehand, and I thought I'd save her from herself."

"You also left this on your desk." Tina brought up a small, crumpled paper bag with a clear bottle neck sticking out of it. "I spotted it when the nurse and I made our final rounds of the building before locking up for the weekend."

Tina set the bag on the desk, and Maryum snatched it up to reveal a quart bottle of Stolichnaya Vodka, which was devoid of all but a remaining third.

"No, no!" Maryum was emphatic as she nearly slammed the bottle back on Tina's desk. "I like my beer and wine, but I've never touched the hard stuff. I've never been drunk in my life, Tina. I'm sure that Hebert and friends planted this shit on my desk to support their story."

"Maryum, I do know that you guys haven't worked well together." Tina was tentative. "I consider that there are reasons for whatever problems we might have with this program...."

"Tina, the problem is that Hebert nearly assaulted a client on Friday, and I reported him to you. Then you get word this morning about me possibly drinking on the job, and it doesn't occur to you that maybe somebody is trying to make me look bad. You're swallowing it hook, line, and sinker, despite the fact that you've never had one problem with either me, or Tracey. What's wrong with this picture, Tina?"

"Maryum, I grew up in an alcoholic household, okay. I remember some of my dad's behaviors when people confronted him about it, and I hate to say it, but....a lot of what you're showing me now, reminds me too much of how my dad acted when my mom railed at him for being drunk so much. I hope that you're not boozing on us, Maryum..."

Maryum didn't hear the rest of Tina's concerns, having bolted from the office in a huff and silently hoping that the woman would try following her for further confrontation. That didn't happen, and for now, Maryum retreated to her office to sulk, quietly rejoicing in the knowledge that she would soon be finished with these sordid, petty people.

The situation was not right, but she was determined to do right, and her first action after sitting down at her desk, was to make a phone call to Starbright Institute. She couldn't speak to the person she'd needed to, the coordinator named on the card Tracey had given her, but did get a promise from the receptionist that her message would be relayed to the head psychiatrist of the program. Maryum was determined to be patient about her efforts to help Dennis, just as her patience was further tested while she prepared her caseloads for the clients who'd arrive in half an hour.

"Morning....Maryum. May I call you that?!"

Hebert walked into the rectangular classroom that Maryum normally shared with Tracey. It wasn't yet eight am, and Maryum had wanted to finish her coffee, as well as organize her class loads for the day. She hadn't anticipated, or desired for that matter, Hebert's company as he pulled up a chair and straddled his huge bulk very close to her desk.

"It's a free country, Hebert. You can call me whatever you want so long as it's not out of my name."

Hebert briefly scratched his nose before resting his hands on the chair top that he leaned his torso against. When Maryum dignified his presence with eye contact, she noticed that he was decked out in a garish green and red tee shirt styled like old prison garb, loose fitting blue jeans with a pair of maroon suspenders across his top, a black beret on his head, and some black leather combat boots on his feet. Maryum wondered, as she eyed him sitting in the chair turned backwards, what his strategy was today, and was this declared war, or what.

"Hey, no spite intended, Maryum." a silver star dangled from his left ear lobe as he raised his head up. "I think we got off on the wrong foot when we started out together and that it don't have to be about....you know."

"No, Hebert, I don't know." she was calm, trying not to sound as angry as she was. "You'll have to tell me how it 'Don't' have to be."

"Look, things got out of hand the other day. I admit, maybe I shouldn't have grabbed Dennis like I did, but you shouldn't have made such a big deal about it, okay? Things would have been cool if you'd just chilled out and not gotten bent out of shape like you did."

"Right. And that would have kept you, Jane, and Sarah from telling that lie on me, I suppose."

"What?" he tried to look surprised. He was a bad actor, and Maryum had no doubt about him ever winning an academy award.

"Hebert, you know exactly what I'm talking about. Telling Tina that I drink on the job, planting a half empty bottle of Stoli's on my desk. Maybe Tina had enough tact not to reveal who reported me, but did you really think I'd be dumb enough not to know what this was all about?"

"Yo, Dupaul, you're getting uppity again. I ain't got a clue as to why you're so down on us. We all work together in this joint and I don't see why we can't make the best of our situation. We ain't got a thing against you, but you're doing your damnedest to keep your distance. I mean, how you think we're supposed to deal with that."

"Hebert, I don't give a damn about how you're going to deal with that." she eyed him icily, keeping a close watch on him, as well as the letter opener near her purse, just in case she needed it. "The reason I came to D.D.E. was to help the clients, and finish my work on my dissertation. I didn't plan on getting on anybody's bad side, but I will not be intimidated, and I have no reason to make the best of this situation, or be nice to people who tell lies on me."

Tension flowed across the desk like pungent cigarette smoke as Hebert and Maryum gazed warily at one another. Maryum thought about pulling out her almost empty pack and lighting one just to blow smoke in his face, but that was when he found his voice again.

"So I guess that's all you got to say, huh?"

"I have nothing else to say except that from now on, unless you stay at least ten feet away from me, I will get a restraining order against you."

He stood up contemptuously, sneering briefly and mumbling something that Maryum didn't bother to listen to, before walking out of the room. If she'd had any illusions of having a halfway decent working elation with Hebert, or any of his 'Associates', they'd been crushed by today's acrimonious summit. She could barely abide the situation any longer, given the rift between she, Hebert, Jane, and Sarah; realizing that Tina was way too indifferent to be really effective; and painfully despairing that someone who needed her help might not get it in the situation she was currently enduring. Even worse, on the following day, Maryum had to deal with these realities again, but without Dennis' presence to help her overcome.

This afternoon, the whole group-instructors, assistants, and clients-were in the facility's multi use cafeteria, watching a movie that someone had rented during one of the training routines that the clients periodically practiced.

The movie was about a bunch of teenaged vampires, who drank blood out of frosted beer mugs, and also practiced the fine art of skinning house cats without killing them. Maryum had never really cared for horror movies, and she questioned the wisdom of having the clients observe a film that might incite some of the less than desirable traits she'd seen some of them exhibit. Then again, she remembered who she was working with, and didn't have to wonder why this was happening. She also missed Dennis, who was absent today due to a scheduled medical exam.

She watched her crew and saw that one of them, a petite blond named Cinnamon Hoffmeryl, seemed entranced by the beginning rainfall as she stood next to a window. Cinnamon was particularly difficult for Maryum to cope with. Twenty two years old, and suffering a sad combination of autism, compulsive eating, and an inability to express herself verbally, Cinnamon was also prone to uninhibited sexual behavior at anytime or place, and Maryum had to keep aware of her other charge's attentions towards the woman. Maryum entertained vague thoughts of Cinnamon being a good friend, or possibly the talk of everyone on campus, had fate been kinder. But now, as she watched the woman with big blue saucer eyes gaze wonderingly at the rainy afternoon, Maryum felt sorrow and a gnawing pain that she might never reach into Cinnamon's world. She'd just noticed that Cinnamon wasn't wearing any shoes, when Jane leaned over to whisper something.

"Uh oh. Looks like Cinnamon's in the mood again." She moved her lank brunette hair from in front of her blotchy, freckled face

"What mood?" Maryum questioned, thinking that Jane looked as though she'd been getting stoned all day.

"You mean you've never caught Cinnamon during a rain storm?!"

"No, Jane. You'll have to hip me."

"Sure." Jane shook her head as if she were trying to wake up. "You see she has her shoes off, yeah?!"

"Yes. I see." Maryum was annoyed, but indulged Jane further, thinking the woman might reveal something important. She also thought that hell would freeze over and became host to next year's edition of the 'Ice Capades'.

"Well, in about two seconds she's going to get naked and go dance outside in the rain." a smile of delicious anticipation crossed Jane's facial landscape.

'Get real, Jane!' Maryum thought as she inhaled deeply and looked down at her watch, just before remembering some of Cinnamon's other proclivities. That was when her ears got flooded with Cinnamon's declaration of independence.

"EEEEEEEEEEEEEE!!!"

Maryum looked up to see the fulfillment of Jane's revelation. Cinnamon Hoffmeryl; naked, squealing, and running for the door.

"Oh, shit!" Maryum rose from her seat, but felt Jane grabbing her arm, even as she eyed the unthinkable. Cinnamon Hoffmeryl; naked, squealing, and running for the door. "Let me go!!"

"Daah, leave her alone!" Jane grinned. "She loves it."

"Let go!!!" Maryum snatched her arm away, roughly brushing Jane's face and forcing a gasp from her coworker before bolting for the door that nubile Cinnamon escaped through.

She'd just made it through the door, getting her last clear sight-Cinnamon Hoffmeryl; naked, squealing, and running in the rain-before getting pelted with the torrential downpour. She was terrified of the prospect of not catching the small, pink figure in front of her before she made it to the wooded areas. Cinnamon ran and delightfully squealed as the rain fell on her naked body.

"Cinnamon! Stop!! Come back here!" Maryum bellowed while desperately running after her, knowing that she might as well have spit in the wind. Futile, it was, almost like her hope that the tall woman walking in the distance wasn't just a wet weather mirage. Futility became reality as the figure ran nearer, dropping her umbrella and hurriedly doffing her long yellow raincoat to reveal a stylish, black, mid thigh length evening dress.

"Tracey!! I need your help!" Maryum bellowed, seeing Tracey grab their naked prey several seconds later. Cinnamon continued to scream, squirm and writhe as Tracey struggled to wrap her up in the raincoat. Maryum reached the two of them and joined in the fray as she forcibly grabbed Cinnamon's kicking legs. When they'd finally achieved a firm grasp on Cinnamon, Maryum and Tracey marched her back to the D.D.E. building, though Cinnamon continued to buck and heave, causing the three of them to fall in deep mud near the center's parking lot, where the tussle became furious as Cinnamon attempted to regain her freedom.

"C'mon, Cinnamon! We're going back inside!" Maryum declared, grabbing Cinnamon's right arm. Tracey had firmly immobilized the woman's left arm with a Jui Jitsu arm bar, while fighting the urge to address the raw sting on the left side of her nose.

"Jeez, Mare! You and Cinnamon picked a real shitty day to go streak. What say we just wait for New Years and go skinny dipping with the Polar Bear Club, huh?!"

Maryum was too angry to laugh at Tracey's humorous aside as the women entered the D.D.E. center's cafeteria, Cinnamon in tense, unwilling tow. The threesome was greeted by the 'Ooh's and 'Ahh's of various clients and co workers as they pushed past the entry in route to a bathroom. Maryum noticed Hebert whispering something in Sarah Goode's ear as he grinned at the sight. Maryum spurned their attention as she steered Cinnamon out of the room. Tracey briefly released the woman's arm to pick up the bra, panties, blue jeans, and purple turtle neck blouse discarded in a frantic row leading towards the door and outdoors. Neither woman spoke a word. Maryum was saving her wrath for Tina once she and Tracey got Cinnamon safely back indoors.

"Tina, this situation will not work!" Maryum bellowed a half second after walking into Tina's office and finding the woman asleep at her desk. "I can't just wink at this crap and not do something about it."

"What....the hell happened to you?" Tina was shocked back to wakefulness by Maryum's sullen confrontation. Eyeing the angry, wet, muddy, individual who stood before her, Tina dared nothing more than a subdued yawn.

"I tried to stop Cinnamon Hoffmeryl from running naked in the rain. It was only due to Tracey showing up unexpectedly that we caught her before she could get buck wild."

"Jesus." Tina muttered. "Is she alright?"

"Cinnamon is fine. But Tracey's dress is ruined. Her hair looks like a swamp after it got flooded out, and Cinnamon managed to rip her nose ring out. Jeff's going to love the sight when he comes to pick Tracey up this evening."

"I should have warned you, Maryum. Cinnamon....likes to get naked in the rain."

"Don't bother, Tina!" Maryum slammed her hands on the front of Tina's desk. "Jane told me all about it in her wonderfully dopey way. I wonder if she's on THC or Acid this time. Even better, you should have seen Hebert and Sarah grinning, laughing and having a good time watching us. They didn't do shit to try and help, Tina."

"Maryum....."

"I'm not finished, Tina!" Maryum leaned further across Tina's desk. "You've got three clowns working here that have no business working with developmentally disabled people. You haven't done a thing to properly instruct them, or correct them when they're messing up. While you were back here napping, your 'Instructors' subjected your clients to a dumb vampire movie and laughed at some pathetic dysfunction. This doesn't work for me, Tina, and I'll be damned if I'm just going to let it slide."

"Maryum, I don't think it's wise...for you to go off on the deep end."

"Then what the hell do you expect me to do, Tina?!" Maryum stood back up and crossed her arms. "This program is not supposed to be some big day care or nursery. Your staff shouldn't be a bunch of stoned, burned out miscreants that I can't trust to act responsibly. I can't even trust you, Tina, because you're more worried about keeping the peace and collecting your fees than you are of maybe dealing with dumb ass Hebert."

"Excuse me." the office door opened slightly and Hebert stuck his head inside; smirking deviously at Maryum. "Ah, the busses will be coming in a few minutes, Maryum. And you and Tracey have bus duty."

"Fuck you, Hebert!" Maryum quickly flung the door wide open and stormed out of the room, thinking it the best way she could exit the scene without somebody suffering a massive loss of flesh and blood. She was too mad to see straight, and the drag of her wet, muddy clothes was making her even crazier. Prayerfully hoping that Hebert, Jane, or Sarah didn't cross her again, Maryum made her way down the hallway and into the restroom, after retrieving an extra sweater and pair of blue jeans she'd brought to the facility several days ago.

She'd run some water in the restroom sink, and was washing traces of red clay from her scalp when Tracey walked into the room. Tracey's red curls were sodden and askew atop her head-evidence of a not so great shampoo with the hand soap on the sink-, and more than matched the perplexed pain radiating from her eyes. She also wore the same yellow raincoat they'd dragged Cinnamon back into the building with.

"You can slow down, Maryum. Tina told Sarah and Jane to take bus duty since we had to catch Cinnamon. Of course, they're pissed off about it."

"My heart bleeds purple cow juice." Maryum vigorously rubbed her scalp before applying a brush to it. "I'm finished with D.D.E. I really don't care what Tina does at this point, but I'm sure that county social services will."

"They'll more than care after I testify about what went down today. I just don't believe this shit." Tracey stared at her reflection in the mirror, drawing a slow line with her fingers underneath the scratches marring her left cheekbone. The wounding wasn't deep, and Maryum didn't fear her friend being scarred for life, but it was heartbreaking to see the bruise besides Tracey's left nostril.

"You should have the nurse look at those. Only God knows where Cinnamon has had her fingers lately." Maryum applied levity, even as she saw Tracey fighting back tears.

"I already did. She said....I was lucky I was just wearing a steel post stud in my nose instead of a ring, and that the post... gave away.....like it did, without ripping me a laceration, or something." Tracey stifled a sob with her fingers across her lips, before hoisting up a plastic bag and pulling out the soiled, torn rag that used to be a purple and black evening dress. "It's not fair, Maryum. I'd planned a lovely evening for Jeff and I. Maybe go someplace fancy to eat dinner and maybe dance......I knew I should have waited till I got back here to put this dress on, but it was just too pretty... for me to leave on the hanger."

She sobbed again, this time not fighting the tears, nor feeling Maryum's firm embrace until she wept with total abandon. Tracey sobbed for many long moments, before composing herself on an inhale, giving Maryum a chance to speak again.

"Tracey, thanks for showing up when you did. I'm not sure what would have happened if you hadn't been there. I'm sorry that this ruined your evening."

"Well...., tonight's not totally shot." Tracey raised her shoulders and sniffled. "Jeff called from Andrews Air Force Base in Maryland this morning. He told me that after six months flying copters over the Mediterranean, he can't wait to get home and sleep in our bed. He also said that he wouldn't mind just a take out pizza and some beer.

"Besides..." Tracey smiled slyly, before breaking from Maryum and flashing open her raincoat to reveal her naked glory. "I can't wait to see his face when we get home and I take this raincoat off."

"Bet!" Maryum laughed deliciously, wondering if Tracey would settle for a quick shower after she and Jeff made it home, or would she ravish him right after closing the front door. Maryum would cherish that moment with Tracey, given it was one of her last happy moments for some time to come.

A day later, she called Langtree County Social Services, informing them of the incident concerning Cinnamon, as well as Hebert's assault on Dennis. She also made another phone call to Starbright Institute, which was located in New Haven, about twenty seven miles south of Langtree.

She'd escorted Dennis to the Starbright Institute complex a day after she'd given Tina her written resignation from D.D.E., and was more than surprised at the ultra modern facility. Starbright had purchased a large former industrial facility on five and a half acres, which they'd converted into an educational and residential facility. Maryum had been told that this was the most complete, technically advanced program available to developmentally disabled adults in the state of Connecticut, and she wasn't disappointed.

On the day she and Dennis came to Starbright, one of the clinical assistants led she and Dennis to the Computer lab, where Maryum came to fully understand just how intelligent Dennis truly was.

"Mr. McClain, this is our computer lab. You're going to spend a lot of time here for the next few weeks." the woman addressed Dennis. She was a short woman, looking slightly older than her mid twenties, and possessing curly black hair that fell below her shoulders atop the white sweater she wore. More slender than Maryum, she paced around while speaking, though she seemed more animated than nervous. Her name was Ellen, and she was trying to make Dennis feel at home. "I'll let Ms. Dupaul place this pointer apparatus on your head so that you'll be able to communicate with us."

Maryum was happy that the woman deferred to her to place the contraption- it resembled a headband with an antenna attached to it- on Dennis. After a cursory explanation about how the mechanism worked, the woman motioned to the computer screen and keyboard that sat on the desk in front of Dennis. Maryum gently guided his hand towards the keyboard, whispering encouragement all along as she placed his fingers on the letters that spelled his name. Unexpectedly, he moved on his own, and picked out a score of letters, creating a message on the blue computer screen.

'HELLO, MARYUM!! GOOD TO BE WITH YOU!'

Maryum nearly gasped, though she quickly replaced her shock and surprise with a fervent embrace around his head and shoulders.

"Dennis, I'm glad to be here too!" she sobbed, knowing that she might have held him closely for the remainder of the day save for Ellen's equally astonished presence in the room. The three of them continued their tour of the center, Maryum walking deliriously close to Dennis as they embarked upon this unusually absorbing day when Dennis revealed the extent of his mental facilities in a way he'd not done during his time in D.D.E. Sometime before Maryum and Dennis left the Starbright Institute, Ellen had purchased two sodas from a nearby soda machine, one of which she gave to Maryum, before innocently posing a question.

"You know, I had a history professor during my freshman year at University of New Haven named Professor McClain. Dennis kind of resembles him. I wonder if they might be related?" she leaned back against a wall and sipped on her soda. Maryum stopped in mid sip, nearly choking on the knowledge that she'd not done enough to find out about Dennis' family background. Thus, not long after she and Dennis left the Starbright Institute, she gleaned whatever information she could get from the group home where Dennis currently resided, then looked up the name of Darris McClain in the New Haven phone book. Even scarier, she telephoned him that evening.

"Am I speaking to Professor Darris McClain?"

"Yes. Who is this calling?"

"Professor McClain, my name is Maryum Dupaul. I'm a graduate student at Langtree College, and for the last two and a half months, I've been working with your nephew, Dennis."

"Miss Dupaul, I don't have a nephew named Dennis that I know of."

"No sir, I figured that you might not be aware of his existence. Did you have a sister named Sofia Zettie McClain?"

An ominous silence haunted the next few moments, before Maryum related the nature of her involvement in Dennis' life, and how she learned of his background. Two days later, Maryum would meet Darris McClain.

Darris and Cornelia McClain were somewhere in the middle of their fifth decade of life, though Maryum thought them both much older. The three of them met in a small, green colored room at Starbright Institute, furnished with only a classroom desk, a small table with a telephone on it, a gray filing cabinet off in a corner, and a leather futon in a pine frame masquerading as a couch. Darris was of medium stature, with shocking white hair, and a nose that reminded Maryum of a sweet potato. He adjusted the tortoise shell glasses that sat above his nose and shrugged his shoulders as if he wanted to take off the gray wool business jacket he was wearing.

Maryum could sense that Darris and Cornelia, she shorter and heavy set, but with a slender nose and dark chocolate complexion in contrast to Darris' own walnut coloring, hadn't been prepared for the phone call they'd received two evenings prior. Then again, Maryum pondered while pouring slow drip coffee into a paper filter, what must it be like to have learned in one evening not only that your long lost sister had been dead for more than two decades, but that she'd also given birth to a severely disabled son who was your eldest nephew?

"Thank you for coming. Would either of you like some coffee, or tea?" Maryum nervously pointed to a nearby hot plate sitting atop a short gray filing cabinet.

"No thank you, Miss Dupaul." he spoke. "If you don't mind, I'd like to know the facts concerning my sister and my nephew."

"I understand." Maryum pursed her lips and looked down at the computer generated papers she'd pulled out of her black book sack. "I tracked down Dennis' birth records yesterday and learned that he was born in a hospital in Richmond, Virginia, on February 15th of 1974. His mother, Sophia…"she noticed Darris wince at the mention of his sister's name. "…was a student at nearby Virginia State University. I'm assuming that she never told you her whereabouts when she went to college."

"You're right, Miss Dupaul." his eyes were as wet as an overflowing water fountain. Cornelia handed him a white handkerchief from her gray alligator purse, and he swabbed his eyes mournfully. "My sister and I left home about the same time. I up and joined the Army.

"The term 'Dysfunctional Family' wasn't the rage back in our day, but it would have fit. My mother had nine children from three different men. My father….left us when I was only five. Then my mom took up with Sophia's daddy just a year or so later."

Maryum noticed Cornelia touching Darris on the arm, and wasn't sure if Cornelia were trying to comfort her distraught husband, or admonishing him not to talk about it anymore. Maryum wasn't even sure she wanted Cornelia in the room at this point, but she wouldn't interrupt Darris as he continued his sad family history.

"Sophia's daddy was named Morgan. He worked the docks in Elizabeth City, North Carolina, and further south. He got kind of frustrated, though, and drank away most of the money he made. He and momma used to argue all the time and sometimes, he'd beat her. He'd beat us too. When I was twelve, he left momma for a younger woman with no children. Momma didn't take that too good, and started drinking heavily herself. When I was fourteen, she died. My siblings and I buried her out in the woods near Roanoke, and we went to live with my grandparents."

"I am so sorry, Mr. McClain." Maryum conceded, suddenly wondering if she really had any legitimate complaints about her own upbringing.

"There's nothing to be sorry about." he assured her. "All of this happened long before you were even born. Anyway, a few years after momma died, some of the older children left home to join the army, go to college, work, or something besides the poverty and misery we'd already been through.

Sophia had diabetes growing up, but she was smart as a whip. Finished high school by the time she was fifteen. She got a job the next year with the local office of the Social Security Administration. Figured out how to secure loans and grants to go to college, and never told anybody about her plans for the future."

"Again," Maryum asserted. "I'm sorry to be the one to tell you of her death. After she died, Dennis was placed in a series of different foster homes before winding up at Langtree College D.D.E. program where I met him. It was just the purest of chance that I was able to locate you at all."

"No." Darris added thoughtfully. "I don't believe that God does anything by accident. You found us because of Sophia's boy."

'Sophia's Boy'

Even after learning the truth about his birth and circumstances, Maryum hadn't thought much about the family she knew Dennis had to have. She knew of the foster homes he'd lived in over the course of his life. Some were good, some were not so good. She often wondered how he attained such intelligence and knowledge given his sometimes chaotic existence, but she'd wondered even more about how deeply she'd begun to care about this stranger who'd entered her life in such amazing fashion. The last few days had been a brand new world of learning and growth for the both of them, and Maryum couldn't imagine how anyone so deeply intelligent had avoided madness in the face of the neglect he'd endured. The memories of his first 'Hello' that afternoon at Starbright remained grafted on her thoughts, and she'd nearly cried when he later wrote on the computer screen, 'THANK YOU FOR GIVING ME A VOICE!'. The sight had been far more welcome than the dark blue sky outside of the airplane window by which she sat. Maryum blinked her eyes, disbelieving and disappointed.

'Damn! I'm still on the airplane.'

A prim, nearly middle aged stewardess with perky blue eyes, passed through the center isle, dispensing peanuts, soda pop, water, and various distilled spirits to the passengers. Maryum raised her eyes towards the blond, blue suited flight attendant as she approached.

"And what would you like to drink, Ma'am?" she flashed an almost sanguine smile.

"I'll take....a shot of bourbon, with a beer chaser."

"Ma'am?" the attendant looked mystified.

"It's called a Boilermaker." Maryum crossed her arms and stared at the back of the seat in front of her. "It's a very popular drink in the Midwest."

For a moment, Maryum thought the woman wasn't going to oblige her, but then the attendant dispensed a can a beer and a mini bottle of Bourbon before receiving Maryum's payment and moving on to the next passenger.

Maryum poured the beer in the plastic cup and emptied the miniature bottle into it before lifting it mournfully to her lips.

"To long life, and for better days ahead."

Taking a long look out the airplane window, Maryum threw her head back, and quickly swallowed the strong, bitter concoction she'd blended. It stung. It burned. Maryum gasped for air, whispering her struggle to regain her breath lest she awaken the sleeping old man in the seat next to her.

The beer and bourbon stung, just like her remembrance of the last few days, memories of the last time she'd given this blessing, as well as the events preceding and following it.

"Maryum, is all this really called for?" Tina tried not to sound desperate as Maryum gathered all of her materials from the gray metal desk near the back wall of the classroom. "Can we talk about this, please?!"

"There's nothing to talk about, Tina. What's done is done. Now you have to talk to county social services. Not me." Maryum was abrupt and aloof as she rose from her desk and walked over to the wall behind Tina to remove the planning calendar and the mahogany framed poem, 'If' that hung beside it.

"Maryum, this isn't the way to handle the situation, okay?! I'm trying to keep an open mind, but you're not making it easy."

"No. I don't intend to make it easy." Maryum turned around and crossed her arms defensively. "You had the chance to do that yourself when I told you abut Dennis McClain, and all I got was laughed at and denigrated. I needed your help when the unholy trio made my life miserable, but you couldn't see past the smoke screen and use your position to make those guys understand how important their jobs were."

"Maryum, social work is a tough field. Turnover rate is sky high and we're lucky enough to get people working here, let alone trying to hang on to them."

"Oh come off it, Tina!" Maryum angrily snatched the framed poetry from off the wall. "You need to get your priorities straight. The purpose for this program is for teaching people skills needed for living. I know that most of the clients here will never be rocket scientists, but they need a lot more than rented videos, MTV, and extended afternoons soaking up rays in the parking lot. Something more than what's going down here as of this moment."

"But, Maryum, your decision to make a complaint to county services only made the situation bad for the college and this program. I know that you want to do your best for Dennis, but was starting all this controversy really the way to do it?"

"I don't know, Tina. But we'll find out soon enough." Maryum reiterated before dropping the poem into a large box atop the desk. She closed it before picking up the box and leaving Tina with one final warning. "And Tina, it's gone beyond merely my complaint, now. Langtree County social services will be sending out subpoenas and all that crap. So I'd advise you not to speak to me again. It might come up in the hearings, and you don't want to face charges of obstruction of justice, or anything like that."

Then she left the D.D.E. building and set her course to wherever the day, and the next day after, would take her. For the most part, it held further involvement in the life of Dennis Williamson McClain.

"To long life, and for better days ahead." Maryum clinked two champagne flutes loaded with sparkling apple cider together and then lifted one to her lips as she placed the other to Dennis'. He smiled. She returned the smile and comfortably touched him on his forearm as they sat together in the guest house on the property owned by Darris and Cornelia McClain. The one acre property consisted of a large wooden white house, and a smaller one which was being renovated and rewired in preparation for Dennis' permanent habitation. The houses were surrounded by lush, green foliage and trees of all kinds, perfect for the children Maryum knew that Darris and Cornelia had never had.

She'd wheeled Dennis into the house by the wooden ramp which Darris had gotten constructed onto the front door soon after learning of Dennis' existence. From there, work had begun on enlarging the confines of the guest house, as well as the main house, to enable Dennis to get around without difficulty. Dennis was examining the computer system he'd been assigned by the Starbright Institute, as Maryum observed the various symbols on the keyboard apparatus that enabled him to project his thoughts on the computer screen. He was enjoying this new way of communicating.

'Yes' flashed on the screen. 'I wish you long life as well, Maryum. You are,' he paused before going further. '....the best friend I've ever had in this life. Thank you for being there.'

"You're welcome, Dennis." she blushed and set her champagne flute down before looking at him meaningfully. She saw the image of Dennis' sentence on screen and almost regretted that before too long, Starbright would also provide him with one of those horrible sounding electric voices. Better for now, she thought, to enjoy reading his thoughts as they were simply spelled out before her. "I just hope that I'm always available to help you when you need me, Dennis."

'As do I, Maryum. At times, I think you are the only one who's ever tried to understand me. For so long, to be aware of so very much, to feel and know as I do, but to be unable to make others understand. Were you not there, I think that I might still be lost inside myself. Do I make sense?'

"Yes, Dennis. And my whole reason for helping you was because I knew you were capable of achieving more than others thought of you." she voiced almost affectionately

'I'm glad.' the screen lit up again to match Dennis' eyes, which were equally bright. 'Tomorrow awaits us, and I'm eager to continue on. There's so much to learn.'

"For sure, Dennis. We all have a lot to learn," Maryum whispered as she raised their glasses again to share another sip of cider.

'I think.....I am ready to go to bed.'

Maryum accompanied him to the bedroom as he commandeered his electric wheelchair to the place of repose. She helped him undress and gave him a bath. Then she kissed him goodnight, before shedding her own clothes and lying besides him in the bed.

Thoughts of that night, as well as the traumatic morning after when Cornelia unexpectedly entered the guest house, returned to the distraught young woman sitting in seat 53B. 30,000 feet in the air, somewhere between her dismal departure from Langtree, and her uncertain arrival in her native Philadelphia, Maryum couldn't rid her thoughts of the wise, intelligent one who'd been trapped in a body that could not give expression to what was within, prior to her entrance into his world. It had been the most wonderful night of her life, and lying beside him, she knew that nothing was ever to be the same again. She'd felt an ecstasy unexpected from the warmth of his heartbeat, a gentle throbbing she felt against her chest that spoke of the life that flowed within him. Maryum hadn't counted on this, or his fragile body responding to her affection as she lay beside him.

"Oh,…God!" she'd whispered when she felt Dennis enter her. She didn't think that he was capable of such, but when he showed her otherwise, Maryum returned the fledgling passion with sweet ministrations of her own. Probing hands sought after the whole of Dennis, and she kissed him with an abandon unlike any she'd shared with her able bodied lovers in times past. It was a wonderful night that should have led to a joyful sharing of the morning sunrise, rather than the ugly encounter that awaited them with Cornelia's arrival upon the scene.

On the flight home, Maryum drank the remainder of the bourbon and beer, and ordered a second one. She drank again, the 'Boilermaker' quickly sending it's inebriating message to her brain. Not long after the plane's arrival at Philadelphia International Airport, Maryum stopped at a lounge adjacent to the terminal she'd arrived in, and ordered a number of straight scotches as she tried to escape the memory of she and Dennis' last night together. But escape wasn't to be hers. Not even as she gathered her bags and walked outside the terminal in search of a taxi cab.

Her eyes blurred by tears, her mind fogged by scotch, beer, and bourbon, Maryum stood on the curb of a sidewalk and tried not to cry. Tried to hide the pain inside of her as well as the knowledge that this time, love had cost her the best friend she'd ever had in this lifetime.

"My friend," she whispered as a yellow cab slowly approached her. "how could I .....let myself lose you?"

5

Wednesday night evangelistic service was always a joyous affair for Rosalie Dupaul, even if it meant driving all the way from Glen Olden, to North Philadelphia. She could deal with the hustle, haze, and squalor of the north side of the city when in route for her spiritual 'Fix', though one night, she hoped not to play so much attention to the broken windows in the abandoned factory next door to the church parking lot.

North Philadelphia Apostolic Center was located on the corner of Phillips Avenue and Fifty Second Street, thirty blocks and more than thirty years removed from the old Church of the Lord Jesus Christ, founded by the late Bishop C.J. Johnson. Schism and personality conflicts erupted during the ascension of Bishop S. McDowell Shelton to the church's leadership after the passing of Bishop Johnson in 1961, prompting seventy or so faithful ones to bolt from the old church on Twenty Second and Bainbridge, to seek hallowed ground somewhere in North Philly. The following years saw a massive increase in church membership and community influence, but North Philadelphia Apostolic Center never strayed from their roots of holiness, heavenly mindedness, and hellbent devotion to 'The Apostle's Doctrine', as Bishop Johnson was fond of saying.

This Wednesday, as usual, the church was filled with music, ecstatic worship, and rejoicing born of hope to rise above the misery and hopelessness just outside the church doors. Hands were held high towards heaven, voices lifted up in song as a crescendo of joyful music rose above the day to day pagan world that most of the parishioners would return to after worship services were over. Rosalie Dupaul was one such worshiper.

Having devoted herself again to the worship of God through the Lord Jesus Christ, the last year of Rosalie's life had surely been better than the almost three decades of sorrow spent with Gerald, time lived in denial of that which she'd fervently believed all of her life. He'd been gone for nearly a year, leaving her free to express the love of Christ which had sustained her though a lifetime she'd spent too much of in denial.

Rosalie was at last free to raise her hands, shout, and sing along with her fellow brethren in Christ. Free to praise God in response to her redemption.

Free from that infidel she'd married, who'd robbed her of joy and chained her heart and hands to something other than the love of Christ Jesus. Safe and secure from all alarm, leaning on Jesus, leaning on Jesus. Leaning on the everlasting arms. Leaning.....

"I want to welcome all the visitors with us here tonight, as we worship God in spirit and truth." bellowed Elder Maltin Nakoosh. Tall, large, and darker than oil, Elder Nakoosh was the young successor to the throne of Johnson, Shelton, and many others following in the Apostolic tradition. Dressed in a white robe and wearing a Kente cloth African scull cap, his full face was already breaking out in a sweat, and he hadn't even started preaching yet. He gripped the pulpit and looked out towards the eager congregation, then snuck a peek at the blue robed choir behind him before addressing the young woman he'd noticed walking into the sanctuary through the center doors directly across from him. "Yes, we are all one fellowship in Christ. One Lord, one faith, and one baptism. And miss, we extend an open invitation to you as well. Please feel welcome to join us as we worship the Lord together."

"Beeeeeeealch!!"

Wantonly leaning against the just closed church doors, the woman's essence of alcohol acquainted everyone with her inebriation. Numerous heads turned in response, getting a glimpse of the one emitting such noxious odor, and spawning whispers which shouted that something was definitely not kosher in the lord's house this evening. The eyes of all waiting not upon the Lord, but beholding the haunted eyes of the disheveled female who'd uniquely announced her presence. Rosalie quickly turned around, and gasped at the sight.

"Maryum?!" she left her seat in the pew, quickly ushering Maryum out of the sanctuary and into the nearby ladies restroom, where the next act began.

"Maryum, what are you trying to prove?!" she angrily ran some cold water in a sink. "You didn't let me know you were coming home, and then you show up here too drunk for words. Have you lost your mind?!"

"Gee, Ma. I've been too busy dropping out of school and avoiding a lawsuit to give it much thought." Maryum ran her fingers through her scalp, before briefly dipping her face into the sink and coming back up for a dripping response. "I also spent the last year or so trying to figure out why you and daddy waited damn near thirty years to finally split up, when you could have just got an annulment ninety days later. Nothing makes a lick of sense, Ma, so I decided to go get seriously fucked up."

"Maryum, you don't understand what happened between your father and I."

"Wrong!" Maryum quipped while vigorously splashing her face again. "I knew that you two were headed for divorce court by the time I was five. Maybe you just had to stay together and be happily miserable....I mean 'Married'."

"Your father and I did what we had to." Rosalie almost sobbed. "We did our best for you. You're being way too ungrateful."

"Yeah! I guess I am." Maryum stood up, wiping her face with a paper towel. "I'm real 'Ungrateful' to expect sanity from you-hooked on Jesus, 'Hallelujah'!-or from Daddy out there in 'Nirvanaland'. Especially now with him busy starting a new generation with a woman young enough to be my sister. My, ...'Big', sister. Oh....shit".

She clutched her stomach before bolting for the toilet in the stall behind them, kneeling over the bowl, and howling passionately in release of everything previously consumed that evening. Maryum faintly heard the parishioners of North Philadelphia Apostolic Center as they sang songs and delivered shouts of praise in the sanctuary she'd just desecrated. Her tortured groans and intense retching were as intense as the 'Amen's and 'Hallelujah's elicited from the worshipers, though she didn't share their enjoyment. And Rosalie could only mourn at the present distress of her unhappy, surviving offspring.

For Maryum, homecoming was a long, incoherent experience of which she had no recall. She didn't remember getting back home, taking off her clothes, or even putting on a pair of pajamas before collapsing on the twin sized bed in the gray walled room that she'd spent the last nineteen years of her life in.

She scarcely noticed the night sounds drifting in through her open window, as the streets of Glen Olden township, a few miles southwest of Philadelphia, had yet to be rolled up and put away for the evening. Out there, cars passed each other on busy highways, local pubs and diners were alive with customers. Even the stray sound of a howling dog from a neighbor's back yard waffled in to Maryum's sleeping ears, but her mind refused her the privilege of waking due to the stimuli outside her bedroom window. It was her ever active imagination which didn't surrender to slumber.

'Where am I?' she questioned, just as the dreamscape delivered her to New Haven, placing her back in the guest house of Darris and Cornelia. She remembered the pale green walls, the wooden floor, the ceiling that ever so threateningly loomed to fall on her. She lay on the bed she'd shared with Dennis, clad only in a ghostly white night shirt, and felt hands reaching down upon her shoulders. Gentle hands touched her, caressed her hungrily as she lay there.

'Dennis?!'

Yes, Dennis stood above her, and looked at her with love touched eyes.

'Standing? How can you be standing?!'
Indeed, he walked around to face her.

'This isn't happening. I know it can't be!, but yes it was. He stood beside her as she breathed and waited. He was tall, and beautiful, and naked as he bent over to kiss her, and then he was gone. Maryum's eager lips found their mark a brick wall in a strange, dark landscape that came to life the instant her lips touched Dennis'.

"No, no, no!! Noooooooooooo!!! she screamed and pounded the wall. All around was darkness, and dreadful fear that she couldn't break through to reclaim her lost love.

"Dennis! Come back!! Come baaaack!" she cried even louder, desperately yearning for him, beloved and vanished behind a dark brick wall that she pounded and beat until her hands bled, staining the nightshirt become prison.

"No!!" her eyes opened painfully to the morning sunlight, and she nearly gagged on the fresh air stampeding into her unprepared lungs. Bright sunlight flooded in through the bedroom window, and Maryum was surrounded in blue and green bedspreads, as well as yellow pajamas. Gray and red wallpaper stared out at her from four walls closing in on her intimate agony.

"Auugh." was Maryum's next utterance, words being overcome by her discovering the miserable flavors lingering on her beleaguered taste buds-too many beers, shots of bourbon, scotch, vomit- and Maryum questioned the wisdom of drinking heavily without brushing her teeth before finally going to bed.

"Please, God, strike me dead before I ever think about getting drunk again." she closed her eyes and shook her head to clear the cobwebs, but ceased doing so when she felt something akin to a trip hammer land in her central nervous system. She opened her eyes again and spotted the framed pictures on the wall above her chest of drawers. They were old pictures, telling stories of times happier than this morning. "I'm serious...God. I can't do this..... hangover shit....again."

She rose from her bed and walked past the wall bearing the pictures, her first destination being the white tiled bathroom two doors down from her room. It might as well have been two miles given Maryum's unsteady gait and nausea, but she arrived there safely and opened the mirror door to the medicine cabinet on the wall. There, she found shaving cream, tooth paste, antacid, laxative, and even an old bottle of hydrogen peroxide, which was probably flatter than a three year old tire. Everything but what she wanted.

"Aspirin. Gott?! Where is the ....damn aspirin? Mother? Mother?!" she raised her voice, only to get quiet immediately after she felt the pressure from her mouth shoot up to the center of her aching head. She determined not to say anything else, lest she screamed for pain, before leaving the bathroom and returning to her room to rummage through a desk next to her chest of drawers. "I hope there's... something... in this desk."

She thought aspirin, Tylenol, or perhaps a Magnum 357, while opening the desk drawer, even as her eyes became drawn again to the medium sized pictures hanging on the wall. Framed in mahogany and sporting pictures of Maryum through various ages, the black and white photographs had survived the ravages of time and bore no hint of the troubled lady who now beheld them. Maryum recognized the girl in those pictures; the naked newborn lying atop soft cotton bed sheets; the ten year old trying to smile despite embarrassing braces; the girl soon to become a woman, adorned in her high school graduation cap and gown. She was that girl. It was when she opened the desk drawer in search of aspirin that the confusion got deeper.

"Oh,...dear God. What is...this?" she whispered half in pain, half in wonder, while discovering an old family album with a gray poster board book cover. An heirloom loaded with pictures she had scarce recall of having ever seen before.

She scanned the old pictures, some of them of her parents, some of them her and Rod, all the while wondering when anyone had the time to make this collection of the various slices of life she and her family had tasted in times past. Her attention was finally riveted to a color photograph taken during a summer's day when she couldn't have been much more than a year old. Amid the foliage and plant life adorning the back yard of their old house in North Philadelphia, stood her very pregnant mother, and her father. They were younger, not as somber as she remembered them being during her childhood, though not by much. Perhaps they were trying to muster some joy in anticipation of the one soon to be born into the world.

"Rod." she whispered tearfully while remembering to take some flowers to Rod's grave at Mt. Lebanon Cemetery, later in the day. "I wish you'd been born into a happier situation."

She looked again at the little girl in the picture, wondering how and why the child was forced to grow into the sorrow she now endured, only to see a similar sadness looking back at her from the haunted eyes of the only person in the picture she didn't recognize. The toddler still in diapers, blue cotton tee shirt, and pigtails had to be her, but this man standing between her and her mother, she did not know.

Maryum looked closer at the man, tall and dark complexioned, with a later than five o'clock shadow on his face, and thought that he resembled a walking memorial stone. His attire of blue jeans, unpolished army combat boots, and wrinkled loose gray cotton shirt, suggested that he was either unworried, or unmindful about starch and steam irons. Even weirder, his head hadn't been combed in a long while, his 'Natural' growing into something more ominous than a mere Afro.

"Maryum?"

Maryum heard her mother's summoning, just as she'd noticed the eerie resemblance she bore to the stranger. Those eyes, those lips, that nose; she eyed her high school picture, comparing it with the unknown person in the middle of her family picture, just before grabbing a white terry cloth bathrobe and returning to the bathroom for a shower. Soon, she was on her way downstairs, greeted by the smell of coffee, which competed with the monstrous throb in her head. Each step down felt like a descent into the abyss, and Maryum was relieved to have arrived in the kitchen, where she sat at the green porcelain breakfast bar adjacent to the stove. Rosalie was cooking scrambled eggs, before looking up to see her daughter. Adorned in a gray morning coat, and wearing a pink stocking cap on her still uncombed head, she spoke softly.

"Good morning. I'm glad you finally made it out of bed."

"I'm not." Maryum admitted, feeling wasted, worn out, and well over the line that said too much.

"Had a bad night, huh?" Rosalie handed Maryum a steaming cup of black coffee.

"Ma, I apologize for last night. I got pretty ugly with you."

"You were drunk, Maryum. Drunk folks can act pretty stupid."

"Maybe." Maryum sipped her coffee, immediately feeling the nauseated resistance of her taste buds. "But being drunk isn't a good excuse. Nothing comes out of a drunk that wasn't already there during the sober, and there are better ways to say what's disturbing you."

"Then I guess I should apologize." Rosalie opened a packet of artificial sweetener, pouring it into her coffee mug. "Your father and I acted pretty stupid ourselves this year."

"But, Ma, you and Daddy had to bury Rod. Whatever went down with you and dad is still no excuse for my acting the ....ass." Maryum apologized. "Excuse me."

"You're excused. So what's this about you dropping out of school?" Rosalie picked up where last night's lurid conversation had left off.

"Oh. The D.D.E. program is under investigation for reports of abuse and mismanagement. I filed two complaints against the program, and things started to snowball when other people came forward with complaints of their own. I....actually have to go back in two weeks and testify at a hearing."

"That's too bad. But it's no reason to be dropping out of school." Rosalie rose from the bar and walked back to the stove to retrieve her scrambled eggs. She brought back a mixing bowl full of the fluffy yellow breakfast and

N. Wilson Enoch

sat it, along with an extra plate, in front of Maryum. "Eat. You need your strength."

"I think...not." Maryum responded dreadfully, her lingering unease announcing that stuffing eggs down her throat would be a really bad idea. "And there's more to it than just my filing the complaints. There was...this guy. This very....special...guy."

"Was he in the program too?" Rosalie wondered, while spooning up a plateful of eggs.

"Yes. His name is Dennis McClain." she put her coffee back on the saucer and folded her arms pensively. "He suffers from severe cerebral palsy and has to use an electric wheelchair to get around in. He couldn't communicate verbally, either."

"Maryum, you didn't get romantically involved with this person, did you?"

"Yes, Momma, I....did. I was instrumental in getting him into a better program at Starbright Institute, where he has access to computers and augmentive technologies. When he was finally able to communicate with me....it was.....beautiful. I mean, he expressed himself like nobody else I'd ever known. And then....things kind of developed from there."

"Wait a minute. This boy couldn't speak? Couldn't tell you how he felt about you?" Rosalie puzzled while looking up from the eggs she'd scarcely eaten.

"He could,..... once we got him to Starbright, and gave him augmentive devices. He told me everything that was inside of him, and I didn't have to guess what his heart was saying.....to me." Maryum rose from the bar and walked over to the kitchen window above the sink. She wanted to behold the back yard, rather than cry in front of her mother. "Things got real complicated after that. The state board began an investigation of the D.D.E. program. The college tried to discredit my testimony, and they got a perfect weapon..... after Dennis and I....slept together."

"What?" Rosalie rose from her seat and joined her daughter at the window. Seeing Maryum's downcast, tearful eyes, she was torn between shouting her displeasure, and placing a comforting arm around the young woman. "You had sex with this boy?"

"He wasn't a boy, Momma." Maryum sobbed, the large vein near her temple rising and throbbing, adding more hangover pain to the heartbreak she suffered. "Dennis was....is....a grown man, with hopes and dreams like the rest of us. He didn't ask to be born into the world with a body that imprisoned him."

42

"Maryum, I can understand you trying to help him, but to get involved with him like that?!" her voice was brittle, and Rosalie's eyes weren't particularly understanding at the moment. "We taught you better than that, I thought."

"Momma," she sniffled and wiped away tears before placing her hands on the sink counter and opening her eyes again to turn towards Rosalie. "How....could you have married Daddy if you didn't love him? Maybe...... I didn't know Dennis all that long, but I loved him. God knows, nobody has ever touched my life like he did. Should I have said no, just because he was....disabled?"

"Child, there's a lot more to the story of your dad and I that you just don't know about." Rosalie eyed her determinedly. "And it's high time you learned that sometimes, you just have to walk away from love."

"Momma, I know that you'll probably always think of me that way, but I wish you wouldn't call me 'Child'."

"Oh yes I will. You're not acting very mature these days, Maryum. You need to start thinking with more than just your glands."

"Point ...well taken, Ma." Maryum surrendered while sitting in a nearby seat. "But that still doesn't answer my question. How....could you marry Daddy if you didn't love him? Rod and I suffered through your wedded misery for nearly three decades, and I'm still trying to figure out why you'd subject yourself, and us, to that."

"Maryum.....your father is the reason I had to walk away from love." she spoke with painful fragility. "I did love your father, a long time ago. But that bastard wouldn't act right to save his life. I couldn't beg him hard enough, or long enough, so I left him behind. I thought.

"I married Gerald back in sixty six, but your father wouldn't let go. And for awhile....."

"Mother? What do you mean? What....are you telling me?!" Maryum's heart was in her throat. "Does it have anything to do with the stranger in that old picture album I found upstairs?"

Rosalie didn't answer, her face taking a sour down turn.

"Mother, who is that man standing above me, between you and Daddy in the old color picture?"

"I should have thrown that damn thing out years ago. Taken that picture and burned it."

"Mother, who....is he? Just tell me the truth."

Rosalie exhaled wearily before answering, wincing at the revelation of things long buried and never mentioned; things that from the sound of her voice, still resounded painfully against the background of long, wasted years and sorrow. Maryum heard, felt, all of her mother's angst, and nearly gasped when her mother at last named the culprit in question. 'James'.

Maryum recalled her parents mentioning James at some point in her childhood, but like the haunted man who'd stood above her in the picture, such conversations remained a mystery that just didn't happen very often. Nor could she ever remember the prefix 'Uncle' placed before his name, despite the realization of him being her father's brother, and now she understood why.

It was still late morning when Maryum took herself out to the porch of the red brick, detached row style house she'd shared with her parents and brother in the years prior to her military service, and college education. She sat in a yard chair underneath the shade that the low roof provided her from the rampage of the already blistering morning sun. Still adorned in her terry cloth bathrobe, her bare feet straddling the cold concrete floor, and enduring a steaming fresh cup of coffee as she held it in her two hands, Maryum contemplated the senseless procession of events and revelations that had marred the last few days of her life.

Pain lingered in her head, like a nightmare of drunken antagonism that wouldn't be pacified in the uncertain morning after. Maryum took another sip of coffee, hoping to push the nausea far from her consciousness, though Rosalie had warned her that at least a day would pass before she started feeling normal again. Certain that she never wanted to have another hangover, Maryum figured that she either had to stay drunk, stay sober, or find some happy medium between those extremes. Then again, there were other thoughts of consequence tugging painfully at her. James was one such, his name a painful drop in the ocean of strangeness she felt hopelessly adrift in the middle of.

James, who she'd never met, but who now haunted her thoughts following her mother's devastating revelation. She now knew that the one who'd raised her and called her name in a loving, devoted fashion all her life, wasn't the one who'd fathered her. A stranger, she thought dejectedly, had loved her mother. A stranger who'd inflicted himself on her mind only an hour ago, even though it felt like a lingering essence that she'd never escape from.

Maryum tugged at the belt of her robe, deciding it was time to go back inside and get dressed before sorting out the rest of the day, as well as her life. She had to find her dad, or perhaps she should call him 'Uncle Gerald', since she now knew all the gory details.

"God, Momma. Why couldn't you have just married my father?! Was trying to make him do right....worth nearly three decades of misery?" she sullenly choked back tears and vomit. The sun was almost at mid sky, and it was going to be a long, hot day.

BOOK TWO

LOST SOULS

6

A cold rain blanketed the southeast end of Baltimore, Maryland, on what should have been the first warm day of spring. Somewhere between the Baltimore-Washington Parkway exit on 33rd Street and the Fort McHenry tunnel, was the row house where James Spencer had settled so many years ago. Nestled on the corner of the only dead end street in the neighborhood, James had liked the place when he first saw it, and bought it outright in '67', while still gigging with the band. The extra cash from he and Cut Throat's enterprises had come in handy, and he was happy to have had a place for the band to crash when they took their tours up and down the east coast. It was even better for him when things got bad after August of '68', and he came there to surrender his soul to sorrow. He'd lived through the rough decade between '69' and '79', and had finally resigned himself to the decline that had come to the neighborhood in the wake of crime and crack cocaine. James beheld the dingy row houses of the street block, and recalled how they'd once reflected the pride and joy of the persons who'd lived in them, loved in them, made their lives-and their families lives-in them. Looking out the window of the two story red brick house that he dwelt in and remembering the better times, he was saddened.

The streets were littered with garbage, broken glass, liquor and beer bottles, rusting automobiles that hadn't rolled in years, and all matter of debris and evidence of the human neglect that now afflicted the community he'd grown to love. He briefly ran his fingers through his gray, dread locked hair, which fell in long tentacles reaching beyond his shoulder blades. He picked up his saxophone from the coffee table, then placed the reed to his lips and blew. His instrument produced a long, low, mournful sound that seemed to bounce off the white walls of the house he shared with her. Jasmine was her name, he reminded himself as he stood up and began walking on the dull oak floors and up the staircase that lead to the room where she'd lay down to sleep so long ago.

Jasmine snored softly, and did not stir on a queen sized trundle bed that had seen better days. James continued to blow his sax as he beheld her, thinking again of the first time he'd seen her, walking barefoot and wearing only a cotton bathrobe and white hospital nightgown in freezing temperatures at two A.M. on a cold February morning in 1969. His bleary eyes had seen many strange sights in Baltimore's infamous Red Light district, but none so astonishing as this sad slip of a girl wandering aimlessly over the cold landscape of East Baltimore Boulevard. Amidst the hookers, hustlers, pimps, pushers, policemen, and other representatives of humanity who haunted the streets that morning, Jasmine was a glaring anomaly and rebuke to the populace at large. Rushing from the greasy spoon diner he'd been eating in, James threw his heavy coat around her, unknowingly pledging his life as a service and bondage to this woman who now slept on the bed in their row house. This woman who'd colored his world with slumber and dreams since that February morning so long ago.

7

Jasmine still dreamt of Dorian, and cherished his memory. She held his face before her dreaming eyes, day in and day out. He'd been beautiful and she'd never forgoten that, in spite of the ugliness that had torn him from her. His touch, so strong and yet so gentle, was like a cool rain on a hot summer's day, quenching the long thirst of waiting and wanting that she'd endured for most of her young life. Jasmine had felt his wonderful hands all across her body and rejoiced with all her heart at the joy he'd raised in her with but a touch.

Dorian Scott was the oldest of five children born to Reverend Joseph and Mrs. Nell Scott. The oldest, and boldest-as some within the Southeastern Missionary Alliance For Justice leadership were known to say. Several inches above six feet tall and dark as a lump of clay, Dorian had always stood out in a crowd.

Jasmine had known him all her life. She'd grown up next door to him in rural North Carolina. They'd been friends and more, but circumstances separated them before the onset of her teen years. She wouldn't see him again until the summer of 1968, a few weeks following the closing of Resurrection City, the poor people's settlement of protest against the federal government in Washington, D.C., as planned by the Reverend Martin Luther King, Jr., before his tragic demise.

It had been a sorrowful spring; tears for Martin, tears for Bobby, unrelenting sorrow over the perceived death of dreams. Hopes raised high, like a toast at a festive New Year's Eve ball, had been thrown down and smashed against the rocks; savagely, horribly mangled and left to rot amidst the landfill of nightmare commonly called 'The American Dream'. That was the prevailing mood which Jasmine discovered upon entering SMAFJ headquarters in Atlanta on that hot evening in July of '68'. A few days later than eighteen, Jasmine had looked forward to coming here. She'd grown up admiring Dr. King, and cried upon learning of his assassination. Like many others, Jasmine longed for, dreamed of, and looked forward to making the kind of world that Dr. King, the Kennedy's, and so many others had given their blood, sweat, tears, and lives for. She would work to make it so. So would Dorian Scott.

"Folks, lets not deceive ourselves." Dorian spoke to an assembled crowd in one of SMAFJ's storefront offices. "A lot of folks in Washington, D.C. just aren't interested in the civil rights and well being of our peoples. Martin's gone, folks. Bobby's gone too. We live in a grim, sad nation that thinks nothing of knocking off leaders interested in justice."

Jasmine heard muffled agreement and even a faint 'Amen' or two in response to Dorian's message as she made her way into the crowded room. Most of the people wore black suits, and other church going wear that seemed out of place on this hot summer evening. She stood against the rear wall of the building, almost directly across from the makeshift podium that Dorian stood behind. Standing between a very dark, heavy set woman adorned in a light blue dress, and a balding middle aged man in a gray suit who fanned himself with a program, Jasmine immediately set her eyes on Dorian. She was beginning to feel the heat beneath her bright yellow and orange flowered dress, and also imagined that many of the listeners were feeling the same. The gray suited man next to her certainly did, fanning himself intently while smiling at the taller girl besides him. Jasmine returned his smile, but just as quickly returned her attention to Dorian, who'd removed his suit coat sometime before she'd walked in and was now loosening his tie.

"I've heard a lot of people tell me, 'I don't want to die, Mr. Scott. I don't want somebody to get crazy with a gun and kill me just because I raise my voice for freedom!' I understand that fear. Felt it too.

"Martin's funeral was probably the saddest I can ever remember attending. I was in Resurrection City the night that the hearse carrying Robert Kennedy's coffin passed by us. Too many people believed that this was the end; that our days of protest and power would soon be over. But injustice remains in the land, and so long as there's injustice, there will be people who fight to end it. My hope is that we won't get weary in well doing. That we keep trying to make things better, and make those who think we are finished with trying to effect positive change understand that we haven't even begun yet!" he paused, the crowd in the meeting hall affirming his fervor with more encouragement and determined 'Amen's.

Jasmine found the room's energy intoxicating, despite the smothering summer blanket that overpowered the window unit air conditioning and the circular fans that failed to make the place comfortable. She was eager to stay all night if need be to speak with Dorian, and was gratified when one of the ministers dismissed the group with prayer, though she found herself unduly engaged with the Reverend J. T. Williams, who'd earlier stood next to her on the wall.

"It's good for young people to be out here carrying on the fight for freedom." the minister spoke ever so enthusiastically as he shook her slender hand in both of his. "Just like Mr. Scott spoke tonight, we can't let ourselves get tired of fighting and struggling to make things right."

"My father always said that." Jasmine spoke as she picked up a paper cup of iced tea from a nearby serving table. "My dad and grandfather always believed it was better to work for our place in this land, rather than be oppressed."

"So tell me," Reverend Williams continued. "...what brings you to SMAFJ, tonight?"

"I start school at Morris Brown this fall. And I'm also a friend of Dorian."

"You are?! Well God bless you, sister." he gave her an affectionate pat on the forearm, but Jasmine would have felt better if Dorian had gotten loose from the throng surrounding him and greeted her with a warm hug. Eight years was a long time to wait to see him again, and she wasn't certain she could settle much longer for another sip of the not too sweet iced tea, and the company of Reverend Williams.

"Well, I have to ask, Miss..." he inquired.

"Simone. Jasmine Elisabeth Simone."

"Pretty name." he didn't miss a beat. "How did you come to meet Mr. Scott?"

"We grew up on farms next door to one another in North Carolina. His mother died in 1960, and his family moved up to Maryland soon afterwards. We've kept in touch and I thought I'd surprise him by showing up tonight."

'Surprise' was a mild word to describe what Dorian felt as he turned from the crowd and spotted Jasmine speaking to Reverend Williams.

"Jasmine?!" his attention was riveted to her, and he made a beeline towards her which more than dented the dense wall of astonished people taking note of their reunion. He could barely speak for the rush of emotions that rolled over him as he embraced her. "My God. You're finally here!"

Whatever else they said that night was scarcely remembered. They'd communicated years of love and longing in their fervent embrace at the center of the room, clinging closely despite the summer heat and the curious looks of the people surrounding them. It had been too long since they'd last laid eyes on each other, and their conversation extended way beyond the moment in SMAFJ headquarters, leading to a Friday afternoon a few days later when they were walking away from the campus bookstore at Morris Brown College.

They'd met somewhere between the English texts and writing materials, and soon after she'd purchased several textbooks for the coming fall semester, Jasmine and Dorian had departed the red brick and glass building, and were walking along the tree lined campus as they discussed their lives and their futures. They settled down to converse on a bench adjacent to a basketball court.

"Jasmine, I know that you're worried, but you have no control over the direction that your father chooses to go in."

"Maybe not," she leaned back on the bench, her eyes small, sad, and mournful as she shared things she hadn't mentioned to Reverend Williams several evenings prior. "…but it hurt to hear my father curse the things we'd grown up believing. He's sure that Elijah Muhammad has all the right answers, and that the Muslims will lead Black America to the Promised Land. All I see is a whole lot of hatred."

"That's sad." Dorian exhaled. "Our fathers shared much wisdom over the years, but learning this would break my father's heart. I've never accepted that we had to learn to hate the whites in order to love ourselves. Malcolm X moved away from that idea towards the end of his life, and Martin didn't believe it either."

"You miss him?" she perked up.

"I'm sad he's gone. I really didn't know him that long, but I liked him. It sucked that we worked in different organizations and didn't get to communicate regularly. I wish he was still here to help me with the Smyrna County project. I'm not sure how much help I'm going to find amongst the leadership at SMAFJ. They took the failure of Resurrection City pretty hard."

She was quiet as the late afternoon sunlight landed on her soft, caramel complexion. Her memories of the innocent childhood she'd shared with Dorian seemed a lifetime removed from the current burdened reality that plagued them both with misgivings about today.

"Dorian, I look forward to this project. If no one else believes in it, I know you do and that's good enough." she spoke expectantly. "I know that your mother is looking down from heaven and loving what she sees."

"Maybe, but Jasmine, I don't know if this country is even remotely interested in approaching anything resembling equality and justice for all people. My mother died eight years ago, painfully remembering some white folks screaming 'Nigger' as my dad took her home from the hospital for the last time. She wanted to live long enough to see a country where her children wouldn't have to deal with that, but she didn't. I'm starting to wonder if we'll ever get there, or if there's any good reason to keep trying."

"I can think of three good reasons." she spoke softly before pointing at three young boys approaching them armed with a basketball. Dorian recognized one of them as the oldest son of an SMAFJ staff minister. Dorian quickly smiled as the boys greeted him, slapping him five on the palms, giggling, challenging, and laughing as one of them bounced the ball in an almost musical cadence. The boys quickly engaged Dorian in a furious game of twenty one, while Jasmine remained on the sidelines, watching them with borderline envy. 'Mr. Scott' as one of the boys called him, seemed a natural on court. He jumped, ran, dribbled and twirled in a magical fashion, enchanting and fluid as a running brook like the ones Jasmine remembered from her North Carolina home. Dorian was poetry in motion as he shared the court with the boys. Jasmine listened and watched as the boys asked Dorian about things pertaining to basketball, and even when one asked him about God. Dorian reminded the child that God was always there, and always ready to give strength and courage to those that needed him. Jasmine smiled, long after the boys were gone, and she stood affectionately lost in Dorian's embrace at mid court.

"Those boys are the reason you shouldn't quit. Those boys will grow up to be men one day, and God help them, the country, and the world, if we haven't learned to live in peace by then."

Then she kissed him, as the horizon of their past began to fade into the instant of today, a lifetime of affection and commitment being renewed in the haze of late summer in Georgia. When last she'd seen him, he was slightly younger than adulthood. Then he was gone. Gone to Baltimore, Maryland, with his father, who wanted no more of life on the cruel North Carolina land under which his beloved Nell lay. Jasmine had mourned the loss of Nell Scott, as well as the loss of Dorian, whom she'd just begun to love. She'd waited eight long years to see him again, and had deliberately chosen to attend Morris Brown in Atlanta, since she knew that Dorian was working down there with the Southeastern Missionary Alliance For Justice. Low and behold, here he was, grown, beautiful, and full of love as she'd wanted, or wished for him to be. Of course, just like their last time together, forces conspired to separate them. This time, Reverend J.T. Williams fired the opening salvo of opposition.

"Brother Scott, why on earth do you want to go down to Smyrna County?!" Reverend Williams was a bit more casually dressed this day, sporting only a short sleeve, cotton white shirt, and a pair of navy blue straight legged pants. He wasn't even wearing a tie, though the veins in his neck were bulging out, pumping blood so furiously that it looked as though they'd burst wide open if he didn't calm down. "Son, I'm sure there's got to be better places for you to try and establish this project."

"Reverend Williams, the land on my father's deed is smack dab in the middle of Smyrna County. I'm sure there might be better attitudes further up the road, but that's beside the point." Dorian leaned back slightly in his folding chair. Again in the storefront office of SMAFJ where he's spoken only a few nights before, Dorian sat alongside Reverend Williams, as the latter uncomfortably fiddled his hands beneath a mahogany desk. Jasmine sat across the room on a church pew beneath the large storefront window bearing the organizational logo. She was also troubled by what Dorian was proposing, though not in the same way, or with the same vehemence as Reverend Williams.

"You're damn tooting there's better attitudes further up the road! Son, they haven't seen a black face in Smyrna County since they hung one in 1932. Them crackers don't give a rat's tail end about us down there. Probably got a sign hanging somewhere saying, 'James Earl Ray: American Hero.'"

"Reverend Williams, that black man they hung in 1932 happened to be my grandfather, but my father never stopped paying taxes on our land down there, and he swore that we were coming back one day.

"My momma died with the knowledge that she was leaving my father and her children in a world full of hatred and evil. But she never told us to give up trying to change this world for the better. As long as she drew breath, she never stopped trying to get people to see that we could make a difference."

"You're not listening to me, man."

"Yes I am." Dorian cut him off. "Smyrna County has some of the best farmland in the southeast. My family owns seven hundred square acres of land down there, and nobody can take it away from us. I've got commitment, capital, and manpower pledged from over twenty different groups, black and white. Not only can we establish a farm, we can create a whole new community based on equality and justice for all. God's love, my brother, will have rule in this place."

Reverend Williams raised his hands up from beneath the desk as he stood up and walked towards the middle of the room. He turned towards the west wall, where a picture of Dr. King hung almost reverently above a framed copy of the last sermon he preached in Memphis on April third of that year.

"Son, I can remember Martin saying things like that." Reverend Williams continued. "He had a big dream that we could all learn to live together in love and harmony. He even believed that SCLC and Southeastern Missionary could patch up their differences and work together in unity. He was my friend and I loved him, but he died behind that dream. He forgot that just too many people didn't share his dream."

"Can that be any worse than living in the current nightmare?" Jasmine unexpectedly lifted her voice, much to the annoyance of Reverend Williams.

"Miss Simone, I wish you wouldn't encourage him any further." he painfully divided his attention between them both.

"She doesn't have to, Reverend Williams." Dorian now stood. "My mind was made up a long time ago. Moreover, I won't let the reality of white men's bigotry rule my thinking and actions. The project has been two years in the making and we're close to fulfillment. We don't have time to try and make new plans."

"Dorian, I got no problem with the project. I just think that you can find a better location."

"There is no 'Better' location, Reverend Williams. It's time for America to realize that all their children have a right to the bounty and resources of the land we live in. If they hate me because I'm black, that still doesn't give them the right to destroy me."

"But they will, son. Nobody had the right to kill Martin, Bobby Kennedy, or his brother." a tear slowly rolled down Reverend Williams' face. "Those three boys killed down at South Carolina State back in February only thought they were protesting an all white bowling alley. I've seen too many good young men die violently this year. I swear, I don't want to see your face on the obituary page."

"I'd sooner die like a man standing up for what's right, than grovel like a slave or sub human. A life spent running from the opposition isn't worth living." Dorian announced, looking affirmatively at Reverend Williams. Jasmine left her seat and stood beside him, even though a small part of her felt the same fear that Reverend Williams had voiced.

Her brave persona aside, Jasmine feared for Dorian's life. Contemplated what might become of him beginning that day in SMAFJ headquarters, on through the establishment, consecration, and commission of the farm project in the fertile farmland of Smyrna County, though she was comforted by the knowledge that what she was doing with Dorian had to be right. It felt as right as the rain which fell on the night in late July, when she and Dorian basked in the afterglow of their first lovemaking, on the trundle bed in one of the corrugated metal structures that had been constructed on the acreage. Dorian was standing in the doorway, clad in a pair of blue jeans and a tee shirt, watching the rain fall on the as yet untilled ground. Jasmine came up beside him, working her way into a comfortable place between his arms where she could look up and kiss him on the side of his neck. She wore only the blanket from the mattress around her, and he smiled.

"Hi, Jasmine. You're awake."

"Of course." she confessed. "As small as that bed is, I still would have enjoyed you staying on it with me."

"Oh." he blushed. "I look forward to the day when we won't have to settle for a small bed in a corner of a temporary building. One day, soon, we're going to build a nice 'A' frame house to live in."

"Can we actually do that?" childlike curiosity was written on her face. She was happy to be alone with him on the project land, even though there had been threats of violence since the first day of their being there. The others involved in the project had returned to their homes in distant places, leaving Jasmine and Dorian alone to enjoy a south eastern Georgia evening, or fight off the rednecks, if it came to that. Then she remembered that several units of the state police were stationed nearby, and there might be some hope of rescue if it were needed.

"Yes, we can. The project's going to need some kind of headquarters once we really get started, and I'm sure we can work a little living space in for ourselves. I only wish that my dad could have come down, but his illness prevented it. I do hope he's well enough to come and perform our nuptials in a few months." his eyes twinkled brighter than the stars in the night sky as he enclosed her slender waist in his arms and nuzzled the back of her head. Jasmine smiled again, thinking fondly of the things he said, could see most clearly as she looked into his eyes. Eyes that she secretly feared she would not look into for very long.

Jasmine hadn't wanted to remember Reverend Williams' somber warning, 'Son....them crackers don't give a rat's tail end about us down there!', but it reverberated in her thoughts like a broken record she had no hope of shutting off. From day one, following the project's dedication, when several pick up trucks passed by with defiant displays of the Confederate Stars and Bars, on to the letters threatening all kinds of malfeasance if, as one of them so deftly put it, '....you niggers don't find another place to dig dirt in!', it became obvious to everyone working in the project that they just weren't welcome in Smyrna County.

"It ain't good enough that these nigg...., these civil rights agitators and communists couldn't leave things alone after they burned down Watts a few years back, and then tried to burn down Washington D.C., when that Negro, King, got shot. No, no!" the voice of a very agitated, presumably very white, man bellowed from the radio playing in the project's cafeteria tent. It was early afternoon, and the sun was an August dragon intent on thoroughly frying Smyrna County before September could make its rainy, cooling rounds. Sixty or so brave souls had gathered underneath the green canvas tent, sharing several tables, and a communal lunch of pasta, salad, garlic bread, industrial strength lemonade, and dire concern for the fate of the project. They couldn't have been encouraged by the further ranting of the nearly hysterical speaker.

"No, brothers and sisters, they ain't near satisfied! Jesus said in Matthew, chapter eleven, verse sixteen, 'We have piped for you and you have not danced!', and they're still not satisfied. Now they've come down to Smyrna so they can spread all this damn fool integrationist insanity. Where is it going to end, brothers and sisters? I can hear the voice of the psalmist crying real loud.

Why do the heathen rage?! Why do the people imagine a vain thing?! I want to know 'Why?!' brothers and sisters. Why, why..."

Dorian flipped the 'Off' switch before the third 'Why?!', much to the pleasure of those sharing lunch with him under the tent. Peter Maxwell, sandy haired and blue eyed, raised his sweaty brow up from the plate of spaghetti he'd been wolfing down, and affirmed his happiness at Dorian's action.

"I'm glad you did that, man. That guy doesn't speak well for the white race."

"Actually, I'm more ashamed that my 'Brother' in Christ doesn't even understand the gospel he's supposedly preaching." Dorian added.

"What really makes me angry, is that this person might be perfectly at home in my native Belfast, were he to change his words from 'Black' to 'Catholic'." came the voice of the Right Reverend Richard Bascombe, fresh from Northern Ireland and still adorned in his black suit and Anglican collar despite the heat. His short gray hair lay limp and moist against his scalp, and seemed the only part of him unduly affected by the scorching summer heat. "Like a lot of persons, over there and here, he doesn't realize how anathema the true teachings of Christ are to the reactionary, separatist drivel that too many of us persist in to our destruction."

"Amen to that." Dorian added while putting some Parmesan Cheese on his pasta. Jasmine left her place behind the makeshift sink and large oil drums converted into a grill and hotplate, bearing a bowl of spaghetti and tomato sauce in her arms while making her way across the hard dirt floor underneath the tent. Stopping at this table and that to dispense the food to hungry people, Jasmine remembered that September wasn't that far away. Fall semester, football season, placement exams, the works, awaited her in not too many days. The better part of a July and August working the farmland of Smyrna County had taught her much about sharing and communing with strangers. Strangers who'd become brothers and sisters, though she wasn't ready to say 'In Christ', as did Dorian, and so many others in the project. Jasmine wasn't ready to pigeonhole her spirituality into any particular religious concepts as yet, nor would she lump Dorian, Peter, and Reverend Bascombe, alongside those who abused the name of Jesus with their racist drivel, denouncing anyone who didn't fit into the mode of White Anglo Saxon Protestant. In fact, she was still thinking about the racist minister she'd just heard on the radio, when the sudden noise of white hooligans reached her ears.

"Hey black niggers!! This here is Smyrna County. Clear out before we run you out!!"

Everyone in the project looked up from their meal to observe four white men driving past the tent, rolling wildly through several stalks of corn and other crops that were just beginning to sprout. The red truck was old, worn down by time and the brutal weight of hatred infecting the men riding in its cab, as well as the two standing in the back, arrogantly waving the Confederate battle flag. As disturbing as the noise of the hecklers was, more disturbing was the sudden breaking of the spaghetti bowl as Jasmine dropped it to the ground. She screamed, and the sound was akin to the tearing of whole cloth mingled with flesh and blood.

"Jasmine?!" Dorian leaped from his seat besides Reverend Bascombe, hurriedly rushing to wrap his arms around her. "Are you alright?"

She sobbed as he surrounded her affectionately. Many under the tent rose up as well, rushing to grant her mutual support in response to the ignorance displayed by the hecklers. Long after the red pick up truck had faded from sight, Jasmine still clung to Dorian, grasping him as though she never wanted to let go.

"Don't worry, Jasmine. They're just a bunch of rebels who haven't figured out that the war ended more than a century ago. They're cowards. We won't see them again."

Painfully, horribly, Dorian was wrong.

Two nights later, the same white men encountered Dorian and Jasmine as they walked together from one of the few local stores that dared permit the project settlers to patronize them. It wasn't a pretty sight.

"Didn't we warn you, boy?!" Dorian was being unduly addressed by the ugliest of the foursome, while two others bodily restrained him. The man spit his chewing tobacco on the ground before striking Dorian hard across the jaw with his fist. "Bingo."

Jasmine struggled against the white man holding her tightly. She and Dorian had only gone to the store to get some soap, and hadn't counted on encountering these angry white men who'd not taken the time to get adorned in their dress white lynching gear. The fearsome foursome had corralled their prey, speed and reckless driving combined to force Dorian and Jasmine to leave the road they'd been walking on, and run for dear life through the woods and trees where the truck shouldn't have been able to follow them. But it could.

"Listen here, boy." the man was still chewing on his tobacco and loading up for another spit as he pulled Dorian by the collar for a closer look. "This is white man's country. Always was, always will be. You niggers need to move on before it's some real bloodshed. Yours!"

"You..."Dorian tried to speak despite his busted lip. Pain from blackened eyes, broken nose, swollen jaw, and other assorted injuries, was almost impossible to break through. "…cannot stop….what has begun. My people, my family…are part of this land, as are you. It is our right…."

Dorian's words were cut short by the sharp impact of an axe handle against his rib cage. It hurt too much for him to say another word, or even think of pretending that he hadn't felt it. A long gasp escaped from him, echoed fervently by the desperate cry that escaped from Jasmine.

"No!! Don't kill him, please!!"

The man holding her, dark haired, smelly, and missing a front tooth, tightened his forearm around her throat. "Now you hush up, missy! Fore we have to get started with you."

"Leave…her alone.!" Dorian elicited through pained lips.

"Right now, boy, I think you better worry more about what's going to happen to you." the first man took off his straw cowboy hat and spit on the ground before addressing Dorian again. "Ways I see it, two things can happen. One, we can let you go so you can get this stupid farm project stopped. Or two, we can hang you from one of these trees so's your friends can get the message. What's it gonna be, boy?!"

Struggling mightily against her captor, Jasmine hoped that for once in his life, Dorian would chicken out. Cowardly submit to deceit in order to save his life. Though she knew it most unlike the Dorian she'd grown to love and care for, this once, she wouldn't have minded that. So long as he didn't die.

"This is….our land!" Dorian doomed himself. "We…will…never be driven…from it!"

A taut rope thrown across a tree with the noose end wrapped around Dorian's neck was the response to his brave, but fatal, declaration.

"This…is….our land! My family's… land. We….will….NEVER….leave it! Jass…."with his dying breath, he called out for her, her whispered name being his last earthly statement. His mind was full of the horrible knowledge that her last memory of him would be his limp, battered body hanging from a moss covered oak tree. Even worse, he knew that the white men would kill her as well.

"Nooooo!! No, no, no!!!" she collapsed, beating her fists on the ground and swallowing dirt with every sorrowful breath. She looked most pitiful to a red headed white man who'd left the other two at the hanging tree, his faded denim overalls bearing a hint of Dorian's lifeblood. The one who'd held Jasmine captive looked up to see the approach of his partner in crime before looking down at Jasmine.

"I reckon we gon have to kill her too, huh?" rotten tooth questioned, as though his foul embrace hadn't been enough.

"Well, she don't look like she'd mind a little roll first, Lige!" the big red haired one spoke humorously as he walked up and grasped Jasmine by the hair. She rose reluctantly, her palms sweaty and caked with dirt and blood. Red hair licked his lips, anticipating a jump between her thighs to cap off his evening, not a stinging face full of rock.

"Gott....damn!!" his eyes were flooded with warm, red blood that blinded him to Jasmine's further mayhem as she turned to bash his unprepared partner, and then returned to pummel the red haired one mercilessly with the large, sharp stone she'd happened on during her collapse to the ground and hid beneath her gray cotton blouse. There wasn't even time to protest as Jasmine rocked the second man into unconsciousness. Of course, big red was still able to loudly complain.

"Clem! This bitch is killing me!!"

Her first blow had smashed one of his eyes, and left the other blinded by a torrent of blood. Nor did he care for long as she smashed the rock into the left side of his head. The duo still standing under the branch from which Dorian hung heard the commotion, saw the unthinkable- 'What the hell that girl think she's doing?!?'-and began running towards her at breakneck speed. Jasmine was ahead of them. Way ahead.

Through the hideous dark of a Georgia forest, Jasmine ran as though hell were chasing after her. She couldn't hear the white men running desperately behind her, didn't hear their cursing or lament, nor knew that they'd abandoned pursuit about the time she entered into Farmer Gilmore's property. His cornfield, to be exact.

"Shit! Ain't no way we go into old man Gilmore's cornfield." the first man spoke in terror.

"But, Clem," the second exhaled, short, fat, and in bad need of a hedge clipper for his wheat blond hair. "...she'll tell the cops if we don't catch her. We got to catch her, Clem!"

"No fucking way! Gilmore is mean as hell, and I'll be damned if I'm crossing him."

"Clem, Gilmore ain't never burned a cross with us. He might even help that girl out!"

"You damn fool! Go ahead and run through that cornfield. Get cut to pieces like she do. Maybe you want to be dinner for Gilmore's hound dog, or catch the business end of his double barrel shotgun. Pick which way you want to die, man! Gilmore might not hate niggers, but he sure as shit hates anybody stupid enough to run through his property."

It was a grim enough decision, chancing the girl's escape, but Clem wanted no parts of Mr. Gilmore. His fat associate was either too cowardly to act otherwise, or silently in agreement.

Dejectedly, almost sadly sympathetic, they watched the pitiful girl as she ran heedlessly through the cornfield. They wouldn't stay around to see her finally end her run. Jasmine was panting bleeding, covered with welts and bruises that screamed vehemently at elderly Farmer Gilmore, who heard his hound howling and his chickens squawking, before exiting his small house to behold the cause of the commotion. His curiosity was shockingly satisfied by the sight of this black girl too horrified to scream any more. He nearly did it for her.

8

It had taken Maryum the better part of three days to recover from her hangover. Her first,

and she swore to God and her mother, that it would be her last. From Thursday to Sunday, she'd felt as though she were struggling with a twenty ton truck rolling through her head and guts. Rosalie had warned her that hangovers were cruel like that. She'd also invited Maryum to go to church with her that morning. Maryum might have been amused at another sight of holy rolling ecstacy exhibited by the parishioners at her mother's church, though the looming reality of seeing her father quieted her faintly humorous introspection. Instead of tripping up to North Philadelphia with her mother, she rented a lime green Ford Taurus sedan and made haste across the Ben Franklin Bridge on highway 676, that would take her into Pensaulken, New Jersey.

She still coped with the reality of having learned that her father, who'd raised her, sang her lullabies, told her stories of the world she'd one day be a part of, changed her dirty diapers, wiped her snotty nose, consoled her broken heart when needed, administered strong discipline when called for, married and eventually walked away from her mother, wasn't the one responsible for her being brought into the world.

"Jesus, ma." Maryum whispered just as a traffic jam developed on the bridge. "I could have gone a whole lot of years without finding this out."

She also could have skipped the potato salad that her mother had packed in a small plastic container for the trip, having eaten a morsel or two after entering the crowded bridge, only to discover that the sunlight through her windshield had dried it out and destroyed the flavor. What wasn't destroyed, was her confusion about this morning's destination.

'Mindful' most occupied her thoughts following the dispersion of traffic and her finally getting across the bridge. She recalled her mother's commentary about her father's new locale.

"He's living in some new age, free love, pacifist, pagan, heathen, commune. I don't mind him leaving, Maryum, but I don't understand how he wound up in that place. Go figure."

Maryum could hardly figure it out herself, questioning everything about what had transpired over the last year. Her parents hadn't been in love when they'd married, and their mutual love and commitment for she and her brother hadn't been enough to keep them from eventually walking away from one another. Maryum wasn't surprised to know this. Indeed, she wondered why it took them this long to split up. But Gerald's conversion to this new religious lifestyle, as well as his eleventh hour remarriage to the woman who bore his son three days later, left Maryum with endless questions, and sheer disbelief.

She'd made it through the intersection of 676 and highway 30, when the second word of consequence came to mind. Brandon.

'My little brother?!' she recalled, thinking in disbelief some three months ago when she'd gotten the post card from her father, announcing his birth. She'd spoken to her dad a week earlier, and Maryum mentally replayed the phone call, all the attendant emotions tugging at her mercilessly.

"Daddy, how can you be getting married again this soon?!" she'd angrily questioned. Wincing at the memory, her hands choked the steering wheel as the sound of her father's apology replayed in her heart and mind.

"Baby, try to understand. Your mother and I tried really hard. We gave it our best shot, but there wasn't enough love there to keep us together. Her heart didn't belong to me, Maryum. Maybe it never did."

"Daddy," she was despondent. *"I don't understand this at all. The divorce was just finalized last month. I've never met Brianne. How am I supposed to act towards this woman you left momma for."*

"Sweetheart, I didn't leave your mother for Brianne. If anything, I tried to keep my distance from Brianne. But things just ....happened, once we found ourselves together in Mindful."

"Daddy, you're calmly telling me that you hope the preacher pronounces you and Brianne husband and wife before she goes into labor. Do you really expect me to be supportive after learning this?!"

Little more than ninety days later, Maryum was on her way to find out how supportive she'd be, as well as to meet her new stepmother, and younger brother. She'd called Gerald on the phone the previous morning, well aware that he really wasn't her father. That also meant that Brianne wasn't her stepmother, and that Brandon couldn't actually be her brother, half or otherwise.

"Oh please, I don't need to think about this right now." she lied to herself while turning off highway 30 to get on to River Road. The area had become more forested, primeval almost, yet she couldn't surrender her mood to the green serenity of the pleasant woods surrounding the road. She focused her attention on the task ahead, knowing she'd need all her faculties to drive the car and arrive at 'Mindful' safely.

'Mindful' was a planned community constructed on 6500 acres of pristine woodland near a crystal blue lake in a northwestern corner of Pensaulken, New Jersey. 'Mindful' was populated by a coalition of devout Buddhists, Unitarian Universalists, ecological activists, organic farmers, vegetarian and non militant animal rights activists, artisans, musicians, and a whole host of people who didn't exactly fit into any particular designation of the American cultural mainstream. Many of the buildings were constructed of materials salvaged from several demolished apartment complexes, and a condemned hotel from Camden, New Jersey, which prompted one newspaper columnist to refer to the community as 'Recyclable'.

Maryum had forgotten her drunken description from the other night, 'Nirvanaland', though she remembered it just before arriving at the stone and glass gate reading 'Mindful', adjacent to the highway and preceding the large parking lot a few yards inside. A large wooden sign placed strategically underneath a newly blossoming oak tree, gave her the first hint of the difference she was in for.

'No automobiles are permitted in the residential, recreational, or agricultural areas of Mindful, without prior permission of the community. Transportation by bicycle, or group bicycle, is permitted. Walking and running are also encouraged.'

"What?" she wondered while reading the sign. Leaving her car and walking several yards away from the parking lot, Maryum spotted sparse gravel roadways leading towards the assorted tree lined expanses, dwelling places, gardens, recreational fields, meeting halls, and other areas of this unconventional community. Large plots of Bamboo, fern trees, and other manicured vegetation greeted her near the front of the community. Moreover, she noticed the absolute lack of noise-cars, buses, heavy machinery and the like-that she'd normally associate with a community of people. A few yards later, Maryum noticed the landscaped area on a nearby hill, and couldn't help scratching her head at the sight she witnessed transpiring. A group of sixty five people, all ages, genders, ethnicities, and even a few seated in wheelchairs, were following the lead of a tall, gray haired man, who was doing Tai Chi movements. Everyone was engaged in slow, fluid movement of their hands and bodies as the leader progressively lead them through the gentle postures of the system.

"Good grief. I think I've died and gone to the Shaolin Temple. Tracey, you ought to be here for this." she mused, suddenly missing her friend and wishing for her company. Her yearning was soon answered by the racket of a bicycle chain, and she turned to see a middle aged man dressed in loose white oversized pants, and an orange tee shirt, riding towards her. The man, slender, with grayish brunette hair, was wearing a blue baseball cap and a smile as wide as the horizon as he slowed down in approach to Maryum. The bicycle was equipped with two wheels in the rear, and a rickshaw like seating between the two wheels. She'd never seen anything like this in the western world, and Maryum started to wonder if running might not be a bad option after all.

"Blessed afternoon!" he exhaled. "Welcome to Mindful. Can I give you a lift anywhere?!"

"Thank you but no." she blushed, forgetting the Shaolin Temple in favor of maybe Shangri La. "I think I feel like walking."

"Walking is fine." he left the bicycle, taking off his cap and revealing a balding pink pate. "It's a great day to walk. If this is your first time here at Mindful, I'm happy to give you any directions."

"Actually, could you direct me to Sankofa Dwelling? My father...and his family live there."

"Well, you're in luck." the man stated clearly. "I happen to live in a single's cell in Sankofa. I'm on my way there, so why don't you hop in the back?! I'd love the company."

'This...is not happening.' Maryum mused inwardly at the evidence of her senses, even as she wondered whether her prospective chauffeur had taken leave of his. Still, she hopped in the back seat, and they got underway. Her driver, who identified himself as Raymond, hummed some music that closely resembled a mantra, even as Maryum questioned who on earth, besides an inmate in custody, would think of their living space as a 'Cell'. That was when Raymond inquired about her father.

"His name is Gerald Dupaul."

"Oh, yeah. 'G'! I see the family resemblance."

Maryum said nothing, hoping to arrive at Sankofa soon. A few minutes later, they arrived at a large, multi leveled, brick and cordwood structure seated in a grove of pine and oak trees. The house was a combination of 'A' frame and contemporary architecture, with three geodesic domes placed at both ends, and in the center of the sprawling, V shaped construct. Twelve to twenty thousand square feet of living space stared her in the face, and the bouquet of flowers, trees, and decorative foliage that surrounded the facility worked to counter the minor warfare that raged inside of Maryum. Riding along with Raymond, she'd done some mathematics in her head, and didn't like the answers. Remembering the phone call of three months ago, as well as the post card sent a week later, she surmised that her little brother had been conceived not long after Gerald had left home. Then she reminded herself; Brandon wasn't really her brother, and Brianne wasn't her stepmother, and Gerald....

'Shit!' Maryum thought as Gerald came through the polished oak door, shattering her momentary attempt at composure when he smiled at her as she descended from the bike seat. Gerald, tall and substantial at fifty one, had a pecan shade complexion, with closely cut black hair and a pencil thin mustache. He was wearing a light blue, Chinese collared cotton shirt, with gray sweat pants and Birkenstock sandals on his bare feet. He moved aside from the front door as Brianne walked outside to stand beside him. Waif thin and not resembling someone who'd recently given birth, the fair skinned woman-most obviously of mixed ethnic heritage-was a head shorter than Gerald, whom Maryum stood eyebrow level to. Brianne had almost translucent, yellow brown skin, and wavy black hair that fell to the middle of her shoulders. Her eyes matched the color of the sky, and her brown, paisley print caftan fell to her kneecaps. She was wearing bunny slippers, but no bra.

'Oh...my....God.' Maryum thought a half second before heartily embracing her dad, whispering, "Hi, dad.", in refusal of the nominal fact of his being her uncle. She'd never be able to think of him as 'Uncle Gerald'. His new wife was another story.

"Maryum," Gerald introduced by gesture. "I want to introduce you to Brianne Jocelyn Koral."

"It's nice to meet you, Maryum." she grasped Maryum's right hand with both of hers. Brianne's voice was strangely sing song, sounding as though she were searching for the right pitch. "Your father has told me all about you."

"Likewise." Maryum was as low key as the sole of her basketball sneakers, not committing herself because she wasn't certain she'd be able to. She also found it hard to stay focused on Brianne's smile with those bunny slippers looking up at her. Brianne then suggested that everyone step inside for some refreshments. Maryum was relieved, for the moment. "That'll work."

They entered a great room furnished with several large futon sofas, and plain wooden tables in the middle of a beige walled room above a hardwood floor. The smell of potpourri permeated the room, hanging plants descended from the ceiling, and there were antique light fixtures spread about to augment the wide windows on the eastern wall. Rows of books and CDs covered the west wall of the room. There was also an entertainment center in the corner at the end of the wall, with a stereo cassette/ CD player and AM/FM radio system, but strangely enough, no television. Things made even less sense when Brianne asked what everyone wanted to drink.

"Actually, an ice cold beer would be nice." Maryum admitted.

"Sorry. Not in stock, yet." Brianne responded. "We've still got a month to go until Vernal Equinox."

"Come again?" Maryum questioned while looking over at her father, who looked mildly embarrassed as he explained.

"The community is still processing part of last fall's harvest of grapes, hops, barley, and other crops designated for wine and beer making. The community grows all our food, and we seldom buy anything from the grocery stores. When we celebrate the change of seasons next month, everybody will get a generous ration of the products, provided they want some.

"I'm actually looking forward to this year's Zinfandel, since I'll celebrate my first year in Mindful about that time."

"Oh." Maryum surrendered, suddenly wondering if she seemed as strange to her father and Brianne as they did to her. "Then I guess I'll settle for lemonade."

"Lemonade it is. Ice cold, too." Brianne affirmed from the kitchen counter. She placed three glasses on a serving tray and came to join Gerald and Maryum on one of the futons. They sipped their lemonade, they spoke, they tried to act normal, but the high pitched cry of a baby was the closest to normality that Maryum had perceived so far, preventing her from asking something akin to 'Why don't we all just chant?!'.

"Oops!" Brianne arose and walked out of the great room, leaving Gerald and Maryum alone for more pertinent conversation.

"Dad....I don't understand."

"Understand what, Maryum?"

"Why her? Why...this?" she put down her glass, the neutral turn of her lips becoming a frown. "This scene doesn't remind me of you at all."

"I know, Maryum." he turned his full attention to her. "It didn't remind me of myself for a long while, but I finally ran out of reasons to say no to joy."

"Joy?" she was almost incredulous.

"Yes, sweetheart. Joy. That stuff that life is too short of for the most part. The last year of my life has been the most joyful I can remember since the time you were Brandon's age and I bounced you up and down on my knee. That meant a lot to me, and there just weren't enough moments like that up until now."

"So you just had to go find somebody half your age and repeat the experience, huh?!?"

"It's not that simple, Maryum. And Brianne is thirty six. That's not half my age." Gerald set his glass on the nearby wicker coffee table. "After nearly three decades with your mother, I was tired, miserable, hopeless, and wanting to kick myself for trying to make the situation work, when we both knew that we should have never married in the first place. After we separated, I unexpectedly encountered Brianne when she came to Temple for graduate school. She enrolled in one of my courses, and told me about this community she was a member of. One thing led to another...."

The sound of soft padding on the hardwood floors, as well as Brianne's whispered singing interrupted Gerald's explanation. Maryum looked to the side of the room and saw now barefooted Brianne walking back into the great room, carrying her infant son.

"Sorry. Brandon is hungry. The boy eats all day long." Brianne unabashedly smiled as she sat in a mahogany rocking chair directly across from Gerald and Maryum. She unbuttoned the top of her dress and placed her son's lip to her nipple. From there, Brandon took over as Brianne settled into a steady, rocking routine while Maryum briefly swept over them with her gaze. She looked back at her dad just as Brianne spoke again. "Your dad tells me you're a grad student at Langtree, up in Connecticut."

"I....was." she demurred, as though she'd fired a gun into someone's skull. Gerald was taken aback by Maryum's tone, sitting up and fixing his eyes on her. Brianne continued to rock as Brandon quietly nursed, but her face radiated overwhelming concern, or perhaps confusion. Maryum felt confused as well. This man could not be the same one she'd called father for so many years. He was never this relaxed, this uninhibited, this....

"Funky, Dad. Everything going down seems so strange and outright... funky." Maryum confessed as she and Gerald took a walk down a tree lined path leading away from Sankofa Dwelling, towards some of the other areas of 'Mindful'. Brianne had stayed behind to make lunch, and Gerald was holding Brandon as Maryum tried not to get distracted by the sights around her. There was a lake nearby, where she noticed several adults sitting near the shore, watching some children frolic in the water, which couldn't be that warm despite several weeks of springtime weather. A fourteen year old girl wearing a sleeveless men's undershirt and bikini panties, was splashing around with three naked toddlers, and seemed to enjoy herself with abandon. Maryum didn't eye them for long, continuing her conversation with her father.

"I was nearly named in a lawsuit due to my sexual activities with a former client in the D.D.E. program. The state is on the college's case for abuse I reported, the college is trying to use my post D.D.E. activities to discredit me, you and mom get divorced, then you turn around and start a whole new family. I mean, everything seems to be spiraling out of control."

"Or maybe it's just flowing along like a river into the ocean." Gerald spoke affirmatively. "I didn't count on Brianne entering my life when she did, or for this little guy showing up either."

Maryum pursed her lips, hoping to appear thoughtful when in truth she was trying not to gag. She was uncertain about her father's counsel, which seemed to amount to him suggesting that she 'Veg' out and observe the happenings affecting her, even if they were chaotic and negative. She also tried not to be resentful, thinking bitterly, 'My mother can't start over like this.', though catching sight of Brandon didn't help. He was a brown little package of a child, with perky blue eyes like his mother, and curly black hair that faintly surrounded his head. Brandon quietly looked over from the security of his father's arms, and Maryum reminded herself that this child had no control or responsibility over how he'd entered the world.

"And I guess I didn't count on learning about your brother, James."

"Then your mother told you the truth about your parentage."

"Yes, but that doesn't change anything, Dad." she reflected. "I don't know James. You're the only one I'll ever call 'Dad'. Everything I learned, I got from you and mom."

"I'm glad to hear that." he almost smiled, but then turned noticeably glum. "But I'm concerned about what you've just told me about your situation."

"Don't worry, Dad. For a time, I thought of remaining at Langtree since I only have a few credit hours and my dissertation to complete my doctorate. Of course, the psych department wasn't too happy with me after all the controversy I started." she exhaled, while catching the sound of the children back at the lake. She briefly tuned around to see that the teenager had taken off her undershirt, as she and the little ones engaged in a water fight. The girl's developing breasts jiggled ever so slightly, leading Maryum to wonder if anyone was concerned about folks running around in a state of undress. But that was before she noticed one of the adults from the shore, a full figured, middle aged blond woman, kick off her sandals, and jump into the water to join the youngsters. Splashing and laughing as her white caftan like dress got soaked due to the aquatic fun. "I decided to leave the college. There was no point in staying around and pursuing my studies there, given how the atmosphere had become downright hostile towards me. I can maybe start over at Temple, or Penn State in the fall semester."

"Lawsuit, legal action, and sexual misadventure are nothing to sneeze at, Maryum." his tone was a bit more fatherly at this point.

"Dad, I loved Dennis McClain." she stopped walking, her eyes more than confessing her feelings. "We made love. I mean real love. The college tried to use our relationship as basis to discredit my testimony. Cornelia McClain, Dennis's aunt, threatened to sue the college if they didn't expel me, but they couldn't do that due to my good grades. They were worried that the state board might think they were retaliating against me. It was....a mess."

"So why didn't you tell me about it?" Gerald breathed heavily as Brandon wiggled against him.

"Dad, I couldn't do that. You had your life to deal with, and none of this was your problem."

"But, sweetheart, that's what I'm here for. I may have divorced your mother, but I didn't divorce you. I may not be the one who conceived you, but I was there for all the moments that followed. I plan to do the same for Brianne and Brandon."

"Tell me about James, Daddy."

"What would you like to know?" Gerald inquired, his big toe painfully kicking a small stone as he and Maryum turned towards the main gathering hall in the center of the community. Their walk had taken them past the lake, scenic gardens, and assorted paths placed between the immense foliage and tree growth of the land. Notwithstanding the variety of strangers and pilgrims wandering about, most of whom greeted them with 'Blessed Afternoon', Maryum concluded that she and her father could have been in a much worse place. Particularly when she, Gerald, and Brandon had arrived at a large, 'A' framed structure constructed of smooth cedar logs and rammed earth, with a gray metal roof. They walked inside the building, which consisted of a large main hall with blue- green carpet, and hundreds of portable chairs, several anterooms that opened to the main space, stark earthen walls, generous glass windows at both of the 'A' frame ends of the building, and artful chimes of glass, metal, and fishing wire that hung from the ceiling. For a moment, Maryum almost forgot her original question, sitting down in one of the chairs as she observed the magnificent, yet strangely simple facility.

"Woah." she whispered. "This is some place. I bet Elder Nakoosh would love to have church in a place like this."

"We'd love to have him, but I suspect that he probably thinks we're stone heathens." Gerald was comical as he searched in his green diaper bag for a bottle to satisfy Brandon, who'd started fidgeting. "You were asking about my brother?"

"I saw his picture in my bedroom in Glen Olden the other day. The one you took when I was still in diapers and Momma was expecting Rod. I noticed something....strange about him."

"Strange?"

"He seemed.....lost." Maryum continued cautiously. "He looked like he was missing in action. You understand, Dad?"

"I understand, Maryum. You were too young when that picture was taken. You couldn't have known my brother and the demons he fought with. It took us a while to deal with having different fathers, but we got over that by our teen years." Gerald hefted Brandon up higher on his chest, as the child consumed the contents of the bottle. "James was the musician of the family. I played basketball and majored in English. Curtis and Regina were the brainy ones who went to MIT and Harvard, but James....that boy picked up every instrument he could find and he played them. Played good, too.

"He was a real ladies man." he smiled. "I envied him for awhile. But when he came to visit after the summer of 68', he'd changed. The day that picture was taken, he told me he was trying to figure out what he was going to do with the rest of his life."

"What had he been doing?" Maryum piped up just as she got a nose full of broccoli, garlic, tomatoes, and other good things on the breeze that kicked in through the open window at the rear of the gathering hall.

"He'd been a member of a jazz band named, 'Axis'. They toured up and down the east coast for a few years, and James was one of the group's stars. He was doing pretty good until just before that weekend he came to visit us. He was hollow that weekend. Something terrible had happened to him, and I knew he wasn't ever going to be the same. I never saw him again after that, although he did send me a postcard from Baltimore a few years later."

"Baltimore?" she wondered as the three of them rose to return to Sankofa, and what smelled like a wonderful lunch.

Lunch consisted of spaghetti with fresh tomatoes, basil, and Parmesan cheese; stir fried broccoli with garlic and almonds; and a fresh salad made of dandelion leaves, lettuce, spinach, wild onions, raw cashews, and some other greens that Maryum couldn't even dream of identifying. Maryum, Gerald, and Brianne washed down their victuals with a big pitcher of fruit punch, and there was no lack of satisfaction. Despite her previous distractions and trepidations, Maryum was enjoying the meal, and for the moment, the company of her dad and his new spouse.

"Brianne, this is really good." Maryum admitted.

"Thanks. Your dad is helping learn how to cook more than just corn flakes."

Everybody laughed, sort of. Maryum surrendered to cheerful levity, even though more than a small part of her thought that this scene might make a great subject for her dissertation once she got reestablished at another college. Her next thought emerged as an almost pointed question.

"Dad, do you still have James' postcard?"

In an old mahogany desk resting in the darkness of the group house's basement, Gerald located the card. His face took on a sad look that blended in perfectly with the subdued illumination of the gray basement. Maryum cut on the nearby light, which showed the trace of a tear rolling down Gerald's cheek. The sight made her wish that she'd left the lights off.

"A little more than twenty five years ago....James sent me this." he spoke sadly. Maryum examined the card, which had the old Dupaul family address in North Philadelphia written in the address column, but the rest of the card was blank, save a brief statement on the left that had been scribbled seemingly as an afterthought.

"Dream. Love, James." Maryum whispered before turning the post card over to see the picture on the other side; the name of the city placed atop a photograph of a street lined with lovely row houses.

"I miss my brother." Gerald was mournful, pain creeping across his previously serene demeanor. "I don't know why he left. I don't know where he is, and I can't figure out why he'd have ever left you behind, Maryum."

"Perhaps it's just as well." Maryum was forlorn, knowing full well her next destination on this road trip just happened to be Baltimore. All that she knew for certain at the moment was that she had a lot of tough questions to ask. Questions she wasn't sure she was ready to ask, not certain she'd understand why she was asking, nor prepared to cope with the answers, particularly if they were answers she hadn't wanted to hear after all.

9

Saul Ravensword was bored.

Two hours into this formal party disguised as a book signing, Saul once again realized just how unimpressed he was with this rich and beautiful crowd who'd gathered together to celebrate his latest literary accomplishment.

Saul swept his blond hair from in front of his eyes and surveyed the room packed with the formally dressed, fawning, adoring crowd that he didn't identify with. He eyed his watch while drinking his cranberry juice, hoping that time would move on and he could depart soon, or that the people he noticed crowding the salad bar wouldn't take away all the veggies before he got there.

Looking down at the formal black suit that seemed to have been sprayed on his slender body, Saul found himself weary at the thought of turning forty in a couple of years, and even wearier at the prospect of enduring more moments like the present.

"You know, I just.....loved.....the way you killed the psychopath in 'Dark Side'." she was blond, model thin, and probably not yet thirty; not quite coherent, and wearing a pastel blue, floor length halter dress. "Having those corpses....slowly stuff him....into.... a garbage disposal....was pure genius."

"Really?" Saul pretended well, but inebriated people didn't impress him. The aroma of Dom Perignon had overpowered any appreciation he might have had for her figure.

"Yeah." she quipped excitedly. "I just....love the way....you wake up sub.... unconscious demons and turn them into....full fledged monsters."

"Well, that's what a good writer does." Saul spoke softly as he and the woman walked towards the center of the large ballroom, hoping that by the time he reached the salad bar, the blond would be gone. Much to his pleasure, she'd departed his presence, but he wasn't pleased with the absence of endive, carrots, tomatoes, cucumbers, and other vegetables he'd hoped for upon finally making it to the food. He'd really wanted to get something else to eat, and he'd rather not have encountered Leonard.

"Saul, I've been looking all over for you, man." Leonard Katzman was fifty three years old, twice divorced, and an editor at American Reader's Press.

Shorter than five ten, almost an eighth of a ton fitting snugly in his black formal suit, with a balding pate surrounded by a long crescent of grayish black hair, as well as a groomed goatee, Leonard fixed his wild green eyes on Saul. He made less than a dent in the cacophonous hordes inhabiting the ballroom this evening, and normally, Saul liked Leonard. Tonight, he'd sooner see the return of the black plague.

"Hi, Len." Saul grabbed a fresh bottle of cranberry juice from a nearby bowl of ice. "Thought I'd see you sooner or later."

"I'm happy to see you too." Leonard proclaimed. "'The Night' is flying really high, Saul. We're number one on the New York Times Fiction best seller list as of today."

"I'm ecstatic." was Saul's droll response. He wasn't sure which scenario was worse; the adoring public drunk on alcohol, or Leonard drunk on editorial power.

"Well, I hate to throw a wet blanket on the party," Leonard responded to Saul's obvious sarcasm. "…but the execs at ARP are getting nervous about your new book."

"I'm not nervous." Saul twisted the cap off the bottle. "I haven't started writing the damn thing yet."

"But can you maybe give me the outline so I can show my senior editor something?" Leonard nervously shoved his sweaty hands into his pants pockets.

"Can't." Saul replied after taking a long sip from the bottle and facing Leonard. "Haven't started writing that either. I'm suffering a little writer's block."

"Saul?!" Leonard exasperated while flinging his hands out of his pockets and adopting a confused posture. "How can you be suffering writer's block? I've known you to start writing your grocery list and turn it into a best selling epic. Writer's block?!"

Actually, Leonard was a poor second in Saul's thoughts at the moment. Catching sight of a tall, athletic looking young lady with tousled blond hair pinned behind her head walking towards him, Saul found himself inspired to perhaps write some poetry. She wore a strapless white chiffon gown, and had exercised the good sense to wear white leather flats instead of heels. Even better, her smile looked genuine, not due to inebriation, and she had a copy of 'The Night' in her right hand. Soreness of thumb and forefinger aside, Saul looked forward to signing her copy.

"Mr. Ravensword, I've been reading your books since fifth grade, and I'd be honored if you'd sign this copy for me."

"I'd be delighted." he smiled while pulling the ball point pen from his lapel. He'd also begun marking in the interior title page before noticing that he'd already cursively scribbled, 'Marc'. "And to whom do I dedicate this?"

"To Marcia. You can also mention my little brother Mark, since this is going in our home library. He's only ten, but he loves your stuff. How'd you guess the first four letters of my name?!"

"Psychic. Esp. I'm a little rusty. A decade ago, I'd have gotten all the letters without asking." he stammered, grateful beyond words that her name hadn't been Laura, or Grace. She laughed, so did he in relief. Then she thanked him before departing, never turning around to notice his fond look lingering on her as she rejoined the party. Leonard was not so inattentive.

"You know her, Saul?!"

"Not personally. She reminds me of an old friend."

"She looks young enough to be your college aged daughter."

"She could have been. Maybe." Saul humored, knowing that the girl, she'd called herself Marcia, had reminded him of another who'd been as inspiring as a lovely summer wind nearly sixteen years ago, but hadn't survived the bracing, icy chill of winter. It was winter to Saul. It had been winter since the ghastly spring of 1979.

"Saul?" Leonard was impatiently tugging at Saul's coat sleeve. "Talk to me, brother. What about your next book?"

"Leonard," Saul continued looking towards where Marcia had walked away to, briefly seeing her converse with another young lady, before losing her all together. "I've got three weeks before my deadline. I'll have the outline ready by then. Have I ever let you guys down before?"

"No. But I've also never known you to have writer's block either." Leonard was vainly trying not to sound nervous, and Saul didn't know whether to pity him, or shoot him through the head to put him out of his misery. Leonard Katzman, Saul lamented inwardly, had to be the only person in New York City, besides himself, who could be at a lavish book signing party-well stocked with great food, voluptuous women, beer, wine, and the finest liquor one could drink-and not enjoy himself. No, Saul thought. Pity would be too kind, but the bullet would cause too many legal problems.

"Well, Len, I'm fresh out of ideas right now. Any suggestions?"

"How about," Leonard fingered his goatee maliciously. "...a story where some embittered ex-husband dreams up a ghoul, or phantom, which goes off and murders his ex-wife and former mother in law."

"I don't think so." Saul swallowed his juice hard.

"C'mon, Saul. I'd love to see something like that across my desk. Maybe you could make it a newspaper report with Elinor's name on it."

"Wrong." Saul curtly faced Leonard again. "I used to be married to her too, remember?"

Saul handed Leonard the empty juice bottle and walked away, leaving him behind to stew in the vile broth he'd made for himself. As little as Saul had been enjoying the party, he was enjoying Leonard's company even less. He made one last pass through the maddening crowd before making a beeline for the door to the bedroom suite adjacent to the ballroom.

Whenever American Reader's Press threw him a book signing party, Saul insisted they get him a suite with a private bedroom he could retreat to when things got too thick. Between the crowd, the signatures, and Leonard's obnoxiousness, Saul needed a serious retreat. He entered the dark suite and cut on the light over the nightstand next to the queen sized bed, softly illuminating the whole room.

'Perfect!' he thought, while kicking off his black leather dress shoes, and tossing his formal jacket on a nearby upholstered white chair. Next came the black clip on bow tie, suspenders, and cuff links, that were discarded alongside the jacket. The room had a blue carpet that Saul's toes sank into as he walked towards the bed, plopping his long, slender body on the bed without pulling back the light blue spread that matched the wall color and contrasted with the white ceiling which his tired eyes stared at.

Saul stretched out and began doing some of the yoga breathing exercises he'd learned over the years to hasten his relaxation and well being, but he didn't close his eyes, knowing that such would be futile.

"Yut, ye, sam, sey."he counted in Chinese, seeking to relax his mind. Tonight had been emotional input overload big time, and he wondered why this couldn't have been one of those average parties where he could have easily walked away, as he'd been able to for so long. Save Marcia's appearance, Saul would have had a decently ambivalent evening, but her arrival had so unsettled him that he couldn't even dream of relaxing.

'Dream' he almost thought aloud. 'I'd give anything to dream'.

In truth, he hadn't dreamed, or even slept soundly since the last spring semester at Boston University, when he'd been rescued from the pool of drunken solitude he'd nearly drowned in by someone who'd inspired him even more than Marcia had. Tonight's vision was too much of a reminder of the all surrounding love that had granted him near salvation almost a lifetime ago, and who's absence had been buried beneath a ton of horror and nightmarish literary endeavor. He had Marcia to thank for the unpleasant reawakening, and he nearly slapped himself when an ounce of ill will surfaced regarding the young lady who'd only wanted his autograph.

"Okay. Let's think of something else." Saul readjusted his pillow to get comfortable, immediately thinking of his encounter with Leonard. Normally, he got along with the guy, maybe even liked him. Leonard seldom bothered him about his work, and Saul couldn't remember a previous time when Leonard seemed so frantic. Then again, none of ARP's other books was doing well at the moment, and he also couldn't remember ever having writer's block either.

It had been nearly nine months since he'd submitted his latest bestseller, 'The Night' to the editorial staff at American Reader's Press. There were some initial worries by the editors that the public would reject the strange novel, dealing with demons which inhabited the shadows, and the terrified, imperfect people who fought them with light of any kind. In particular, Saul remembered Leonard's lamentations.

"Saul, nobody is going to seriously believe that a one eyed stripper with V.D. and false teeth can find enough intestinal fortitude to fight off snarling demons straight from hell."

How wrong, Saul snickered, Leonard and the editors had been. The books smashing success gave him an ounce or two of relief, while he could scarcely feel sorry for Leonard, who was now dealing with both the less than stellar sales of ARP's other authors, and his estrangement from Elinor.

"I've done my time, old man. You can have her now."

Indeed, he'd been freed from the pangs of separation guilt and court ordered alimony, but he lamented his continued inability to write, or maybe even fall asleep. It had been a long time since he'd slept, or could enjoy what minute slumber he'd experienced when his body just quit on him. The numbness and fatigue of insomnia were never more than an inch away from his awareness, and they plagued him horribly at the moment. He turned on his side in order to get more comfortable, but the bed, despite looking pretty, felt as hard as a rock. Saul remembered a similar situation when he and Leonard spoke about 'The Night' few months ago, after its initial publication, and early success.

"I'm glad sales are picking up, Leonard, but the book's a piece of shit."

"Saul, you can't be saying stuff like that." Leonard arose from his desk at American Reader's Press offices in mid Manhattan. "What if the New York Times Book Review has a bug planted in my office?"

"I wonder if I care anymore, Len." Saul sat dejectedly, staring out of a window towards the western horizon. The view of Central Park, its lush green trees sprawling and thriving amid the overgrown metropolis surrounding it, was just below the panoramic rectangle of glass in Leonard's office. It was probably the only thing about the place that Saul liked besides Leonard; sometimes.

"You do care, man. Why do you think you bust your hump to churn out the scary mess you unleash on the public every year?"

"Good question, Len." Saul turned his head towards his friend and editor, giggling at the sight of Leonard's pink short sleeve shirt, gray pants, blue socks, and brown shoes. Saul couldn't help thinking that Leonard looked as though he'd gotten dressed in a dark closet.

"What's so funny?" Leonard inquired as he walked towards Saul.

"Sorry, Len." he thought quickly. "It's just that I think I did some of my best writing when I was still in college."

"Maybe you did." Leonard's response was surprisingly restrained. "But you're not in college anymore."

"I know that, Len, but I honestly enjoyed the writing I did back then a whole lot more than I do now. It made me feel.....alive."

"You were younger, Saul." Leonard copped a squat on the corner of his desk while briefly burying his face in his hands. He peeked out at Saul between fingers before rubbing his goatee and letting his arms drop. "We were all younger. God, I wouldn't mind being twenty one again."

Saul smiled weakly. Age wasn't the issue, though he wouldn't have minded a return to his twenties so long as he didn't have to surrender everything he'd learned since that time. The real issue, he considered some months later in the luxury suite of the hotel, was who he'd lost in the spring of his last semester of college.

Saul hadn't wanted to think about Marceleen again, but Marcia's appearance had unexpectedly brought the former's memory back to fore, and disrupted the fifteen year process of denial that Saul had erected to keep the pain and sorrow at bay. He also reminded himself that Marcia was not his long lost friend, nor responsible for the pain he was now inflicting himself with given the tumbling down of the artifice he'd thought kept him safe from memory all these years. Real life, as in the sounds of party guests, the smell of alcohol and flesh as the mingling of myriad people continued on through the night, was what haunted Saul at the moment. Real life reminded him that there was love, and loss, and pain that wouldn't vanish just because he tried to pretend it wasn't there.

"Well....I could go visit a graveyard. It would be quieter than here." he mused, faintly detecting the sound of piped in music from the ballroom, just before realizing the shocking change of his reality.

"What? Where in hell...am I?!" Saul elicited as he sat on the soft green grass of a place he'd never seen before. Sunlight stung his eyes as they adjusted to their sudden departure from darkness. "Oh...boy. Somebody really put a Mickey in my Cranberry juice."

Gazing at his surroundings and wondering how he got there, Saul was convinced he was in some kind of garden. A well kept garden with flowers, hedges, trees, and colorful bushes of all kinds surrounding stone monuments, which were placed throughout the well tended landscape. Horseshoe shaped, tall black obelisks, statues of cherubs, flat plaques resting at the rectangles of freshly disturbed earth. He knew, shockingly, just where he was now.

"Graveyard. I'm in a Goddamned graveyard!"

He walked around a bit, spotting odd names and dates on the various headstones, granite and steel monuments that surrounded him.

"Leonard, this is not funny." he muttered urgently. "I swear, next time I see your face I'm going to give you such a headache. May God strike me dead...."

A flock of snow white doves suddenly flew across his path, and Saul began to think that maybe Leonard had nothing to do with this at all. Leonard just wasn't that creative. Frantically, Saul looked over in the direction the birds had come from and then he saw one white dove, sitting alone atop a gray headstone.

"This is getting too weird." Saul scratched his head as he looked at the bird, who beckoned him with its steadfast gaze. Saul wondered about that as he wandered closer, enjoying a brief literary flashback,-'Once upon a midnight dreary, as I wondered weak and weary'-thinking of Edgar Allen Poe's sojourn with the raven, but this wasn't a poem. This was the real world, wasn't it?

Saul continued on, still uncertain about what he was doing, or how he got there, or even if he wanted to stay. It was tempting to find the quickest way out of the cemetery and hail a taxi, but something compelled him to keep walking towards the bird. His stocking feet felt the dampness of the morning dew as he approached even closer to the not too fancy stone atop which the bird preened and cleaned itself.

"Hey, fellow. Sweetheart, maybe?" Saul reached out to touch the bird, but the dove frantically flew away, leaving Saul to raise his hands in defense against the flapping wings in his face. He cursed inwardly, even while grabbing hold of the headstone in order to keep from falling over backwards. His hand felt a groove. His fingers were embedded in what felt like a large 'B', so he walked around the front of the headstone to see what it said. He nearly fainted at the sight.

'Beloved Daughter, Sister, Friend. Marceleen Carla Goldberg. July 16, 1957-March 23, 1979'

"Goldie? Oh my God." he whispered, his eyes suddenly flooded with hot tears as companion to the long buried heartache and sorrow he'd spent too many years trying to repress.

"Goldie?!" he fell to his knees in front of the headstone, feeling his face drop to the dirt as sorrow and grief fueled his mortal venting of the desolation he could not control, that seemed to last long enough for the sun to rise, set and nightfall to crash upon his grief.

"Wait...a minute." Saul sat up in the darkness of the hotel suite he'd lay down in nearly six hours ago, somewhere far removed from the graveyard where he'd cried endless tears over Marceleen's grave. Now he was bathed in cold sweat, and even more, there was a warm body beside him.

"Aww, Jeez." he moaned, quickly running his fingers through his hair and looking frantically to the side. "What the hell did I do this time?"

"Mmmmmmmmmugh." she stirred, rolling to the side so Saul could get a good look. It was the blond again. Her pastel blue dress was rumpled from the drunken sleep she was rising out of, and Saul knew that she was in for the hangover of the century. He carefully checked himself-shirt still buttoned, pants zipper still pulled all the way up, no sexual smell-to be certain that nothing untoward occurred in the middle of the night.

"Hello?" he reached over and touched her on the hip as he spoke, only to detect the unsavory residue of cranberry juice, onion dip, roast beef, turkey, and honey ham, on his taste buds. He might have said 'Yuuuuck!', but he thought discretion the better part of valor in order to save her from the sound of his distress. "Good morning."

He could see the earliest rays of the sun as they cascaded through the louvered blinds. They made striped pattern of light and shade across her face and highlighted the woman's platinum blond hair, which he hadn't noticed the previous evening. He couldn't help noticing now as she threw off the cover and turned towards him in utter surprise.

"Wha...?" she uttered incoherently. Her eyes were redder than paint and a hint of alcohol floated about her body aroma. Saul might have considered her a lovely sight to wake up to had he felt rested enough to believe he'd slept. The tightness of his back and neck, as well as the weariness behind his eyes and sinuses informed him that if he'd slept at all, it was only long enough to have that weird dream. The blond, on the other hand, had probably slept like the dead. "How....did....I get...here?!"

"Good question." he mused humorously. "I'll have to ask myself that sometime."

10

James Spencer stood beneath the scaffolding between two buildings and the construction of a new bank building near Baltimore's old city hall, as the rain fell about mid afternoon. Soft rain descended on the black streets and gray sidewalks as people made their way through town during the lunch hour, many passing by the solitary man as he blew his saxophone in a somnolent, sleepy fashion. Decked out in an old pair of blue jeans, unpolished black combat boots, and a green army issue raincoat with parka, James was hardly conspicuous. His black saxophone case was on the ground next to him, open for donations from those being entertained as they walked along. A few people tossed coins in the case as they passed by. Some dropped paper money, much to James' delight.

"Thank you." he smiled as a long haired young man with a silver ring on the left side of his nose pulled quarters, nickels, and pennies from the pocket of the leather bombardier jacket he was wearing, depositing all of them in the saxophone case. His other hand was in the back pocket of the blue jeans worn by the similarly dressed woman walking alongside him. James smiled as they walked by him, figuring that longhair nose ring probably wasn't searching for a hundred dollar bill back there. The woman's smile was as beautiful as the absent sunshine, and her gold locks reached down almost to her waist. James continued to play, even while looking down at his open case to see the meager take.

Probably five hundred or more people had passed him in the hours he'd worked the corner, though he'd probably gotten contributions from only a tenth of them, if that many. A few of the folks had actually stuck around to listen to his melodious labors. The people were like the rain; randomly making their acquaintance, gathering around in pools and puddles, or just floating on to whatever destination their busy feet carried them. Most of them passed on without leaving James a token of their passage, coin or otherwise. He laughed when a memory intruded on his musical output. He could almost hear Cut Throat's voice, imagining what his old friend would have said had he looked in the till.

"That's chump change, man! You talking ten cents on the dollar once Uncle Shithead gets his cut. So how the hell you think yo' black ass is gonna go to college, pay rent, and eat too, once the tax man gets finished with that pay check?!"

So spoke Matt 'Cut Throat' Allen to James, as they sat together in the Melody bar, the most popular juke joint in the predominantly black 'Backyard' district of Chester, Pennsylvania. James was halfway through a tough semester, having second and third thoughts about returning to Temple University to complete the academic year. He'd also endured a tough day of slinging hamburgers and French fries at the local 'Willies' fast food restaurant that had recently opened on the corner of French street and Sixteenth, conveniently accessible to both black and white communities. James had applied for a job and got lucky. At least he'd thought so until the pressures of work and academia had gotten the best of him.

"Cut Throat, hip me to something I don't already know, okay?" James took a long swig from his bottle of Miller High Life beer. At twenty two, James was tall, smoothly dark complexioned, and possessed short cropped black hair that seemed wavier than it should have been. Clad in dark blue pants, a blue wool sweater, the white shirt and black bow tie he'd earlier worn to work, James tried to stand his ground. "I got to hustle in order to pay the rest of my tuition, if I decide to go back to school. How else am I going to get over, short of doing illegal stuff like you and Surrender?"

"Oh, puh-leease!" Cut Throat threw back his bald head before slamming the scotch from his shot glass down his throat. His face contorted in a grimace as he swallowed. His big lips pursed over gleaming white teeth, Cut Throat toyed with his pencil thin mustache while looking sternly at James. "Man, if you was even close to getting over, I guarran-damn-tee you the feds would be trying to get your black ass behind bars! Point is, you ain't going nowhere they don't want you to!"

"Cut Throat is a little psychotic, but he's right on time." spoke Surrender. Short, fair skinned with red hair and scary amber eyes, Surrender was the meanest of the group when he had to be. "White man in America is a mother fucker. They kill their own if they think he's getting' out of line."

"JFK." Cut Throat remarked while tugging at the collar of his white turtleneck shirt and pouring another round of Jack Daniel's into his and Surrender's shot glasses.

"And you know they had to kill Malcolm." Surrender continued his tirade. "White folks ain't ready for black leaders who can actually 'Lead' the folks."

"Excuse me, but I was in Audubon Ballroom when it came down." Michael interjected. Easily the muscle of the group, Michael raised his almost six and a half feet tall body up assertively in his seat. "The guys who did Malcolm...were brothers."

"No brothers of mine." James looked over at Michael, almost envious of the massive gray blue dashiki that covered his three hundred pound girth, and wondered if his friend was having nightmares about the trauma of last February twenty first. "Mike's right. We can't blame the white man for that one."

"Maybe not, but there was ten million cops, T.V. cameras, and even reporters with microphones on the premises a minute after the shooting was over." Surrender was almost livid. "They even rescued that dog, Talmadge, from the crowd before they could tear his ass up. Now just where the fuck were they before all hell broke loose?!"

"Guys, we're getting off track here." Michael's big hand tightened around his glass of orange juice. "We know that LBJ isn't playing around with the Viet Cong. He's ready to commit some serious warfare in Southeast Asia, and when the draft gets started, we young black men are going to be the first in line to get dragged away."

"Yeah." Surrender calmed down. "Sorry bout' that, Michael, but the shit ain't right. If I was rich and white, or able to run the football, maybe I could get in on that college deferment."

"That's not why I'm still at Syracuse, Surrender." Michael added. "My knee is too torn up for me to ever worry about playing football again, but my grades were good enough to keep me in as a student."

"Lucky you." James muttered and looked around before taking a sip from his beer. Someone in the bar popped a quarter in the juke box, bringing forth the sounds of Meridian Sax, a local musician who produced his own records. The blaring saxophone and the raspy singing loudly sounded through the bar as Cut Throat tapped his fingertips on the table top. Michael smiled, and moved his head with animation to the steady beat. James remained ominously reflective before speaking again. "Mike, I wish I could say the same, but sometimes I think I'm just wasting time trying to stay in school to get better with my music. Still can't read notes worth a damn."

"Man, you already play the sax better than Meridian Sax ever dreamed of. Plus you sing better too." Cut Throat spoke before hefting his shot glass and guzzling.

"Look better, too. Meridian Sax is a ugly mother fucker." Surrender chimed in, though James continued his lament.

"Michael, I envy you, man. At least you know what you're doing in school. Right now, between Rosalie thinking I might do well in music education, and my partners in Axis wanting to hit the road, I'm kind of lost. I do know that I want no parts of anybody's classroom."

"Then don't." Michael affirmed. "You shouldn't go back just because somebody thinks you should be a teacher. You can do a lot with a degree in music performance."

"Yo, Michael," Cut Throat spoke up again. "I'm glad you're pointing all this out for my man, but that's beside the point."

"And what is the point?" Michael was serious, putting his glass down on the table and giving Cut Throat his undivided attention.

"Point is, James don't need to go to school to learn nothing about music. He's already the best there is." Cut Throat reached for the bottle again, refilling only his shot glass this time. "You're right about him not going back just for Rosalie. That chick is too much in love with Jesus for me to think she's ever gonna love James serious. Plus he had to work day and night for two years just to afford tuition. If he goes back to Temple next semester, he might as well sell his soul, or promise his first born to the tax man just to pay the bill. He can't buy no decent clothes, or take some babe out to see a movie. He can't even look at a sticker on a car, or think of scoring some...."

"Dope?" Michael eyed Cut Throat and Surrender seriously. Ever the athlete, Michael had never touched drug or drink. "Tell the truth, Cut Throat. Did dope ever do anything good for you?"

"It's gotten me money in my pocket, man." Surrender announced defensively. "A few more big scores like the one from last week, and like what's going down tonight, we be looking at easy street."

"You're also looking at cops and competitors breathing down you neck every moment of the day and night. How does it feel to always be looking over your shoulder?"

Good question, James reflected on Michael's solemn inquiry. The mood had turned borderline gloomy as the four friends passed a few more words between them before hefting their respective drinks for a final swig. Another reminder that the world they lived in was changing drastically before their eyes. James and his friends had grown into the reality of a life of adult demands; not to mention sadness at the recall of carefree youth, boyhood pranks, fun and misbehavior devoid of serious responsibility, or consequences.

Indeed, that meeting in the Melody Bar was the last time the 'Fearsome Foursome' would ever get together for friendly camaraderie. Not long after leaving the bar, the foursome split up. Cut Throat and Surrender went their way to attend some nebulous meeting related to their illicit trade. James and Michael made their way to the Greyhound Bus terminal, where Michael was about to board a bus bound for Syracuse, New York, and the remainder of his final spring semester at Syracuse University.

"James, I'm concerned about Cut Throat and Surrender." he admitted in the outside terminal of the bus station. He'd donned an olive green jacket, and had a black colored duffel bag slung over his right shoulder. "Nothing good is going to come of what they're into."

"No." James muttered, unwilling to admit that Cut Throat and Surrender had asked him to accompany them that evening, and even more, that he'd almost gone along. "But I understand where they're coming from. They don't know anything else but where they've been all their lives."

"They can learn. I did." Michael wearily exhaled. "I mean, Surrender ought to want better than what happened to his father. Can you imagine being named after the last thing the police said to your dad?! His mother thought it was funny. I never did."

"Maybe Surrender didn't like it either, but what else is he going to do, Mike?"

"He can start thinking outside the box, James. Until last November, I thought my hope and salvation was on that football field. Then I spent a week in a hospital bed, thinking for sure my life was over, before my English professor came to visit and gave me my paper from the last test I'd taken before the football game. I got an 'A' plus."

"Woah!" James laughed. "The highest grade I ever made in English was a 'C' minus, and I had to beg for that."

"You don't have to beg, man. All you got to do is work hard. Here I thought I was killing myself with all this study, but it helped me stay in school after what went down, and I'm this close to a BA in English. And I know you're capable of doing good, also. Just follow your heart and do your best."

"You're right, man." James noticed Michael's continued seriousness, which he found more than a touch unnerving. "I just know that I can't say I want to do anything other than blow my horn. I love music, man."

"No problem with that. You love Rosalie, too?"

"I don't know, Mike. I mean, I do...., but I'm not sure where this is going." James stammered, haunted by the tortured relationship he shared with Rosalie, who would as soon seduce him as lead him to the foot of the cross. "I don't agree with how Cut Throat said it, but he was right about Rosalie's religion. I never believed that stuff, and I know that I wouldn't change just for her sake."

"James, you shouldn't let anybody make you go anywhere you don't want to. Not Rosalie, and especially not our buddies. You showed real wisdom in not going with Cut Throat and Surrender tonight."

"You knew?"

"James. Who do you think they asked to go with them first?!"

Then they laughed, though they both knew that the laughter couldn't last forever. Not that they'd ever had a bad moment laughing before, but there was finality to the brotherly love and laughter this evening. A realization grounded in something colder than the night wind surrounding them in the breezy terminal of the bus station. A whiff of difference, definitely not the aroma of fried chicken that flowed from a nearby grill, reached James as he embraced Michael. Something in the air smelled foul. A grim essence of foreboding filled the night, and was fulfilled the following morning with the news of Surrender's death.

Surrender had succumbed to the vicious street wars between the various factions vying for the dope trade in the Backyard. James didn't learn the whole story, but he knew that Cut Throat and Surrender had stepped in some very bad waters, leaving the foursome a grim trio.

A few mornings later, drizzling rainfall pelted James, Cut Throat, and a few other assorted mourners, as they watched a mahogany coffin slowly lowered into the cold, wet ground. The family, the minister, and the other mourners retreated to their vehicles not long after the minister uttered his somber eulogy-"I am the resurrection and the life. He that believeth in me shall not perish, but have everlasting life."-leaving James and Cut Throat alone at the grave sight long after the black limo carrying the family, and the other assorted cars driven by mourners, were out of sight.

"For the brothers....that ain't here. Goodbye, Surrender." James mourned while pouring a bottle of Mogen David Twenty Twenty inside Surrender's not yet filled grave. Cut Throat remained silent, the falling rain splashing and splattering upon his bald pate as his eyes remained on the dark earth that Surrender made his premature bed in. 'Devastated' was a mild word to describe James' state of mind as he looked over at Cut Throat, who appeared to be holding back an avalanche of rage and violence that would flow unchecked if he didn't keep a lock on it.

"Cut Throat, how bad was it?" James walked over and stood besides Cut Throat, opening his umbrella to cover he and his soaked friend. They stared painfully at the box which contained their life long friend.

"Bad enough." he rubbed his face to clear away the moisture, then rubbed his right eye as more rain, this time from inside, rolled down his cheek. "The boy had too many holes in too many places to even think about surviving."

James' vivid imagination painted a grim moving picture of Surrender's body being suddenly filled with invasive holes as the bullets struck him. He imagined the final pain of Surrender's demise, though he had more sympathy for Cut Throat, who no doubt bore the shame of having been quicker to hit the sidewalk; of cowering fearfully as his partner and friend took the brunt of gunfire aimed at the both of them. If imagining were this terrible, James only wondered how bad being there must have been.

"We need to get out of here." James offered, putting his arm around Cut Throat, and feeling it roughly thrust away.

"I can walk, man!"

They did. Away from a rainy graveyard in the northern part of Chester, Pennsylvania, on to a diner only a few blocks away, where they ordered coffee and further discussed their circumstances.

"I'm serious, Cut Throat." James eyed his friend severely, not even cutting his eyes to peek at the black coffee he was sipping. "I don't want to be standing over your grave like I was for Surrender."

"They maybe you ought to try catching that Greyhound that took Michael away so you can transfer to Syracuse. I hear upstate New York is lovely this time of year." Cut Throat surrendered a touch of sarcasm. His voice wavered between a white flag raised from a bombed out foxhole, and a low grade grumble that foretold further grim tidings. The greasy spoon diner he and James sat in was moderately crowded this afternoon, but James looked around briefly, noticing no one but himself and Cut Throat wearing black. Cut Throat aimlessly spun his spoon around in the nearby sugar jar, making no effort to place any in his coffee, which by now, had to be cold enough to ice skate on. His next words only added to the chill.

"Besides, I'm starting to think that our 'Buddy' really don't give two pop bottles about us down here. He's chasing that almighty sheepskin real hard, James. Notice he couldn't get down for the funeral."

"Come on, Cut Throat. Since he lost his scholarship, you know it's costing his family an arm and a leg for him to finish school. His mother didn't tell him about Surrender until yesterday afternoon, just to make sure he didn't try getting down here. Besides, he did send flowers and a card by Western Union."

"Yeah, flowers and cards. How 'Sweet'." Cut Throat wasn't pacified. "What about friendship, huh?! Where was his big ass the other night when they gunned Surrender down?"

"Probably the same place I was." James stared bullets at Cut Throat, raising the angst in his voice. "Man, you can't turn this into a reason to hate Michael. You know that if he'd been there, he'd have done anything to save Surrender's life, or died trying. Mike might be big, but he ain't Superman, and bullets don't bounce off his chest."

"I'm sorry, James." Cut Throat's recalcitrant voice maintained a low grade grumble. "Right now, I just don't know what the fuck to do. Out on the street, they didn't call me 'Cut Throat' because of my good looks. But now my partner gets capped right in front of me, and I didn't do diddly shit but watch him die. I mean, what's that going to do for my rep?"

"Hey, damn your rep, Cut Throat." James whispered angrily. "A friend of ours is dead behind the same stupid shit that killed his daddy. You can't be so lame as to be more upset about what them clowns in the street think of you than you are about what happened to Surrender, can you?!"

"Unlike you, college boy," Cut Throat dropped the spoon on the hard linoleum table top before warily eyeing James. "I still got a life out there in those streets. I got people who depend on me to keep em on cloud nine. Up until they did Surrender, we ruled the neighborhood. It was our kingdom, man."

"Yeah, Cut Throat. Some kingdom. You making a living off of death and misery. Now somebody's Bogarded your territory, and you're scared shitless. How does it feel, your highness?!"

"You know, you can be a real bastard sometimes." Cut Throat exhaled sullenly while sinking back into his seat at the booth. "You think the shit that happened to Surrender just don't hurt, huh?"

"That's how you're acting, man."

"I'm sorry you think that, brother. Maybe I don't act as bad as it hurts, but I can't lose my mind crying. This is the wrong world to get mournful in. I get weak, I wind up just like Surrender."

"Cruel world, Cut Throat." James slurped his coffee to cover the sound of a sniffle.

"You got a better one? And, no, I'm not following Jesus like your lady does."

"Don't worry, man. I'm not going there either."

Instead, James told Cut Throat of the music group that he and six of his classmates were forming. Axis was the name they'd chosen, and their brand of music was somewhere between folk, rock, jazz, rhythm and blues, pop, and a whole host of other stuff they could find to fit into their own melodic fusion. James' eyes lit up as he gave Cut Throat the information, his enthusiasm rising sky high as he laid out the plan. It sounded good, Cut Throat thought, but he couldn't imagine why James was telling him about it since he couldn't play or sing a lick.

"We need a manager, Cut Throat. We got enough musicians. We need somebody to scare us up gigs."

Thus was born Axis Productions. Cut Throat spent days calling and visiting promoters, disc jockeys, bar and club owners, armed with cassette tapes of the band's music, and occasionally his 357 Magnum, or an ounce of good dope, if such were needed to persuade folks to give the band a chance to play. James and his musical partners spent nights making music while Cut Throat spent days doing the promotion, balancing the books, and making sure everything worked in the band's favor. After a few rough months, the band began making a profit, in spite of their being a fusion type band that didn't do top forty, and didn't have a recording contract. Yet.

For the next two and a half years, Axis toured up and down the east coast, making music, making love, making mayhem, and leaving a grand melodic menagerie in their wake. Of course, Cut Throat managed to persist in criminal behavior, hooking up with major drug suppliers, even managing to get James into the illicit trade. James never used, but he wasn't above being Cut Throat's lookout, right hand man, or enforcer, when the time came for big scores and deals. He simply made one request of Cut Throat; that he never use the house that they'd purchased in East Baltimore as a place to stash the dope he'd continued to deal. Cut Throat honored his buddy's request, even though he at one point labeled it 'Chicken-shit'.

Despite the madness, James stayed above it all by immersing himself in his saxophone and in the endless parade of women who served as surrogate for Rosalie, whom he missed terribly.

James could scarcely hide his yearning for the simple girl who wanted only to love him and lead him on to redemption through Jesus, whom she also loved. James remembered his brother telling him, "You better grab her before I do. I think she likes you."

Gerald had been right, James realized one night in Harlem as he serenaded an eager crowd in a bar called 'Fats', somewhere on 125th street, and several blocks west of the Apollo Theater. It was a crowded night, people dancing and drowning in the smoky center of the night club. Rivers of scotch, vodka, and fine champagne were flowing between the island tables of the establishment, and above them all on the mountain like stage platform, was Axis, providing the music. James blew his saxophone for dear life, just as he'd always done.

The tune, 'Abraham, Martin, and John', deftly made it's way through the brass chambers of his alto saxophone, though James was tempted to paraphrase the song's last verse with a pertinent question of his own.

'Has anybody here, seen my old friend Matthew? Can you tell me where he's gone?'

Sadly, the answer to that question had been uttered less than two months ago in a federal courtroom in Trenton, New Jersey. A grim faced judge had inquired of the clerk of court, requesting the woman to read the jury's decision.

"On the charge of possession of a controlled substance with the intent to distribute, we the jury, find the defendant, Matthew Robert Allen, guilty as charged."

The judge sentenced Cut Throat to fifteen to twenty years in the maximum security unit at Rahweh, New Jersey, shortly after asking the defendant if he had anything to say.

Cut Throat said nothing. James knew that the only reason he was still playing for the crowd at 'Fats', instead of maybe the one at Rahweh, was because of Cut Throat's silence. That, besides the heat of late summer, troubled him.

It was early September of 1968. A long, hot summer was fading into an uncertain autumn. The band was chugging along with a new pianist, as well as a string bass player who wasn't quite in step with the rest of the group yet. They would have to have to have a nice long practice session soon, James thought, while scoping out the toe tapping, finger snapping, and general enjoyment of the crowd.

After Axis finished the set, James indulged in a Bloody Mary while sharing a table with the club's manager, who named the place after his own incognito moniker. Spiffily dressed in a gray sharkskin suit to match his graying hair, he inquired of Axis' most recent transitions.

"I hear Cut Throat got sent up the river." the man played around his bone white teeth with a toothpick. "Rumor, or fact?"

"Fact, man." James brought his glass up for another hit of the red libation. "He sold a pound of Horse to the wrong guy. Feds sent him to Rahweh to do a double dime stretch."

"So how come you didn't get sent there alongside him?" the man's face suddenly became as grim as the dark side of the moon, the only hint of illumination being the whites of his eyes. "I know that you're as deep into this dope game as Cut Throat was. Deep as I am."

"Was as deep." James responded warily.

"Point is, James, you were in too deep. How in God's name did Cut Throat get busted and you didn't?" Fats questioned, his eyes taking a more stern appearance.

"Listen, Fats, ain't no way I'd try to cut a deal to save my own skin if I knew Cut Throat was gonna fry." James declared defensively, his voice the barely repressed boom of an erupting volcano. "Nobody likes a snitch, man, and shit for sure I don't appreciate you accusing me."

"I'm not accusing you..."

"Yes you are! Don't even play me like that, Fats." James shot back. "The reason I'm not in jail, or you and your associates for that matter, is that Cut Throat got involved in something we didn't know about, and wouldn't have gone for. He was also too loyal to take anybody down with him behind his own bullshit. I didn't rat on nobody, man. I'd die first."

"Hey, James. Chill, okay?!" the fat man leaned back in his seat and interlaced his fingers on the table in front of him. "Peace in the valley, brother. Best way we can keep from joining him down there at Rahwah is to be cool and not draw attention to ourselves. You guys getting a recording contract was cool, but you know you got to keep your nose clean for the foreseeable future, dig?"

"No problem." James took another sip of his Bloody Mary, this time emptying the glass while somberly thinking of Cut Throat's ordeal, the hassle of keeping the business end of things together, and his realization that recruiting Fats as a possible replacement manager was not happening. At this point, he figured things could only get better. They had to.

"James Spencer?"

James turned to his right to see a dude looking almost too young to be in the club, standing at the table beside him. Where, James wondered, had this kid come from. Fats had an unspoken, 'Jesus F. Christ!' look on his face at this sudden intrusion on his and James' domain.

"Who's asking?" James warily looked at this young guy who addressed him. Tall, gangly, and fair skinned, the man's red hair was cut in a tight crew cut. His eyes were an almost golden shade of amber, and they locked on James uncomfortably. Despite the spit shine polished black shoes, neatly pressed dark blue suit, and matching tie over white dress shirt, the kid looked way out of place.

"My name's Cordell Mosson. You don't know me, but your band came to my home town, Norfolk, Virginia, last summer."

"Yeah. We did." James affirmed. "What about it?"

"Actually, you knew my sister, Mr. Spencer." the kid reached into his jacket lapel, causing Fats to slide out of his seat and stand up defensively. James was also unnerved, but Cordell set them both at east by pulling out two photographs. "Her name was Alicia Mosson."

"Nope. Afraid that name don't ring any bells."

"Maybe her picture will." Cordell reverently placed the hand sized portrait on the table besides James empty glass. James said nothing while scanning the face in the photograph, but he had known her. At least for a night he had. Alicia had the same smooth, fair skin complexion as did Cordell. Her own red locks struggled for freedom beneath a high school graduation cap. Yes, James had known her. Like a lot of fine female faces and bodies he'd racked up and known in the past two and a half years. Still, he pleaded ignorance, whereas Fats was not so moved.

"Listen, Caldwell..."

"Cordell." he affirmed, never taking his eyes off of James.

"I don't know what you think you're doing, but you need to move on, pronto!"

"I think I may have....seen her when we hit Norfolk." James groped for words, understating the truth in order to placate this kid, and maybe even calm Fats down. "But then I see a lot of babes when we tour."

"Then you should see this 'Babe'." Cordell tossed a second photo on top of the table, this one of a naked girl of about four to five months, splashing around in a plastic tub of bath water. She was a beautiful child who bore the unmistakable dark complexion and brown eyes of a dark skinned father. James knew who the moment he saw the photograph.

"Cute kid. What's her name?" James questioned.

"You bothering me, Cordell." Fats was not pleased. "You better make your point real fast."

"Ease up, Fats." James picked up the baby's picture and eyed it carefully. "I'm sure the dude don't mean nothing by this."

"Yes I do." Cordell contradicted, adding an edge to his already uneasy presentation. "I want to acquaint you with your handiwork."

"I said she's cute. I didn't say she's mine."

"Hey. Enough of this bullshit." Fats spat out his toothpick and started walking towards the young man. "Either you hit the bar and start drinking, find a woman and get out on the dance floor, or get your ass out of my club, Cordell."

"She's yours. You were the first guy my sister ever made it with...."a pinprick of sorrow floated on Cordell's voice as his eyes remained on James, though Fats had moved close enough to touch, though not affectionately. James recalled Alicia from the Main Event; a crowded, smoky, juke joint that he'd not wanted to play in. Cut Throat hadn't wanted to book the group in that place either, but the band needed the cash at the moment, and the show there introduced James to Alicia.

He remembered Alicia, a tall, redbone girl, who waited tables, sold cigarettes, laid whiskey down for thirsty patrons. Beautiful, red skinned, 'High Yella' child working her way through Norfolk State U. She was nervous, shy, tight in the hips, and unsure what to do as he caressed her gently, but boldly, beneath the sheets in his hotel room.

"....and you were also the last, Mr. Spencer."

"The ....last?! I was? Oh dear God. Oh....God?!" James whispered, not needing Cordell to fill in the blanks. Fats' voice did the next breaking of any consequences, summoning his bouncers to 'Escort' Cordell out of the establishment. The young man didn't flinch as the two burly men grabbed him, but his eyes remained glued to James, who was suddenly distraught as he stared at the photographs on the table top. Cordell vanished like baloney between the large, black suited figures darker than Pumpernickel bread, and was swept away from sight and out of the club quicker than a laxative to constipation. It was a strange scene, the patrons of the club beholding two burly black men hauling this sorrowful appearing young man-who didn't struggle with them- out through the front door. James would see none of it, being too bound to the golden lady and baby child in the photographs on the table in front of him. Remembering Alicia all too well, James took a deep breath and sighed sorrowfully, so unlike the sigh he'd drawn from the girl who'd gamely submitted to his seduction. To her, it was the beginning. Maybe love, maybe more. To James...

"Oh my....God." he trembled, struggling not to start screaming. Fats rejoined James at the table after seeing that his henchmen had evicted Cordell from the property.

"I'm sorry about that, James." he reached down to grab the photographs from off of the table. "Let me get this shit out of your face."

"No!!" James forcibly slammed both palms over the photographs and glared at Fats. The eyes, Fats thought in a fear filled instant, were way too crazy for his tastes. James reminded him of a cornered, wounded animal, who's lifeblood was seeping out profusely and leaving a crazed trail of pain with each step.

"Okay, man." Fats backed off defensively, seeing the devastation behind James' barely coherent eyes. "You want another drink?"

"Yeah. Get me a double. Hell. Get me the whole fucking bottle."

Such began James' drunken, incoherent odyssey, his vain attempt at running from the knowledge of what he'd wrought. On those rare nights he was able to sleep, Alicia's beautiful face was the last thing to grace his mind, only to fade too soon into the morning when the memory of her mournful brother returned again to remind him that save his 'Love Jones', an innocent girl might be alive today. The wound had left naught but ashes in what was supposed to be his soul.

James thought of that night in Harlem, more than a quarter century later, blowing his saxophone on a street corner in Baltimore. He wondered what ever became of Cordell after they'd bodily tossed him out of the club. James figured that any bruises he'd received that night would have long since healed, though he imagined Cordell's sorrow would remain. James also considered that Alicia's daughter would be the second child he'd fathered and not known. He wondered why life had to so often be cruel, until he reminded himself of his part in the cruelty.

Alicia hadn't deserved to die, and Cordell shouldn't have had to confront the one responsible for her fatal pregnancy. A lot of things shouldn't have happened, James concluded, as he blew his final note and closed his case after sticking his meager earnings in a black cotton shoulder bag, before he began walking back towards the row house in southeast Baltimore. He kind of wanted it to stop raining, but he didn't really mind. Somebody had to cry for Alicia. It might as well have been God.

N. Wilson Enoch

A four mile walk through the wet, misty Baltimore streets wasn't merely James's way of keeping in shape. It was also the only way to get back to his house since he didn't own a car, and didn't want to spend any of his take on the public transit. He'd become accustomed to his daily treks to play his music. He didn't worry about leaving Jasmine alone since he could depend on the Primeaux kid to stop by on the way back from school and let him know if anything untoward had occurred. Besides, there were enough potential roadblocks and delays within a few blocks of the house for James to wonder if he'd get home before dark.

"Spen....cer!!"

James turned around at the familiar sound of his friend, Street, who shuffled his feet in carefree fashion. James threw the sling of his saxophone case across his shoulder as Street broke into one of his classic smiles, hiding the fact that he just might be on the verge of running for his life. A long, tall drink of water who's head was habitually shaved, who's brown eyes had 'Yellows' rather than 'Whites', Street often appeared not to know where he was headed. James occasionally grinned when he considered where Rosalie would have said Street was going.

"Hi, Street. How's life?"

"Usual, my man. I keep ripping and running to get over. Long as the high price of thrills don't go down, I'm looking at big, large life. Know what I mean, Spen...cer?!"

"Whatever you say, Street." in truth, James suspected that his friend had made some chump change of his own, selling something other than music. "I still think you could do a lot better than pushing those rocks, man. I hear that the trade is very dangerous."

"Shit. Only if you don't watch your back." Street rummaged through the left pocket of his Navy pea coat, and James sadly observed the emergence of a plastic vial containing a chalky white rock and a hollow glass tube that Street deftly handled between his fingers.

"Yo, Street. You really aught to wait till you get home before firing up. Getting busted would really wreck your day."

"It's cool, Spen...cer. Cops don't come here to East side anyway."

James said nothing else, knowing better than to demand anything of someone about to do major narcotics. Instead, he cast his eyes on the gray landscape as Street placed the white particle in a hole in the middle of the tube. They walked on the wet sidewalk past rusty, parked cars, and aged tenement buildings that seemed older and wearier than the earth itself. James heard the crackle of Street's cigarette lighter and a moment later, he smelled the acrid, detestable, smoke of free base cocaine. He hated the seductive lie of crack cocaine use, and as they walked along, James wondered if it were

94

possible to introduce his jovial acquaintance to a larger world of lovely colors that were real, not filtered through a haze of mind numbing smoke.

"So how's she doing, Spen...cer? She still sleeping, or what?"

"Jasmine's always sleeping, Street. She's been sleeping since shortly after the morning I met her."

"Yeah. Very weird, Spen....cer. You sure that chick ain't dead?!"

"She's alive. She's still breathing and hasn't started to rot, decay or smell bad, so I guess she's still just sleeping."

"Whatever. Two and a half decades is a long time to be sleeping." Street shook the pipe to clear it of ash after taking his last inhalation, appearing disappointed that his smoke didn't last very long. "I'd a looked up from my coffee at Watkin's Diner and saw some chick walking around half naked and barefoot in freezing weather at 2:00 A.M., I'd probably go home and do some serious dope after I called the paddy wagon to take her away. Why for you choose to put her up, man?!"

"It's about devotion and responsibility, Street." James bordered on whimsical. The rain had stopped, and he could see the sun returning, transforming the gray sky into blue. "Jasmine didn't tell me the whole story, but I think she was running from people who'd murdered her boyfriend. They were seriously in love. She might have been dreaming about him this morning."

"Oh, yeah?"

"She cried." James exhaled as he stopped at a street corner, the magnitude of his last statement overcoming him all at once. "I've never seen her cry before."

"Man, you ain't never seen her do anything but sleep. Maybe she's getting ready to wake up."

"Maybe." James reflected as he looked at Street.

"Sounds like you gon' need another line of work once she gets up. Maybe get back into the game. I could use another man on the corner."

James thought of shouting 'Hell no!'. He'd already been there, remembering Cut Throat, Surrender, Fats, all the pimps, players, pushers, and dealers of where he'd once been, and not wishing to join those amongst the quick, the dead, and the incarcerated.

"I don't think so. Keeping a constant eye on my backside don't sound like much of a living, Street."

"Oh puh-leeasee!" Street blurted out, reminding James of an earlier scoffer. "Neegroe, explain to me what's so great about your current situation, baby sitting this sleeper?!"

"Keeps me honest." James smiled while tugging at the saxophone case sliding off of his shoulder.

"Honest, shmaunest! You're only a couple of inches away from retirement age, Spen...cer. Either you got some stocks and bonds hid away somewhere, or you just look forward to standing on street corners and blowing your sax when you're ninety."

"Maybe I'll tell you about it one day." James quipped, just as he observed the emerging sunlight, as well as the neighborhood children being let out of school busses and other people coming out to converse and congregate on the local sidewalks and streets. James was happy about that. It forced Street to re pocket his smoking utensils. Even he couldn't know if one of his neighbors was a narc.

A few steps further down the road, James stood on a street corner not far from the brown brick row house he shared with Jasmine. Normally, he'd have felt good about taking his weary self inside, but today was not normal. Not withstanding Street's ominous suggestion about Jasmine-'Maybe she's getting ready to wake up.'- he was also perplexed by the car he spotted just outside the house. A lime green Ford Taurus sedan was parked on the street in front of the house, and a young woman clad in blue jeans and a green nylon jacket was walking in the vicinity. Tall, with the hood of the jacket pulled over her low cut hair, she seemed deeply introspective as he saw her. He wondered who she was, and as he quickly crossed the street and approached her, he figured that she wasn't just some stranger in search of directions to the nearby interstate.

"James Spencer?" she immediately locked on his eyes.

"Who's asking?"

"My name is ...Maryum Dupaul." she slowly deliberated. "My mother is Rosalie Dupaul. I'm...your daughter."

BOOK THREE

BEGINNINGS, AND AN END

11

The longer James looked at the woman, the more he became aware of his past rushing up to forcefully confront him.

He and Maryum had retreated to the sparsely furnished beige living room of the row house, and James recognized the unmistakable relationship of Rosalie's soft brown to his own deep ebony on Maryum's face in the room's muted light.

"I apologize that I don't have any coffee or tea to offer you." he stammered. "How was your trip down from New Jersey?"

"I've had worse trips." Maryum confessed while sitting on the aged blue couch. She might have added, 'But none more bewildering', while watching James lean against the faded beige wallpaper and eye her as though he'd never wanted to in the first place. "Please....sit down. I'm nervous enough as it is."

"Thank you for your honesty." he whispered while walking over to sit in a loosely upholstered brown chair diagonally across from where she sat. James interlaced his fingers while looking this woman in the eyes. "How did you find me?"

"When I got to town, I went to the main post office and asked if they could tell me the postal facility this card was mailed from." she reached into her denim knapsack and pulled out the post card and placing it on top of the coffee table between her couch and his chair. "I got directed to a fire station a few blocks from here. One of the firemen told me that most of the old neighborhood was gone, but he also mentioned having seen a strange man hanging out on the street corners blowing his sax, and also walking into this house when they'd had to deal with another emergency in the area. I figured that it might be you."

"I sent my brother this card nearly a lifetime ago. How is he?" he picked up the card, looking at it briefly and hoping to ignore the bright fire of Maryum's eyes.

"Divorced. He and Momma finally split up after twenty eight years. He remarried and has a baby son named Brandon."

"How's your mother?"

"Why didn't you marry her?" Maryum was painfully unrestrained. "I grew up wondering why she and my dad got hitched, since they didn't seem to get along. Then Momma told me about you when I was hung over one morning last week. If you weren't going to marry her, why couldn't you just leave her alone?"

"You don't mince words, do you?" James reflected. "Your mother was always straight to the point, too."

"You didn't answer my question."

"I didn't have to." he exhaled, while looking away from the card and engaging Maryum's eyes again. "A lot of things in this life I didn't have to do. Lots of things aren't worth trying to wake up."

"No no. That's not good enough." she gripped the side cushion of the couch for support. "I need a better answer than that. I don't even know what to call you, or why I came looking for you."

"Maryum, don't make yourself crazy because of me." he dropped the card back on the table before daring to relax. "I walked away from your mother a long time ago. We were in love....once."

"I know. She said that you wouldn't do right to save your life."

"That's....half right. Her family wasn't too crazy about me dropping out of college and playing full time with the band. Your great grandmother never much cared for me either. Things just...fell apart, and Rosalie married my brother in 66'. I didn't count on you coming along, but then I didn't count on me and Rosalie still carrying on like we did. She probably wound up marrying Gerald because I got her knocked up...with you"

"You say that so casually. Like maybe I was an afterthought, or an accident."

"Look, Maryum. I don't know what you want." he stood up and walked towards the doorway at the end of the room, turning around to face her again. "I don't know if you came here to guilt trip me, or if you're looking for a missing part of yourself, or whatever. You were barely talking and still had a diaper on last time I saw you. We don't have much past to talk about."

"No. But you and my dad do. He misses you." she purposefully turned her head to meet his eyes. "He didn't think I should come here to find you."

"Maybe you shouldn't have." he walked through the living room door to a hallway adjacent to the kitchen. "Would you like a glass of water?"

"You got any scotch?" Maryum crossed her arms and leaned back in the not too comfortable cushions. This wasn't going well. A million and one stupid questions came to mind, 'Why for?', 'What the Hell?!', and other ruminations entered her thoughts as she sat and fumed. She wondered if she was accomplishing anything worthwhile by confronting James like this, torridly reminding herself, 'He's not my father!.' She could have saved the energy and time, she thought, but she'd have remained haunted by the mystery of this man who conspired in her birth, then abandoned her to grow up in the shadow of gloom from Gerald and Rosalie. It was all too confusing, and at the moment, her main concern was whether or not James was a teetotaler.

James did have a bottle of something tucked away in a corner cabinet of his almost bare kitchen cupboard. It was the only thing in that particular cabinet, and James figured that it was time to go buy what meager odds and ends he could get for the ten bucks and miscellaneous change he'd budgeted for food this week.

The kitchen, a glum square with bone white cabinets and a dull plastic counter adorning one side of the room, was awash with the late afternoon sun. The walls, decorated with brown and white wallpaper, looked as though they were in sore need of painting, or papering. One day, he figured he'd get around to doing what needed to be done. Then again, he'd said that five years ago when Street, who was then commemorating the birth of his fourth or fifth child, gave him the bottle of bourbon. Beyond the four or five shots he'd swallowed with his friend, James hadn't drunk any of it. The label had long since faded from yellow and black to light brown and dull gray. The liquid lacked any pungent smell upon James' opening the cap and pouring it in a glass. He wasn't worried about the condition of the libation, though he could almost predict Maryum's response.

"Ugg! Ah....what exactly am I drinking?" she paused, the liquid hitting her throat like rainwater mingled in dirt.

"Some very 'Old' Grand Dad. A friend of mine gave it to me five years ago to celebrate his becoming a father again. I guess I should have maybe stored it someplace else."

"You two should have killed it. Then again, prior to last weekend, I'd never drank anything stronger than dinner wine." she stood up and walked past the living room chair in, settling at the window and observing the street scenes below. Sundown approached. The environs became less crowded. A mother's voice was raised-"Boy! You better get in this house! It's getting dark outside!"-street lights clicked on, and the sky above registered the red fade of dusk. "Do you have a garage in the back of the house?"

"I do."

"Good. I need to take the car off the street before the natives get restless."

Maryum quickly went outside and drove the rental car to the side street adjacent to the row house, before finding the double wooden doors built into the rear. At first sight, she wasn't sure the car would fit inside, but after a brief struggle with some rusty chains surrounding the handle, Maryum slid the doors open before driving the car into the dank cubicle.

Spying a few old boxes on the floor of the garage, as well as spider webs and ancient dust all over the place, Maryum steered her sedan to a safe location inside the small rectangle before cutting off the ignition.

"Phew!!" Maryum inhaled the funky air; mold, mildew, rust, corruption, that assaulted her nose the moment she exited the car. She also detected a hint of old, dirty motor oil, probably left over from the last time anyone did automotive work around the place. She stepped in it a moment after closing her car door.

"Damn!" she reached out for any hope of support as she began slipping, furtively grabbing something that jutted down from the low ceiling. Something strong enough to hold her weight and made of metal, for which she was glad, having found it with her hand and not her forehead. It was too dark for her to see much of anything. Only a small flicker of light from the still opened garage doors shown in to break the darkness, and Maryum came face to face with the wall.

The wall, dark and oppressive, was all she could see in the dim light. This wall was darker than dark. The landscape around her was even darker. Like a bad dream repeating itself unexpectedly.

"God....dammit! I'm in ...." she flustered while attempting to regain her balance and releasing her support. "a garage. I'm in a....garage. Aww... shit!"

All she'd wanted to do was get the rental car off the street, but now she found herself desperately confronting the wall in the garage. She was horrified, suddenly remembering this set of forlorn bricks and mortar from a previous evening and wanting no more of it.

"Okay." she straightened up, locating the oil slick on the concrete floor, as well as the metal light fixture she'd grabbed hold of, before walking back towards the garage double doors. There was light, though very sparse given the nearness of dusk, which led her back to the alley way through which she'd driven into the garage. Maryum had considered finding a door back into the house through the garage, but she wanted no more of that wall, since it reminded her too much of her barely forgotten nightmare.

"James?!" she clumsily called as she reentered the living room through the front door. Maryum knew she had to call him something. 'Uncle James' didn't seem quite right, but 'Dad' was out of the question. The couch on which she'd sat was empty, so was the chair that James had plopped down in. The room had no light fixtures, and was growing dark with the sunset.

"James? Where are you?"

He was gone again, just as he'd been gone all the years before, when her father had fondly spoken of him, and her mother responded to such talk with frowns and disdainful faces. She wandered into an adjacent hallway between the kitchen and what appeared to be a dining room. Beyond the empty dining room, lay the bland, sparsely adorned kitchen that James had gotten the equally bland bourbon out of. In between all three rooms, was a staircase that Maryum hadn't noticed when she'd first entered the house.

"James, are you up there?"

The mellow sound of a saxophone intruded upon Maryum's eardrums, causing her to look up the staircase and walk towards the sound. The tune, sonorous and thoughtful, drew her increasingly with each step.

"James?"

Following the sound of the saxophone to the top of the stairs, Maryum came to a hallway separating the two sides of the second floor. To her left, in the only open door of the three rooms surrounding her, a light glowed. Inside the room stood James, blowing his sax while leaning against the bare white walls, and hovering like a mother hen above a sleeping woman lying on the trundle bed.

Maryum didn't know whether to ask 'Who?', or 'What?', as she spied the sleeper James lovingly stood over. The woman was little more than a whisper beneath the beige sheets of the bed, breathing softly as the air moved ever so slightly through her flared nostrils. The hair, black with many strands of gray, looked to have been immaculately kept. The face was unlined, with smooth cinnamon skin that gave no hint as to the woman's true age. Moreover, her eyes moved rapidly beneath the eyelids, telling Maryum that the woman was enjoying a wonderful dream, or enduring a horrid nightmare.

"James, what's going on?"

He didn't answer at first, only bringing his eyes to meet Maryum's after he finished playing his music. James slid the reed from his lips and looked reflectively, first at Jasmine, then at Maryum.

"I should have waited for you in the living room so we could have come up here together. Maybe prepare you for it." he shrugged his shoulders.

"Who is she, James? Your wife? Girlfriend?"

"I really don't know." he scratched beneath his chin, his fingers becoming tangled in the gnarly whiskers. "I do know that her name is Jasmine. She'd been in some trouble before she ran into me."

"I don't understand. You don't know this woman?"

"Not....really." he hesitated while turning from Maryum to retrieve his saxophone case from a nearby brown folding chair.

"So why on earth are you serenading and tending to her? What's going on?"

"It's a long story, Maryum. Twenty five years long."

'Twenty five years?'

Maryum's baby browns opened wide with rapt attention. Twenty five years ago, she was still just a young toddler, and wouldn't have remembered the young man she unwittingly posed beside in a family photograph. Nor could she understand the man grown older and standing before her, holding a saxophone and relating his nebulous connection to this sleeping woman who did not stir, but whose closed eyes were rapid beneath eyelids that didn't conceal their motion.

"James....I don't understand."

"I don't either." he confessed while dismantling his horn. "Maybe I could explain if you give me some time. I have a spare bedroom, an extra cot, and some clean sheets if you want to spend the night."

'Twenty five years?'

Maryum couldn't remember twenty five years ago. Could barely remember much beyond the here and now, or four days past when she'd first seen the haunted eyes belonging to the stranger in her mother's scrapbook.

"Maryum, you're welcome to stay for dinner. Ain't much in the ice box, but it's enough for the two of us."

Maryum looked in James' eyes, and could find no trace of the haunted, frightened man who'd stood beside her on that late summer's day so long ago.

"Maryum?"

"No." she snapped to. "Thanks for the offer, but.... no. I've......got other appointments to keep here in B-More."

She weakly smiled and promised to visit again before finding her way back to the garage through a door in the kitchen, leaving the kitchen light on to shine through the doorway since she sought to avoid the wall again before getting back in the car. Upon returning to the highway, Maryum's smile faded, dropped into a dour depression that mirrored the dark lanes of Highway One, on towards downtown Baltimore. The more she wondered about what she'd witnessed, the worse her confusion grew, her questions became a tangled web of 'Why?' that she had no hope of answering in the current moment, if not lifetime.

She felt bad about telling James a half lie. Yes, she had other appointments and people to see in Baltimore, but not this evening. She could have stayed. Maybe even spent the night as James had invited, but she didn't dare.

Having taken a long, scary look at Jasmine, Maryum knew that she would not permit herself to fall asleep under the same roof.

12

Saul lay atop the smooth, leather covered table of his favorite masseuse while trying not to think about encroaching deadlines, troublesome editors, and adoring fans who bordered on psychotic. He also thought of Elinor, who he once loved for maybe ten seconds, but hadn't grown to hate, as had Leonard, who'd subsequently married and divorced her, succeeding in the loathing that he just couldn't muster.

"Aw, ease up, Leonard." Saul unintentionally grunted, much to the dismay of the woman standing over him. Her name was Ling Mai, and she was a certified massage therapist, as well as a student of Chiropractic.

"Excuse me?" she mused with confusion.

"I'm sorry. I was thinking out loud, and it wasn't directed at you." he apologized while lifting up his head to look at her, following her gentle urging with her fingers and turning over on his back as he tried to relax. "My editor is giving me a hassle, but you're doing just fine, Mai."

"Good." she grinned, her faintly accented voice seemed almost musical. "Don't worry about your editor, Saul. Just relax. Let it all go and 'Relax'."

'I wish.'

He felt bad about Mai finding herself on the wrong side of his mood, and briefly wondered if canceling today's session with her might have been a better idea.

"God, you're tied up in knots." Mai's unusual lapse in professionalism was punctuated with a nervous smile. She normally did her best to just work her hands back and forth over his tense muscles, but today, Saul was beyond tense. The muscles surrounding his neck and shoulders resembled a hard knot of cord, causing him headache and pain to no end. Still, she oiled her hands again and began ministering to his abdomen as Saul observed her fluid technique.

Ling Mai was tall, somewhere between five foot nine and five foot eleven. Her skin was porcelain smooth and without flaw, unless one counted the small mole on the left side of her face next to her lips. Her black hair was cut in a Dutch Boy coif that softly surrounded her face. Ling Mai's big eyes were marginally slanted, and dark like coal. Saul appreciated the view, surrendering himself to her strong hands and fantasizing about experiencing the rest of her body on his as he closed his eyes.

'Oh, yeah!' he almost voiced, imagining her muscular, strong, and naked as she straddled his hips and firmly rubbed more oil onto his thighs, rib cage, his neck,.....other places.

"Well." she blushed. "It looks as though my massage is having… an effect on you."

"Oh." he mused with embarrassment, even as he quieted his fantasies and submitted to the rest of her massage. "I guess you are. Sorry about that."

"Don't apologize." she slid down to his legs and feet, leaving the mid torso along. "A good masseuse can receive two inadvertent complements form the one being massaged. The other being that they fall asleep beneath your fingers."

Saul would definitely have preferred slumber to arousal. He'd been with Mai for nearly a year, and while she'd managed to sooth his aches and pains, as well as foster some sense of relaxation, he'd never fallen asleep beneath her fingers. It had been long since anything, much less someone's touch, had put him to sleep.

Thirty minutes later, and only slightly less tense than beforehand, Saul had left Mai's Greenwich Village loft, and headed uptown for the meeting he truly dreaded. He'd not seen Leonard since the formal book signing party a week ago, and frankly, he wasn't in a hurry to see him again. He'd previously had vague thoughts of cancelling the session with Mai. Now he almost wished to be back on her table again.

'More massage?' he smiled, recalling who he'd actually said that to in the painfully distant past, when a late winter's day into spring would dissolve into the winter he continued to endure even now.

"More massage, please?!" he recalled looking up into Marceleen's beautiful blue eyes, which had inspired him immensely, and eased the pain of living. Love waited just around the corner; he knew that every time she smiled at him, just as she did while they sat together on the green of Boston University during the last day of class before spring break, 1979. His involvement in a tutorial program he'd volunteered for in Baltimore, Maryland, would keep him away from her for the next two weeks, and David hated it. Marceleen, on the other hand, was on her way to paradise.

"Why, David, I do believe you're getting addicted to my touch." she smiled, rubbing the muscles of his neck and shoulders.

"It's nice. You're nice. I can't think of anything else I'd rather be addicted to."

She wrapped her arms around his shoulders while burying her nose on the back of his head, quietly contemplating the regimen they'd shared for the last six months-daily swimming, weight training three times a week, bicycling, running, raising doves-and rejoicing in the benefits; David gave up drugs and drinking, and they both enjoyed the blossom of friendship and love that had followed. He could feel the warmth of her smile, the depth of her affection as it rested on him, even as he sensed the tint of sadness included in her demeanor.

"I really wish you could come with us. I hear Greece is really nice this time of year, but I'm going to miss you."

"Likewise. And I honestly wish maybe we were going up to Reading together, so I can meet your folks. I've already been to Greece." he stumbled, hoping she could read between the lines he wrote with his voice, praying she could discern the script written on his heart. "Besides, I'm going to catch holy hell feeding those birds without your guidance, before I leave tomorrow morning."

"Ha!! You'll do just fine. Besides, you turned me on to Camus, Voltaire, and Shelly. But, I'll still never understand Hendrix." she laughed while gently prodding his sweat suited thigh with the heel of her bare foot. Dressed as they were, he in gray sweats; she in cut off blue jeans, white tee shirt, an open blue paisley vest, a red bandana tied around her neck, sans shoes and brassier, David enjoyed their being so funky. She grabbed his hand and stood up. He followed suit. Off in the distance, some street blocks away, David glimpsed a red 1976 Ford Mustang convertible. The car was driven by Gina,-captain of the swim team, Marceleen's closest friend- and would take Marceleen away from him.

"I think I see Gina driving up." she walked not so briskly to the center of the campus green, bringing David with her as they walked near the Sherman Student Union Building, the University Information Center, and the Mugar Memorial Library. He paid no attention to the neo colonial and contemporary red brick and brown concrete edifices, the clear blue sky around them without a trace of cloud, or even the green grass beneath their feet. David only had eyes for Marceleen.

"I love you, David." her voice mellow as a shower on a summer day. Gently, longingly, she almost whispered. "Hope you know that. I can't think of another way to tell you....what I know."

"I....can't either." he smiled, kissing her and drawing her comfortably closer into his arms. His fingers were lost in her long, frizzy blond hair, and he prayed that his embrace would convey the message of his feeling better than his lips, still unready to say 'I love you.' There was still too much pain of days past he hadn't broken through; too much agony to be salved, though he imagined that she'd be patient enough to wait as he found his way. He was happy, for now, to hold her close in his arms and kiss her affectionately.

Amid the green grass, the approach of warm temperatures, and even the gawk of curious classmates walking past, David Green and Marceleen Goldberg embraced for the final time. They thought only for the semester. They didn't care, nor did they hear the sound of the car's horn blowing until it occurred for the third time.

"Hey, Goldberg?! C'mon!!" a small, lithe, dark haired girl sporting a gray tee shirt and granny styled glasses was hanging out of the driver's side of the Mustang convertible. Marceleen and David broke their embrace long enough for her to turn towards the road from where the car was approaching.

"Damn." David muttered as he pulled at his gray sweat pants, feeling a twinge of regret and jealously, but feeling more unspoken affection to accompany Marceleen on her journey.

"Got to go." she kissed him again, turning to gingerly sprint away as she went to join Gina in the car. Impulsively, she did a series of three cartwheels when she was far enough away from David and came up laughing, much to his delight. Her eyed her wonderful, womanly figure, and was more than eager for the sight in full symphony, which awaited him in a fortnight.

David never saw Marceleen again.

She vanished in the night, leaving David to turn towards darkness deeper than the drugs and drink she'd helped him escape from. David disappeared, much like the hysterical woman whose account Saul read about in an old newspaper microfilm from 1969 at the 40th Street branch of the New York City Public Library.

The Baltimore Sun, a newspaper he might have briefly glanced at when he'd visited the city in 1979, related the tale of an escaped patient from a Georgia mental hospital, who'd stolen one of the doctor's cars and driven all the way up to Baltimore. The mystery, he pondered, of this young coed who'd been involved in a southern farm project, witnessed a murder, stolen a car and drove all the way to Baltimore, before finally parking the car at the front gate of the cemetery where the murder victim had been buried. Then she disappeared. It was interesting, but Saul soon abandoned his exploration in the library, walking to Central Park and going to the midst of the urban garden, despite knowing where he had to go next. He really didn't wish to see Leonard today.

Trees were beginning to bloom in the park; forsythia blossomed, its pink flowers were just gaining the courage to rise above winter's chill that was only a few weeks past. Spring, he thought, was just another season. Regardless of how green the grass got, how high it grew, or how bright the sun shined, Saul couldn't enjoy the coming of spring. Such angst was evident when he finally arrived in Leonard's Manhattan office. After entering the gray granite sky scrapper and stepping on to the elevator, Saul reluctantly pressed the button to take him to the seventh floor. He knew that Leonard wouldn't take it well when he admitted to still being unable to write anything of worth.

"Jeez, Saul. This is getting way too serious." Leonard sank his head into his hands as he slumped over his desk. "But first, I need to apologize for all the crap I said to you last weekend."

Saul was uncomfortable in the plush brown love seat adjacent to the wide window offering him a full view of Central Park below. He chose not to sit in the white chair in front of Leonard's desk, since Leonard seemed more frazzled than sincerely apologetic.

"Saul, I talked with the editorial board this morning; explained that aside from your bestsellers, American Reader's Press probably wouldn't be much more than a piss poor subsidy house. They....kind of saw the light."

"Really?" Saul dead panned gently.

"Yeah." Leonard exhaled cautiously before looking Saul in the eyes. "The board decided to give you until June to produce an outline."

"How kind of them. I should probably send them a thank you card from my padded cell, eh Len?"

"Saul, I'm sorry, okay?!" Leonard was trying to recover. "I tried to convince them that you needed some serious time off, but all they're interested in right now is keeping the booksellers happy."

"And what about the authors?" Saul stood up, shoving his hands in the pockets of his white cotton slacks. He turned to the window and looked out of it so longingly that Leonard feared his friend might try to jump through it and sprout futile wings.

"I...can't answer that." Leonard stammered. "Nobody thought to address the issue."

"Well somebody should have. I'm burnt out, Len. I'm tired of going to the well of nightmares, okay? I spent an hour at the 40th Street library, looking though old newspapers, magazines, and even encyclopedias looking for some inspirations. I found bumpkus, man." Saul turned to face Leonard, his eyes sad and sullen. "There's enough horror in the world, Leonard. I really don't feel like adding to it anymore.

"The only thing I want....is to start living like a normal human being again. I want to write good stuff for a change."

"You do write good stuff, Saul."

"Oh give me a break!" he approached Leonard's desk. "Fucking vampires, serial killers, psychotic kitty cats, good stuff?! Ancient curses? Fucking headless ghouls roaming the countryside and decapitating people to replace their own cranials, good stuff?! Bullshit!! I don't think so, Len. I've dredged up every ounce of dread, slime, and horror I could think of and I'm tired. I just don't want to write this shit anymore."

The silence was almost unbearable, and Leonard could see the livid manifestation of slaughter, nightmare, desecration, and perhaps an undiscovered doorway to Hades, or worse, that lay behind Saul's tortured gray eyes. Leonard shuddered while taking in his halted breath, barely wanting to open his mouth.

"Saul...it sounds like you need to get laid. Maybe take a long vacation, get a good night's sleep, or something like that."

"Maybe." Saul sat in front of Leonard's desk, his eyes closed as if he didn't want any further input, or better, not to look at Leonard again.

"Yeah!" Leonard continued with animation. "That sounds like just the ticket. Poor slob works like a dog for over a decade, then decides to take a two week vacation in the Caribbean. He meets a beautiful love goddess on the beaches of St. Croix. They spend a night together, having great sex from midnight to sunrise before drifting off to sleep. He wakes up a few hours later and finds himself alone. I mean, he wonders what happened to her, but he really doesn't give it much thought until he walks into the bathroom to take a shower."

"And then?" not that Saul was interested, but Leonard was on a roll, and it would be pointless to stop him.

"Well, you could provide the next idea. You could put that imagination of yours to work and maybe turn this into some erotic horror story, make it a kinky 'S&M' story, or some other weird twist on the erotic level."

"And what would you do with it, Leonard?"

"In my story, he opens the bathroom door and screams when he sees the woman sitting butt naked on the toilet, and slit wide open from the top of her crotch clear to her sternum. She's got an ear to ear smile on her face and her eyes are looking towards heaven. Plus, the walls, ceiling, and floor have all sorts of religious and occult symbols painted in blood all over them. It gets worse when he raises his hands to cover his eyes and sees that they're covered with blood that wasn't there before he stepped into the bathroom. What do you think, Saul?!"

"I don't think you heard a word I said." he calmly retorted while icily rising from the chair and walking out of the room. He heard Leonard's desperate calls-"Saul! Wait up, man! I was just joking, brother. Okay?! Saul?!?"-but he didn't respond, being fed up with Leonard and possessing not an ounce of sympathy for his erstwhile friend. Another bomb had fallen, he thought grimly, while taking the elevator down to the ground. The scorched earth of another marred friendship added to the already painful day. Leonard was the latest disappointment, and not even the fizz from the brackish soda pop he'd purchased from a sidewalk vendor could convince Saul otherwise. He'd considered going over to the coffee shop just outside of the building where American Reader's Press was located, maybe drown his sorrows in a tall cappuccino, but decided against it. He wasn't in the mood to possibly be recognized by a rabid fan and get mugged for an autograph. Bitterly, Saul swallowed more of the soda pop, contemplating his last sentence to Leonard.

'*I don't think you heard a word I said.*'

Leonard hadn't listened at all, Saul realized. He still felt the same a few hours later while lying in the king sized bed of his luxury apartment in Manhattan.

The apartment, a spacious efficiency with a luxurious master suite and bath attached, was Saul's refuge from the world outside, so unlike the beautiful red brick colonial on a wooded acre in Long Island, where he'd shared four years of marital chaos with Elinor. Such, he reasoned, they might have spared one another save the fears of middle aged loneliness, biological time clocks, and other nutty notions inflicted on his generation.

He'd wanted the Hamptons; she'd wanted the inner city where she was a social worker. They compromised, picking the suburbs and an unlisted phone number, but it was probably the last thing they successfully accomplished together. It was also, ultimately, why he purchased the apartment.

"Damn. Did I have to think about her?" he whispered just as the telephone rang, prompting him to consider cursing out whoever was calling. He settled for letting his answering machine handle it instead.

"Saul, it's me. Leonard." the voice was nervously low key. "I can't go back to the editorial board with what you told me, man. You got to give me something better than what you said before you left today, okay? Call me. We'll have lunch or something, huh?"

111

13

Save some residual subconscious sense of piety, Maryum might have disregarded the Gideon's bible she'd inadvertently knocked to the floor upon awakening when her battery operated alarm clock buzzed on at approximately nine A.M. Given her sleep deprivation of the last few days, Maryum didn't welcome the brittle buzz emanating from alarm sitting besides the bible on the bed stand.

"Awwwwwwhhw...doo doo!!" her arm swept out from under the blanket as she reached to turn off the mechanical maniac screeching unmercifully. Her motion sent both the alarm clock and the Gideon's good book crashing to the brown carpeted floor, and also precipitated her unhappy scramble from the hotel's queen sized bed in pursuit of the still screaming alarm clock. "God....damn. God... diddly, diddly, damn!"

She reached the dwned alarm clock and hurriedly pressed the red button to silence the infernal machine. She took a quick look at the plastic monitor face as it changed from nine A.M., to one minute later, while tugging at her oversized navy blue tee shirt with the bold white letters saying 'LANGTREE', on her chest, just as she was hit by the mid morning sunlight, and the unsettling sight of the bible sprawled open and face down on the floor.

Picking up the bible, Maryum briefly glanced at the verse in Proverbs- 'Vanity. All is vanity, saith the preacher'-before abruptly closing the book cover. Her next fast action wasn't vain, as she ran to the bathroom after feeling the subtle tingling between her legs. If it was what she thought it was, Maryum would sooner be sitting on the toilet than staring at a page in the scriptures that she didn't find all that holy just now.

A shower left Maryum feeling better, though she didn't feel relieved at the arrival of her period; she wasn't pregnant, but then she wasn't carrying Dennis' child, either. Hurriedly putting on a clean pair of blue jeans and a red sweater, Maryum regretted that she'd be denied the chance to bear even a small part of her lost love inside of her. That reality nagged at her, as she made a long distance phone call to her mother.

"Ma, I'm at a motel on Russell Street in South Baltimore called the Harbor Inn. It's over near the maritime industries and the big power plant near I 95."

Seated on the bed, Maryum glimpsed through the phone book, turning pages until she found the listings for the University of Maryland, Baltimore. 'Bingo!', she thought, while Rosalie distracted her from the search.

"Oh Lord. First you go to that commune with Gerald and his love child." Rosalie wearily declared. "But what on earth are you doing in Baltimore?!"

"I'm going to see one of my professors from Langtree who got a job here at the University of Maryland a few years ago. Maybe he can help me figure out what to do next."

"I hope so." Rosalie continued from the other end. "And I hope you haven't had your head stuck in a liquor bottle this trip."

"No, Mom. Daddy and Brianne have to wait for the Spring Equinox Festival to get their ration of grog. And James only had a five year old bottle of bourbon that tasted too flat for jazz." she heard her mother exhale mournfully on the other end, before growing silent. "Momma...?"

"I'm still here." Rosalie hesitated. "How is James?"

"He's....here, Momma. It's a long story and you're probably not going to believe it. I'm not sure I'm ready to even try explaining. Not yet."

Not that she could explain anything at this point. The traumatic thoughts of her last encounter with James came to mind, haunting her even after she'd hung up the phone, eaten a breakfast of oatmeal, grapefruit, and strawberries, and taken to the road in her green rental car. Maryum remained painfully confused. Supposedly, she was going to the University of Maryland to look up her former instructor and old friend, Dr. Quentin Braxley, and maybe inquire into the possibilities of a transfer there. But her journey had taken a strange turn after she'd met James and Jasmine. She remained clueless as to what would follow next, hoping for a rescue from the strangeness via her appointment for the morning.

On the outskirts of downtown Baltimore, the campus of the University of Maryland sat on several large city blocks. Red brick and dark glass buildings decorated the landscape where Maryum parked her car. She found a space near the Thurgood Marshall Law Library before dropping seventy five cents into the parking meter, and walking towards the center of campus, fervently hoping that Dr. Braxley would help her move beyond the nothingness she was currently plagued with regarding her future.

Dr. Quentin Braxley had a corner office in the psychology building that sat a few block north of Westminister Hall, the old church where Edgar Allen Poe was buried. A fitting irony, Quentin thought as he sat at his mahogany desk and read the most recent Journal of the American Psychiatric Society, featuring a story on drug abuse by famous figures of history. Edgar Allen Poe graced the magazine's front cover.

"Edgar old boy, it's too bad we couldn't have met one hundred and sixty years ago." he snickered, briefly entertaining notions of what he might have done had Poe sat in on one of his twelve step counseling programs.

"Dr. Braxley," the voice of his secretary came through the intercom on his desk top. "Ms. Dupaul is here to see you."

"Yes. Thank you, Gina." he immediately sat up and closed the magazine. Quickly straightening his black neck tie, Quentin ran a comb through his totally gray hair, cut moderately short around his balding brown scalp. "Send her in."

Maryum entered the office and it was all she could do to keep from flying across the room into his arms. Yes, he was fat, balding, with a potato nose, and blotchy dark skin unevenly toned across the whole of his body. But right now, Dr. Braxley was the best sight her sore eyes had laid eyes on.

"Hello, Quentin." she walked over and grasped his hand affectionately. "Been awhile."

"Too long, Maryum." he smiled. "This is most surprising."

"I know." she responded, sitting down in front of his desk, where he'd prominently displayed a photograph of himself shaking hands with Dr. Martin Luther King, Jr., at Mason Temple Church of God in Christ, in Memphis, Tennessee, on April 3rd of 1968. "I hadn't planned on coming to Baltimore, but circumstances necessitated I find you, ASAP."

"Yes. I imagine your blowout with Langtree was most difficult." he mused. "I know that mine was."

"Well, that's one reason I'm here, Quentin."

"Oh?" he walked around to his seat and nervously tried to straighten up the clutter on his desk. Maryum didn't need such a gesture on his part, and happily, he sat back down and interlaced his fingers in front of him before focusing his whole attention on her.

"I met my biological father for the first time, yesterday."

"Maryum, who's hand did I shake at your graduation two years ago?" his bushy gray eyebrows raised up in a horseshoe.

"Technically, you met my Uncle Gerald." Maryum was annoyed at having to reveal this. "James, my dad's older brother, and my mother were responsible for my conception."

"So.... how are you dealing with it, Maryum?"

"I don't know....yet. It's not like I have any loyalty to James simply because he fathered me. In fact, I'd never even met him until two days ago. I'm not even sure why I bothered to find him since my main purpose for coming to

Baltimore was to talk with you. Right now, my whole life is like a bad road map and I wish to God I knew where it was going to lead me."

"That depends on where you plan on going, Maryum." Quentin was relaxed, but direct. "Regardless of what went down, I hope you know where you're headed."

"Quentin, I wish you'd still been at Langtree this year. My late night phone call last week didn't do justice in describing the situation." She'd reached inside the left corner of the blue cotton jacket she was wearing to retrieve her pack of Camel cigarettes, when she noticed him eyeing her warily, almost as though he were saying 'Oh no you don't!'. Out of habit, she offered him one.

"Sorry. I quit six months ago." he affirmed. "I always thought Camel's were too harsh anyway."

"Then you wouldn't have liked what happened at Langtree last month, either." she placed the cigarette back in the pack, not noticing an ash tray nearby, and suddenly realizing that a stray spark might have set the whole cluttered office afire. "So many folks tried to cover their asses over what happened in D.D.E. that I thought of purchasing toilet tissue for everybody in the psych department."

"Which brings us to the matter of your sexual adventures with Dennis Williamson McClain." he uttered firmly, much to Maryum's surprise. "Yes, I learned about it from talking to the coordinator of the D.D.E. program. Ms. Monroe, I believe her name is. Given the vagueness of our conversation last week, I figured that there was more to this than you were telling me, Maryum, and I wondered when you were going come clean about it."

"Quentin,...I was honestly going to tell you about it today." she stumbled, feeling betrayed that he'd inquired of this with anyone at Langtree, as well as stunned by his ability to hide his critical intentions. "And not to sound defensive, but it really isn't the huge deal that the college is trying to make of it."

"On the contrary, Maryum, it's a major factor in this whole situation. Reporting the shortcomings of the program was all well and good, but you shouldn't have slept with your patient."

"Oh please. Quentin, I am not a psychiatrist....yet. Moreover, I wasn't even working in D.D.E. when all hell broke loose. What happened with Dennis and I had nothing to do with what was going on in the program."

"Maryum, don't try to kid a kidder, okay?" he was patient, controlled even, as he opened one of his desk drawers and pulled out an ash tray. "You are a graduate student in psychology with grand ambitions of becoming a first class head shrink. That means prescribing medicines, doing therapies, supervising patient routines, and caseloads ad infinitum. Do you really think any self respecting medical board is going to hand you a license after the fiasco at Langtree? Particularly, if it turns into a mess where some folks wind up doing jail time?"

She hardly perceived the gray glass fixture as he slid it within reach of her fingers, but a half second later, her automatic smoker kicked in and she pulled out one of the cancer straws. She looked down long enough to put the cigarette to her lips and light it before locking again on Quentin's unflinching gaze.

"Maryum, you are the brightest student I've ever had in any of my classes. The whole psych department at Langtree was a carton of burnt out light bulbs by comparison."

"Thanks." she exhaled her first intake of blue smoke turned white. "I needed that."

"It wasn't a compliment." he grew more serious. "The point is, you shot yourself in both feet and stabbed yourself in the back by getting romantically involved with this former client. With you bringing down heat on Langtree D.D.E., didn't you consider the possibility of the college using your ill timed liaison with your client to discredit you? I also guess that getting discovered never occurred to you, no? Now, did I ever tell you, or any of my other students, to do stupid stuff and not cover your rear ends?!"

"Dennis' aunt and uncle were supposed to be gone all weekend." she muttered, while flicking cigarette ashes into the tray. "He forgot to pack a full supply of insulin and they came back a day early. Diabetes runs in his family."

"I didn't ask about anybody's medical condition. I want to know your rationale for what occurred between you and the client."

"Quentin, I'd worked with Dennis for nearly three months. I'm the one responsible for getting him into the Starbright Institute, where he's flourishing, thank you, and not being warehoused in D.D.E. Once he had access to augmentive devices I got to really communicate with him. Got to know his thoughts, listen to his heart. We talked every day...."she trailed off into a sob, covering her mouth with her hand before looking into Quentin's dispassionate eyes.

"In other words, you got emotionally involved with your charge. You stepped over the line that separates you from the populace you're trying to serve." he stood up and lightly pushed back the chair with his rear end. Exhaling as though he were too pooped to pop, he looked profoundly disappointed. "Maryum, you can't permit yourself the luxury of involvement with your patients. Yes, I know he wasn't your patient since you're not a doctor yet, but you'll deal with this again somewhere down the road. Trust me. God help you if it happens after you've established residency or a practice somewhere."

"Thank you, Mr. Spock, for reminding me that I must remain in control of my emotions." Maryum tersely crushed her half smoked cigarette into the ash tray." I guess you think that I have to learn to totally divorce myself from my feelings about people and their lives while acting as their therapist, huh?"

"You summed it up pretty well, Maryum."

She wanted to scream, but she hadn't come this far just to emote and fall out all over Quentin's desk. She almost desired to scratch his eyes out for having contacted Tina Monroe, even as the rational part of her mind came into play, and she remembered having never heard Quentin say anything that didn't make a whole lot of sense. She also dreaded facing the reality that he might be right about all of this, and that knowledge brought forth a small tear. She tried to hide what was going on inside of her, only to abandon the pretense when Quentin presented her a tissue.

"Need this?"

"Thanks." she sniffled before crying out loud, feeling precious little comfort at the feel of Quentin gently grasping her free hand while she dried her eyes with the other. The tissue was soft, comforting. More than her friend had been prior to this moment.

"I don't mean to be unnecessarily hard on you, Maryum, but you have to understand how important it is for you to place your client's welfare above your own feelings. Someone more cynical than me would ask who you thought you were saving; that young man, or yourself. Psychiatry can be a terribly cruel discipline if you truly care about the people you work with, and sometimes, we must take drastic steps to avoid getting into situations like the one you've just lived through. It's never easy, Maryum, but it's essential if you're going to stay saner than your patients."

Long after she'd departed from Dr. Braxley's office, Maryum remained mindful of their conversation, even while munching on a hot dog and some French fries in a nearby campus eatery. She considered all of the voices she'd heard of late, advising, admonishing, or painfully upbraiding, as was her mother.

"Even after Gerald and I were married, that bastard wouldn't leave me alone."

Maryum tried not to think of her mother's vehemence and bitterness, sipping on a soda pop as she looked around the not too crowded student delicatessen. Maryum sat at the bar and paid little attention to the few student bodies-assorted blonds, brunettes, and deadheads-inhabiting the nearby tables and booths. She caught brief snippets of conversation; Nags

117

Head, Cancun, Jacksonville, Ocean Beach, debauchery, sunburn, etcetera, etcetera, etcetera, and didn't begrudge them their vacation from school, though she did wish that the eatery had something a little stronger than root beer for her to sip on.

Her visit to Dr. Braxley had been a brief respite from the other matters that clawed at her attention, but Maryum wasn't sure her thinking was any clearer in the aftermath. A week after her acrimonious departure form Langtree, Maryum was still doing what she'd been doing from moment one; sullenly eating or drinking something to hide from the pain and knowing all the while that she couldn't.

"You can't hide from yourself, Maryum." her father had said to her as they walked along the tree lined path between the group house he shared with Brianne, Brandon, and twenty other people in Mindful, and the community hall that she'd fairly swooned in upon entering. He'd been at peace that day, so unlike her embittered mother, whom she could barely stand living underneath the same roof with.

"Daddy, everything seems to be spinning out of control. I can't make heads or tails about what's going down." she told him. She'd been near tears, looking into his love filled eyes and knowing that he'd wanted to fold his arms around her. But he was holding Brandon as they walked the path and the only comfort he could afford her was his voice.

"Sweetheart, there are things that we have control over, and things we can't even dream of controlling, no matter how hard we try. The point isn't just knowing the difference, but acquiring the wisdom to act accordingly regarding those things, to the benefit of everyone concerned."

Maryum contemplated her father's words that afternoon. She nearly yielded to the sunlight, blue skies, the scent of flowers, sweet herbs and incense which wonderfully flavored the air. But Maryum felt woefully out of place in the joyful quietness of a community consciously seeking peace, and had a sinking feeling that she might never accomplish that for herself. Acceptance of her father's happiness was one thing, but Maryum wasn't ready to gleefully surrender herself to such contentment with all the turmoil relentlessly slapping her upside the head.

"What on earth do you think you're doing?!"

The words,-brittle, haunting, and anguished-returned to Maryum's thoughts again, turning the taste of lunch into wormwood. Maryum had wanted to forget everything about Cornelia McClain, especially the horrid sound of her whiny, high pitched voice, which unexpectedly shattered the communion she'd shared with Dennis.

"I don't know what's going on here," Cornelia wore a dress similar, if not identical, to the same black dress she'd worn on the morning she and Darris had

met Maryum. *"but you can make damn sure we won't stand for you molesting this child."*

"He's not a child, Mrs. McClain." Maryum pleaded as she scrambled to put on her panties. "He's a full grown man who...."

"Miss Dupaul!" Cornelia's hands were on her hips now, a scowl adorned her dark face. "I think you'd better get dressed and get out of this house."

Maryum struggled for words, wondering how much of a point she could make standing there in Dennis' bedroom, wearing nothing but her gray panties and a grimace. She beheld Cornelia furtively yanking the covers over Dennis' frail, naked frame, as well as the fear and pain on Dennis' face as he scrambled his attention between the two women. The sight was not pleasant.

A week later, all Maryum could think of while departing the café and abandoning her half eaten frank and fries, was her last sight of Dennis in deep despair at her hasty, unhappy departure. Just another reason to detest Cornelia, who Maryum almost wished to have sliced up on her plate, rather than her hot dog.

The neighborhood where James lived was not very far from Maryum's hotel, and in driving there, she thought of yesterday's meeting-if it could rightly be called that-with Jasmine. She pondered James' circumstances, wondering how anyone could live in the same house with someone for twenty five years and not be well acquainted with them. Nor could she understand any possible connection, or maybe attraction, that James held for this woman he lovingly serenaded with his saxophone while she slept.

Driving along the roads of the east Baltimore neighborhood, Maryum wondered if James was at home, but even more, she questioned his reality, and sanity. Perhaps she wondered at her own grip, given her intense interest in someone who'd only been a stranger in a photograph a few short days ago. Something about his demeanor, staid, quiet, not at all alarmed or defeated about his lowly circumstances, was very unnerving to Maryum. She kept in mind that James was her dad's brother, and it was eerie that both of them had a kind of peace that eluded her. She stepped harder on the accelerator as she turned the last curve before arriving on the street where James' row house lay.

It was nearly sundown as Maryum's rental car rolled down Black Street. She slowed the car as she passed the house numbered '4102', remembering that James lived at '4216'.

'Maybe I should just go back to the hotel.'she thought seriously, just as she began speaking the addresses she passed. "Forty one ninety eight; forty two hundred. Forty two....twelve."

She caught sight of the familiar brown brick of James' row house and was minded to turn onto the side street and park her car in the rear garage, when she saw a light go on in the second floor window, accompanied by the ethereal silhouette of a person in the midst of it. Maryum noticed the long, straight hair, the slender figure standing at the window, and suddenly cared nothing about the road.

"Who is she, James?"

Maryum's mind echoed her inquiry of the day before, and she recalled him knowing nothing besides the woman's name and what little of her story she'd related to him. There were too many questions as Maryum peered into the window and realized for certain that she was looking at Jasmine.

"Oh my…. God." Maryum took a turn into a nearby driveway and made a 'U' turn, departing the street and leaving herself no time to ponder the matter as she streaked heedlessly down the road. She wasn't prepared to see this woman awake, and seriously wondered if she ever would be.

14

The last time Saul was in Baltimore, he was still David Green, and Baltimore Washington International Airport was little more than a traffic jam in the opposite direction his sixty seven Rambler with the rebuilt engine was headed. He couldn't have afforded to fly in and out of BWI back in 1979. When last Saul had seen this part of the east coat, he'd been a happy camper like the six students he'd noticed while sipping a cappuccino in a terminal café.

The students were dressed in a variety of sweat clothes, denim pants and jackets, baseball caps, Birkenstock sandals, army boots, and the like, as they sat and stood together in a row of seats, conversing and checking their camping gear. He overheard one of the boys, a strapping six footer with flaming red hair and large jug ears, talking about the granite cliffs near where he hoped to pitch the group's tents. He also heard the resulting groans from the rest of the group, and grinned at the response of the petite coed, sitting lotus style on the floor, who wore a green vinyl Pancho over her ragged denim pants, brown hiking boots, and had a blue bandanna covering her curly black hair.

"Oh gag me, Shawn!" she playfully stuck her index finger in her mouth. "Bad enough we'll be between 'Redneck' North Carolina and 'Inbred' Tennessee. Now you want us to camp out on a rock?!"

Amid the resounding group laughter, another student-long legged, with waist length honey blond hair rolling down her back-ceased stuffing a cheese croissant into her mouth long enough to correct her friend; informing everyone that 'Inbred' was actually in West Virginia.

Vicariously enjoying the student's camaraderie, Saul fondly recalled having had his last good time as a college student in Baltimore. He'd spent most of his last spring break in this city, tutoring inner city children in an English department project that he'd actually not wanted to get involved with. He'd have waited patiently in Boston for Marceleen's return, but she'd encouraged him to go since she didn't want him worrying about her for the next two weeks.

Saul smiled as he sipped his cappuccino, observing the curly headed young woman, only to see her stare at him with apprehension. She quickly turned away from him, and the thirty yards between Saul and the young woman suddenly became an open air barrier, leaving Saul sad as he drank his frothy java from a safe distance. Maybe the girl recognized his face and was too terrified to say anything about it. Or worse, he shuddered to think of her inadvertently reading the foreboding behind his eyes. Grimly, he wondered if the camp out would end happily for these young folks, or were they in store for the kind of news that greeted him upon his return to Boston University in the spring of '79'.

Forsythias, Goldenrods, Dandelions, and a variety of other flowers had begun to blossom in the two weeks since David Green had sat with Goldie on the university green. The sight and smell of the foliage excited his weary senses as he walked to his dorm room. The drive from Baltimore had taken nearly ten and a half hours, and except for three hours in a New Jersey rest area, David hadn't slept since waking up the previous morning. Still, his lack of sleep wouldn't hinder his laboring as the Hummingbird's understudy this morning.

"Tonight, our eternity begins. We celebrate this love, without end. Oh well….." David warbled a tune currently inhabiting the Billboard 'Top 40s', certain that Freddie Hayes would suggest he only 'Listen' to the music from now on, were he to ever hear this horrible rendition. "My heart will melt into yours. We will love, forever more. Oh....love!"

He paid little attention to his classmates walking alongside him this morning, figuring that most of them dreaded the return to classes on Monday. A few carried suitcases, no doubt filled with dirty clothes they'd neglected to wash during spring break. David carried nothing but a dozen red roses wrapped in light green paper as he trekked down the street to reach his dorm room in the red brick South Campus Residential Area, which was scheduled to close for renovation at the end of spring semester. Which suited David fine, since he and Goldie had planned to move into a loft downtown at the end of the semester anyway.

"Yoo, hoo!! Davie boy's home!" he chirped upon opening the front door of the dormitory. Looking into the almost empty lobby, David saw only Mr. Chance, the gruff, cigar chomping janitor buffing the terrazzo floor and looking at David as if he'd lost his mind. David smiled at the crusty Septuagenarian, tall and unbowed despite his age, who's thin gray hair was packed underneath a beige fishing hat. Mr. Chance possessed an even thinner frame, which never the less was strong enough to handle a buffer machine, or pick up a car battery in one hand, as David had once observed in a parking lot. Today, Mr. Chance was wearing olive green coveralls and brown work boots that had looked better two sole replacements ago.

"I swear, Green." Mr. Chance released the handle on the mechanical buffer, shutting down the machine and pulling the cigar butt from his lips.

"Why da' hell you got to be coming in here makin' all this noise on Sunday morning?!"

"Well, I got my reasons, Mr. C." David looked carefully over the floor before holding the flowers teasingly in front of Mr. Chance's face. "Besides, you didn't think these roses were for you, did you?"

"Do tell?" Mr. Chance commented while crossing his forearms atop the buffer's handlebars. "So when's her parole date? Oops! I meant, who's the lucky lady?"

"You'll see." David chuckled and started backing out the door. "Guess I'll go around to the side entrance, huh?!"

"Be my guest. Oh yeah, Freddie Hayes is looking for you. I think he's somewhere in the hall." the old man muttered as he shut his machine back on and went back to his task. He waited until David had closed the door and was out of sight before unleashing the sniffle and moan he'd hidden. Mr. Chance released the handle again, this time bringing the back of his hand up to his eyes and hastily wiping away the tears that stung his cheeks before he resolutely clamped his lips together, and cut his buffer back on again. The world, Mr. Chance knew, was sometimes as rough and ugly as the red fiber pad that furtively stripped old wax from the floor, but he wished that David could be spared that knowledge in the way he was about to get it.

David somberly eyed his dorm room, thinking that he wouldn't be living there much longer. Four walls of blue and gray concrete with a light brown tile floor, David had spent the last three and a half years trying to make the place habitable. He cut on his black Sanyo boom box, filling the room with Goldie's beloved Haydn, as he went about trying to straighten up the place in anticipation of her eventual visit. There were dungarees, blue jeans, white socks, and sweat clothes strewn about, waiting to be washed. He spied a pair of used underwear beneath the unmade twin bed he normally slept in.

"Oh dear. I have to do better than this." he muttered while bending over to pick the clothing up. Everything else looked clean and not dusty. There was no visible dirt, and mercifully, no trace of body odor, despite the unkempt condition he'd left the place in a week ago. The small coke mirror, which had been given a bracket and now sat atop his white dresser drawer, bore no trace of its former illicit employ. His posters- one of the late Jimi Hendrix, his impassioned face surrounded by thick smoke from the reefer he held in his fingers, the other of an Orangutan posing behind steel bars above the bold caption 'HARD TIME'- weren't leaning for a change. He and Marceleen would probably argue about him keeping the Hendrix, or so he thought.

"Dave?"

David looked up from his labors to see Freddie Hayes standing in the room's doorway. Freddie, all of six foot four, darker than midnight, and sporting a five inch Afro hairstyle, had latched his soulful brown eyes on David as though his life depended on it. David always thought that Freddie would have made a great point guard on the basketball squad, had he not been so dedicated to playing bassoon with the university orchestra.

"What's happening, Fred?!" David took a hip tone at Freddie's sudden appearance. He dropped his few articles of clothing in a nearby wicker basket and walked over to Freddie, hand outstretched for a handshake. "Yeah. Old man Chance said you were looking for me."

"Are you alright, man?" Freddie's long face turned increasingly serious as he gazed at David.

"I'm right as rain, Freddie. What's the haps with you?!" David detected a weird detachment in Freddie's demeanor, and wondered if his friend and former dope smoking partner was maybe doing some bad acid. The two clasped hands, but Freddie was distracted by the roses that sat in a clear glass vase full of water on David's desk. Blood red roses.

"I guess you don't know." Freddie looked back at David, his eyes now sad.

"Know what?"

"I think you better sit down, Dave."

"Freddie, what's going on?!" David inquired with a grin, noticing how Freddie's dark blue tee shirt and bell bottomed blue jeans seemed to fit him like a shroud. "What's got you so bent out of shape, man?"

"Dave, I still think you should sit down." Freddie walked into the room and sat on the bed while David leaned against the wall next to his desk. Freddie still couldn't break his sight from those roses.

"Dammit, Freddie, just tell me!"

"Marceleen's dead." Freddie's voice sounded as lifeless as its subject matter. David stared at Freddie for a long moment, not believing what he'd just heard and feeling as though he'd been struck with an ugly stick. Then he looked down at Freddie, hoping for some sign of ill humor before crossing his arms.

"You're bullshitting, right?! Please tell me this is a real bad joke, Fred."

"I wish I could, Dave." Freddie moaned. "But I wouldn't joke about something like this. I know she thought I was a bad influence on you, but I liked her. She was....good people. She shouldn't have died ....like she did."

"What....happened, Freddie?" David's skin began to crawl as he slowly sank into a sitting position on the desk.

"She and Gina and ....Ruthie, I think...."Freddie was nearly sobbing. "were driving down to Philly so's they could catch their plane the next morning. They decided to drive all the way down in one night, and made it to New York City. Then they stopped for gas at a self serve in Harlem. Two dudes walked up on Gina while she was pumping gas, beat her up, and took the car. Ruthie was in the restroom. Marceleen was in the back seat asleep.

"The dudes drove off from the station and Goldberg woke up screaming. They pistol whipped her to shut her up. Cops found her two days later somewhere in South Bronx. Goldberg had been raped....stabbed about seven times, and....had both of her eyes shot out....with a twenty two pistol."

Those words were the last David heard before he started screaming and picked up his wooden chair from under the desk to send it through the room's glass window. Next went the chest of drawers, being viciously pulled from the wall and smashed to the ground. David then grabbed the small mirror, flinging it out into the hallway before mindlessly confessing his anguish.

"NOOOOOOOOOO!!"

"Woah, Dave!! Chill out, man! Tearing up the room ain't gonna bring Goldberg back!" Freddie pleaded before hurriedly rising from the bed, which David flipped against the wall. David didn't hear Freddie, or some of his other dormmates, who'd rushed down to the source of the commotion. All David heard that day was the grim revelation of Goldie's death, and the sounds of his own screams.

Sixteen years later, David Green was long lost in the aftermath of sorrow and anguish over the love that had been denied him. Love like the blood red roses, which ironically, had survived the rampage. But David died that day, and in his place, Saul Ravensword had risen like an obscene Phoenix, feasting on the carrion of sin and evil that plagued the world in which he lived. The one thing of David's that had survived the blasphemous resurrection was the memory of Marceleen's smile; a smile not unlike those worn by the cheerfully alive students, who'd long since gotten on their flight to wherever, leaving Saul to briefly remember a time and sorrow that was uniquely his own, and that he hoped would remain so.

Once outside the terminal, Saul looked for a taxi cab when he spotted a nearby vendor trying to make a buck.

"Yo, Holmes." the man called to Saul from behind a makeshift display of flowers and bouquets in white plastic buckets of water. He was a tall, swarthy Hispanic man, with long black hair tied in a ponytail, a mustache and goatee, and wore a white apron over his blue coveralls. "You look like you need to buy some flowers for that lady you all dressed up for."

Saul smiled, presuming that this guy was seriously out to make a buck. He knew his simple ensemble of blue dress shirt, gray pullover wool sweater, gray tie, matching pants, and gray felt raincoat, were hardly deserving of this salesman's hype, but he walked over to the man's stand, remembering red roses.

"I'm actually here on business." Saul ambivalently stated while looking at the variety of roses, posies, baby's breath, lilies, and other assorted flowers on display.

"Well, why not grab some for your secretary, or that next power lunch?! Flowers are a whole lot better than rollovers, hostile acquisitions, and leveraged buyouts. They can also soften the blow if you're about to wack some unsuspecting CEO, with a severance check, hey?!"

"Okay." Saul laughed. "Sounds like you know the corporate world pretty well."

"Graduated Summa Cum Laude from Columbia U., School of Business in 1987." the man snorted, briefly squeezing his nose with thumb and forefinger. "Was an MBA working with a marketing firm in New York, till we got acquired by a bigger advertising agency in '91'. They downsized and I was the first to hit the door."

"That's too bad." Saul opened his wallet, pulling out a twenty dollar bill.

"Nah! New York is a sewer. Don't miss it a bit. Not getting rich selling flowers, but I also run a communications gig on the side. I do okay, and I get to see my wife and kids more often than when we were in NYC."

Saul reached down into a bucket and grabbed two of the bouquets, before handing the man the twenty, as well as a white business card and one of the bouquets.

"Give this one to your wife and let her know how much you love her."

Saul left the vendor and hailed a taxi,-one of those ugly gray 'BWI Limousine Service' sedans-to take him to downtown Baltimore.

The vendor was amazed at Saul's generosity. Looking at the business card he'd just gotten, he wanted to kick himself for not noticing the amazing resemblance this guy had to one of his favorite authors, as well as wondered when the man had time to scribble a note on the card.

'Hey, maybe I can convince you to manage a new publishing house down her in B-More. Once I get my head on straight, I'll be looking for you. I trust you'll be on the job, okay?!

S. Ravensword'

"Oh, man!" he lightly smacked himself on the forehead, making up his mind to be at BWI everyday until Saul finally did show up again.

Baltimore.

The last decent night's sleep Saul remembered getting was in a sleeping bag parked on the floor of a local high school, where he and his buddies in the literacy project had bunked during the two week duration of the program. He'd been a humble student volunteer back then, tutoring children in their ABC's by day, and making excursions to East Baltimore Boulevard by night.

The strip, the red light district, combat zone, the gut; remembering names from the recitations of his academic comrades in arms that spring, Saul had nostalgic pains akin to labor that ended in stillbirth.

"Driver, I've got a reservation at a hotel in the Inner Harbor." Saul spoke to the cab driver in the seat ahead of him. "But could we take a trip through East Baltimore Boulevard first? 200 block?"

"No problem, sir." the man-short, way past middle age, with a balding head-spoke animatedly while keeping his eye on the highway. "Too bad you couldn't have caught it twenty five years ago. Now there was a place, buddy! Live burlesque shows, real dancing girls. They could even take all their clothes off back then. Now the cops make em wear G. Strings and pasties."

"The ides of March."

"What?"

"I was down here during spring break of 1979. Some buddies and I went down to the strip and took in some of the shows. My buddies got trashed, while all I drank was orange juice and seven up. Still, I had a good time."

"Trust me, bub, the place has changed since you last visited. Nowadays, ain't nothing on East Baltimore Boulevard but hookers, pimps, cheap pizza, and peep shows."

Much had changed since Saul was last in Baltimore, though he wouldn't fully appreciate that until after sunset, when he took a walk over to East Baltimore Boulevard.

Ten minutes into his sojourn, walking along the crowded, but lonely street, Saul glumly considered that he could have stayed in his hotel room. Had he been researching another horror novel, Saul imagined that he'd write a hideous tome detailing grim fates for the scantily clad women who looked at him enticingly as he passed by. It was cool enough for jackets and sweaters; Saul wondered why these women persisted in wearing only lycra body stockings, mini dresses, midriff baring combinations of tank tops, and hot pants, along with even more revealing wear.

"Sex still sells." he whispered, conscious of a pair of mascara wearing eyes locked on him, and a hint of tongue, wicked and pink, slithering out from lips he was certain would call out to him. The woman, tall like a pine tree and dark as hot chocolate, wore a body hugging, lime green dress with interconnected slits down the sides and sleeves, revealing bare flesh beneath. Her long black hair cascaded wantonly down her back, accompanied by hazel eyes that seemed to arrive by contact lenses rather than genetic express.

Saul knew this routine too well; pay for play, dollars for attention, a moment's company for a few bucks. The way this woman focused on him, Saul figured that she'd make her approach, once she'd determined whether he was an undercover cop or not. He looked away and stopped walking long enough to face the marquee of a strip joint.

"Goldie's?!" he thought with amazement while eyeing the black letters placed atop the white lit screen. The silhouette figures of naked dancing girls next to the club's name were amusing since he knew that they weren't permitted to dance totally nude anymore. That reality almost deterred him from walking into the brown brick storefront, but he wanted to escape this woman stalking him even more than he wanted not to go inside.

"I'll have a Cranberry juice." Saul looked into the rough, weather beaten face of the bartender. The man, somewhere before fifty, with a short blond haircut and bushy mustache, looked at Saul as if he'd ordered a Molotov cocktail.

"Best I can do is O.J. We don't get much call for Cranberry juice around here."

"Then how about whatever you use to mix Bloody Marys with?"

"No problem." the man went to the expansive wood cabinetry behind the bar as Saul gloomily observed him pouring a can of V8 vegetable juice into a tall glass. Three dollars and eighty five cent later, Saul faced the stage lights towards the center of the dark room. He joined the assorted patrons; young men, old, and in between, seated at various gray tables situated in front of the hardwood stage. He eyed a nubile young woman, naked except for the little green pasties adorning her nipples, and a slip of green G String glued to her crotch. It hid the womanhood underneath in a taunting fashion as the woman gyrated her smooth hips exotically in his direction.

"Damn." Saul muttered before sitting at the only empty table he could find near the dancer's stage. "I can't get nudity to save my life."

He sipped, he stared, he almost felt embarrassed for this beautiful young woman gyrating on stage while these guys, himself included, ogled her like a piece of meat. She reminded him of another woman, also blond, blue eyed with bodily perfection, he'd seen in another club. Only then, in 1979, he could tell she was blond all over without actually having to ask her.

"Hello." a softly feminine voice wafted into his hearing. Saul turned his head and saw the woman in green again. She was still tall, dark, and lovely, the same hazel eyes flashed at him, this time aided by the red and blue light that popped on and off from the club's ceiling. "Is this seat taken?"

"No." he smiled not too enthusiastically as she sat down beside him and opened a small pocket book which contained a mirror and compact. She quickly touched up her lipstick, all the while eyeing Saul in a manner that told him the pitch was right around the corner.

"Would you like to buy the lady a drink?"

"I thought you'd never ask." Saul quipped while pulling a dark billfold out of his coat pocket. The woman smiled as he pulled out a twenty and caught the attention of the waiter nearby. The woman ordered a scotch and tonic, while Saul ordered another vegetable juice. The woman took a long sip before looking lustily at Saul.

"I'm Saundra. I'm great company, as you'll find out if you stay long enough. And I also dance. Privately, that is."

"I'm Saul. I write."

"Oh." she purred, while patronizing with her eyes. Saul wondered if she was listening, or just trying to sucker him in for more. "Anything I might have read?"

"Well, my current book is called, 'The Night'." he didn't miss a clip. "I've published nine novels so far, three collections of short fiction, and a book of essays based on my readings of Poe, Lovecraft, and Saki."

"Then I bet you're probably rich and famous." she cooed between sips of her poison. Every inch of her looked the part of pre paid attention as she sat flirtatiously close, inching ever closer, but not touching him. Saul knew that this was sham and pretense. Had he worn a pair of tattered blue jeans and a grimy tee shirt, he figured that she wouldn't have given him the time of day, much less her undivided attention.

"I do alright."

"So what kind of stuff do you write?"

"I write horror stories." he'd waited for her to ask that. "My first novel was called, 'Loverman', and it was about this guy who thought he was a real stud, when in fact, he was possessed by the spirit of an Incubus."

"Incubus?"

"A male demon possessed of a particularly fierce and fatal sex drive. My protagonist, the poor slob, runs around bedding any woman that moves, but he doesn't realize that the ejaculation of the Incubus causes a woman's vagina and uterus to rupture. And once the woman's dead, the demon takes over this guy's mind and causes him to further mutilate his victim's corpse. The only person who realizes what's happening is this three year old girl, who because of a freak in her genetic code, is the only person who can detect the demon's presence....." he paused for emphasis while watching Saundra slowly lower her glass from her lips. "...and only she can safely have sex with him and give him the child he wants so badly."

"Oh." she gagged gently, trying not to reveal how deeply the revelation disturbed her. "Sounds...interesting."

"My second book was called 'Maggot Brain'."

"Eeeeeeeuuu! I can't imagine the story behind that title." Saundra tried to sound amused, but she could barely conceal her budding revulsion.

"That was the title of a record album belonging to one of my college buddies. The story is about a nerdy computer analyst who doesn't get along with his co workers, and gets fired for making an error that costs his company several million dollars. He's quite bitter and spends the next couple of weeks playing with his home computer, drinking heavily, and reading some ancient writings called 'Chronicles Necrodemon Deus'."

"Is this like 'The Book of the Dead', or something?" she interrupted him, trying to salvage her grip on the situation. "I've read up on lots of occult type stuff."

"In that same vein, yes. But 'Necrodemon Deus' is my own fictional creation."

"Well, you know..."she smiled nervously before he cut her off.

"In my story, the supernatural nature of the chronicle causes this guy to write a bizarre computer program that causes people's brain cells to turn into parasitic, flesh eating creatures if they're unfortunate enough to be viewing monitor screens hooked up to the computer network. Things get worse once he gets access to the city's computer systems and communication lines. All sorts of gross, horrifying things come on people's television screens. Telephones carry obscene messages with demonic voices on them; city transit and traffic lights star running amok..."

"Uh, Saul!" she reached out and took his hand for the first time. "This all sounds interesting, but I do more than listen. I can also give you a private dance, totally nude, in one of our back rooms. Provided you don't tell the cops, that is."

"Hmmm, that doesn't sound like such a bad idea." he indulged her, watching her exhale, relax almost, before he spoke again. "I do need to find inspiration for my next novel. I'm thinking about visiting Edgar Allen Poe's grave, though I doubt that they'll let me into Westminister Hall after dark. I imagine that I could conceive an interestingly grim story concerning a woman, or women, who work the sex trade. Maybe even work AIDS, VD, or some other malevolently sexual angle into my composition. Of course, my heroine in 'The Night', was a one eyed streetwalker with false teeth and a chronic case of Syphilis. I probably shouldn't go to that well again."

All the while, Saul looked at her with cool, unemotional eyes that didn't betray an ounce of what he was feeling. Saundra wasn't that good.

"Ex....cuse me!" she quickly released his hand and pushed herself away from him. Far away. Turning her horrified, disbelieving eyes away from him, Saundra knocked over the remains of her drink while running away from Saul. She bumped into several patrons in her mad dash, almost knocking over a waiter, and finally being caught by a younger blond woman who'd cast more than a passing glance at Saul. Saundra grabbed her compatriot by both shoulders, giving her a firm warning, briefly glaring at Saul before slashing across her throat with pressed together fingers. Saul lifted his glass, smiled and winked at both women in a charming fashion. The blond woman's eyes popped wide open, and her face became redder than the lacy camisole and sequined bikini panties she was wearing. Then both women bolted from his sight, which suited Saul fine. He'd only wanted to drink his V8 in peace anyway, though he almost regretted not taking Saundra up on her nude dance offer.

"Naaaah! Her legs were too skinny for my taste, anyway."

Four hours past midnight, Saul was guzzling a bottle of mineral water as he sat on the ground next to Edgar Allen Poe's grave sight in Westminister Hall on Lafayette Street, adjacent to the campus of the University of Maryland, Baltimore. He'd had to climb over an iron fence to achieve his goal, as well as evade certain shady characters trafficking in substances illicit, inebriating, and illegal enough to land one in prison for a very long time. Fortunately, he hadn't noticed any monitors, or alarms to announce his intrusion. No distractions, no disruptions, no one hassled him as he sat and contemplated his presence in this city, and his solitary communion with a long dead mentor.

"You know, Edgar, were a cop to approach me right now, he'd probably figure I was trashed on one of your favorite libations." he mused, eying the almost empty green glass bottle before turning to the white stone obelisk monument that sat in the church's courtyard. "Sixteen years ago, I thought about getting ripped when I was last here in your city. Just to be in with my buddies at the end of the project. I told myself, 'Goldie will never find out.', and I knew I'd be sober again by the time she got back from spring break. Unfortunately...."

He stopped for a half second, his mournful remembrance intermingling with the stillness of the early spring morning. This was the city, he thought. There should have been some sound other that that of his tell tale heart.

"...she would never have known anyway. If I'd believed in God, I would have cursed him to his face when I found out about her being murdered. I thought about getting ripped after that. Maybe going out and downing a case of beer and chasing it with vodka. My friends wanted to take me out drinking after I tore up my dorm room. But, no. I decided to let her death hurt for a long time. Put my bitter imagination to work. I wound up hiding from the pain by churning out gut wrenching horror stories.

"I channeled my anger at having lost her by filling the world that took her from me with my own demons. Funny thing though. In the end, I lost more than a part of myself. I loved her, Ed. Never took the time, or got the chance to tell her." he stifled a tear, knowing that if he started crying, he'd probably never stop.

"No, I didn't try to sooth the pain with booze and opium, though I don't knock you for trying to. I just wonder, Ed, does lost love always make you so crazy that you almost wished you didn't have to go on living? You think that maybe Marceleen and Lenore are upstairs wondering just how dumb we are,-or at least I am-pining like lost puppies?"

There was no answer forthcoming from the alabaster headstone that Saul stared at. No sound erupted from the ground under which Edgar slept peacefully, and above where Saul brooded menacingly like the Raven of yore that quoted 'NEVERMORE'. Saul almost muttered that for fun, but he knew that dead folks had no sense of humor.

"I almost envy you, Ed. At least you're getting some good sleep. Then again, you're dead. I'm not there....yet."

He finished his bottle, all the while realizing that he'd been in too many graveyards of late; from his brief dream of having seen Marceleen's gravestone, to this moment at a stranger's memorial in the dark early morning which had yet to turn to sunrise. His heart reminded him of a graveyard, but Saul had no clue as to changing it from the death haunted stopwatch ticking inside of him. Short of stepping off a twenty story building, or eating the wrong end of his thirty eight revolver, Saul didn't see the likelihood of it ending for him. He was too loathing of pain to slit his wrist, and suffocating in a car full of exhaust fumes didn't appeal to him.

"I better stop musing on suicide before I start actually start thinking about it seriously." Saul contemplated while depositing his empty bottle on Poe's grave sight. He also placed the previously purchased bouquet of Roses beside it; much like the mysterious stranger, whose single rose and bottle of Cognac, had become famous every year on Poe's birthday. After a few deep breaths, Saul stood up and slowly made his way out of the cemetery. On to the city streets, empty save for a few vehicles driven by late night riders, early birds, and people working the graveyard shift. Saul thought about a lot of things; life, love, and tombstones predominant among them. He'd never even laid eyes on the grave sight of the closest friend he'd ever had, and here he was in Baltimore, toasting a total stranger he had nothing in common with, save their respectively macabre writings.

The morning droned on. Saul walked. How much of the city had he walked across, he wondered, or even how many times had he crossed the same path in his endless, aimless meandering. The questions rested in Saul's mind like a slow mordant hum.

"Hummmmmmmmmm." he hummed quietly, thinking that it was foolish to worry about who might hear his meditative sounding. He had much to meditate on, and even when he ended his hum, Saul could hear another hum, this time, loud and clear, moving rhythmically to a musical pattern. A sound from a saxophone had become the hum, and drew him increasingly closer.

Saul continued walking, until the sound lead him to a furthermost corner, somewhere between the business district and the poorer environs near the edge of town. Somewhere near the street corner facing the train tracks, Camden Yards-the fancy new baseball park-and a drab red brick tavern, there stood a man. A dread locked man, wearing gray sweat pants, a denim jacket, and dull combat boots. The man blew his saxophone, and Saul kept walking towards him. The song he played, long, low, and enticing, reminded Saul of the sound of his soul oh so long ago.

15

"Come back for a visit." Brianne had smiled the afternoon Maryum departed from Mindful. As the two women walked the path leading to the large parking lot, Maryum wondered if she'd ever met, or known anyone like Brianne. "Gerald and I would love to have you back when the community celebrates Vernal equinox."

"I'm sure it will be a blast." Maryum uttered calmly, hoping she could get away before Brianne caught on to her sarcasm. "But I'll probably still be in Baltimore trying to get my life sorted out. You never know."

"No. No one ever knows for certain, Maryum. Life takes some strange turns." Brianne reached behind her head and gently pulled her semi kinky hair into a bun. "Occasionally, I have to pinch myself to make sure I'm here with your father. I mean, wife and mother weren't exactly on my 'Must Accomplish' list before departing this life. But now, I don't think I'd have it any other way."

'Get fucking real, Brianne!' Maryum struggled not to scream at this woman walking beside her, spouting what sounded like the drivel of the century. She eyed Brianne, whose reddish brunette coif now resembled dark ice cream atop a golden cone, and could scarcely bear looking into those peaceful blue eyes. 'God! This woman is even smiling!!'

A week later, sitting alone in her motel room, hardly enjoying a bottle of wine and a small box of take out chicken, Maryum seriously wondered why Brianne had returned to her thoughts.

"Maryum, I know all of this may seem strange to you." Brianne laid her hands on Maryum's shoulders.

"Understatement." she nervously confessed, fighting the urge to tell Brianne not to touch her.

"Please try to understand. The last thing 'G' and I wanted was to cause you pain and confusion. He loves you very much. And I love him as well. I'd really like to be your friend, Maryum. I'm sure you'll never call me, 'Mom', and I wouldn't dream of trying to go there."

Again, Maryum didn't verbalize what came to mind-'No shit, Sherlock!'-but her exact response was a lot smoother than what she'd thought. After a perfunctory kiss on the cheek, Maryum bid Brianne farewell and retreated to her rental car to avoid totally losing it for the sake of her insanity. Start the car, bolt down the highway at breakneck speed; such Maryum desired. Observing Brianne from inside the vehicle, she was also tempted to sit quietly and wait to see how long the woman would stand there and smile at her. Instead, she cranked up the ignition and quickly vanished from the physical traces of her father's strange new reality, though she knew that she'd never get so far away that she'd escape her own thoughts, and at the moment, Maryum thought she'd walk down to the liquor store.

Once outside, Maryum wondered if she were still in Baltimore. A moment after she closed the door, every trace of light vanished from sight. No streetlights, or lights from other hotel rooms were visible. No approaching cars on the highway. Nothing shined. Everything was darker than dark.

"Damn! What the hell is going on out here?!"

Everything was gone. No gas stations, no billboards, nothing resembling normal space and time existed anymore.

'Get back inside!' she thought, only to find the doorknob missing when she reached behind her. Maryum looked at the ground to make sure it was still there and noticed her bare feet above a shiny black floor. A smooth, reflective floor that revealed the black robe she'd not put on before walking out of the room.

"AAAAHHHHHRGH!!!" escaped from Maryum's throat as she collapsed to the ground. At least there was a ground. Maryum couldn't be sure of anything else. Her wail was the only sound in the void, the nowhere she suddenly found herself lost in.

"Wait..." she raised herself up on her hands and knees, looking at the bleak, dark landscape, and hoping desperately not to cry out again. "I ....am not lost! Or frightened, or....or,"

She was all of those, and more. Maryum figured she could either continue screaming and losing her mind, or she could stand up and try to figure out where she was. She slowly rose to her feet in time to see the wall again.

"Oh...no!" she turned around, vainly hoping to see the hotel, but the wall confronted her again. That same wall which that held her beloved sad hostage, and had breathed down her neck in the garage the evening she'd parked in James' place.

"No, no, no!" she shut her eyes, but the wall came bursting through anyway, her traumatized mind relaying the sight; telling Maryum it was still there. She wanted to run, but every direction she turned, the wall was there, silently taunting her, begging almost, for Maryum to come and vainly assault it again. Maryum ran, not knowing where, nor caring. She had to get away, but it followed her. In front, behind her, at all sides surrounding her. Blocking her path and daring her to do anything but scream again.

"What?!" Maryum rose from the hotel bed, noticing her spent wine bottle, as well as the box of ravenously devoured chicken which sat on the night stand next to her bed. "Boy, what a weird dream. I need to stop drinking that cheap shit."

She climbed off the bed and walked to the bathroom, an ugly reminder of chicken flesh and eighty nine cent wine lingering on her taste buds. 'Wash my face, brush my teeth, clean up', was her predominant thought as she passed the partition wall separating the sink, tub, and toilet from the rest of the room. She didn't count on what she'd see upon looking in the mirror on the wall above the sink.

"Jesus." she moaned, beholding the dark landscape inside the mirror and knowing that closing her eyes again would be pointless. Then her ears got into the act. The music, romantic, surging, evocative, began to play. Maryum turned from the mirror and saw the same brick wall, this time laid out in front of her like a pathway underneath a dark sky suddenly lit up with a million stars and strange lights.

"Follow the yellow brick road...."she almost sang as she walked towards where she heard the music. "Different story. I'm definitely not in Kansas, anymore."

Maryum still wore her tee shirt and loose fitting blue jeans, but for all she knew, she was probably in East Hades, somewhere. The strangest dream of her lifetime found her walking along a dark road towards music, underneath a night light show that could only be a dream. Or so she hoped.

A few hundred steps later, Maryum found herself at a central place beneath the skylights overhead. A place well illuminated and seemingly the source of the music which she'd followed. She stopped long enough to catch sight of them dancing.

"Who?!" she ran to the patio as she eyed the duo dressed in black, dancing and twirling. Long, flowing robes adorned both of their lithe, slender bodies. Maryum wasn't there yet, but one look at the man, even from a distance, and she knew him better than her own soul.

"Dennis?!" she cried, not believing the sight, nor understanding how he could be so mobile. Maryum had gotten close enough to enter the patio when her legs ceased moving. She froze, unable to move another step as she helplessly watched Dennis share a wonderful dance in the arms of this stranger.

"Dennis? Dennis?!" she felt foolish and impotent as she beheld her beloved dancing away from her in the arms of another. Maryum felt her heart almost burst with her next scream, desperately crying Dennis' name, even as he remained engrossed with his new dancing partner.

"Who are you, bitch?! What are you doing with my lover?!?" Maryum expressed her hurt at being locked into seeing-no, she was dreaming, wasn't she?-Dennis and this woman dancing in the strange light. Maryum stared, hoping to see the face of this interloper who faithfully kept pace with Dennis. Her bare feet caressed the ground below as she embraced him even closer. Then they pulled further away, and the woman's tresses began to take on a life of their own, making her more of a wanton mystery.

"Oh no... you don't!" Maryum affirmed, gaining strength and resolve enough to break through the inertia that held her bound. Tear her away from him, Maryum thought. Reach out and grab this woman before she ran off with the one she loved. "Who...are you?!"

Her hand reached the back of the woman's robe and violently pulled her away from Dennis. 'I want to see your face!', was all she thought before gazing into eyes that didn't lie.

Jasmine's eyes.

"Would someone answer the phone?" Maryum groggily asked upon awaking, finding herself still in her room and underneath the covers of her bed. She was horrified at the sight of the bed spread discolored by reddish yellow froth with bits of brown flake and a trace of red wine lying ominously in the space besides her pillow. "Damn. I have to... get sick before.... waking up?!"

She got off the bed, noticing that her regurgitation resembled a bloodstain with major attitude problems. It had caked up all over the side of her face and even found its way to the tee shirt she was wearing.

'Great! First my period. Then that damn wall again.' she thought, before answering the phone at the third ring. "Hello?"

"Hi, Maryum. It's James."

"Hi." Maryum wearily sank back onto her mattress, and covered her eyes with her free hand, while responding to the unexpected intrusion on the other end. No, she told James, it wasn't a bad time to call. No, she didn't have anything planned for today and she'd be happy to have a lunch date downtown later this afternoon. Besides, she knew she needed to try and eat something, as she requested the restaurant's address. Lunch with James didn't seem like the worst way to waste a day, and for all she knew, she might even get something out of it.

She also believed in the tooth fairy, and that Bill Clinton didn't inhale.

BOOK FOUR

REACQUAINTENCES

16

Come morning, East Baltimore Boulevard was almost dead. Saul observed the contrast to the previous evening, when the street had been crowded with people searching for a thrill, hustling for a buck, or whatever might have floated their boat on this particularly lustful thruway. He and his new found friend-who'd stopped at a pay phone to contact his daughter-, were among the few populating East Baltimore Boulevard, which now resembled a side road in a graveyard.

"The place is called 'Crazy John's', and it's in the middle of the red light district on East Baltimore Boulevard." James spoke to Maryum on the other end, certain that she'd just woken up given her groggy response. "You can't miss it. It's between a couple of peep shows and some strip joints. It's got a big yellow marquee and it's across the street from the Gayety Theater. Yeah. 1:30 will be fine."

He hung up the telephone, and then noticed Saul sitting on a park bench adjacent to an orchestra shell overlooking an amphitheater, handling the black saxophone case as though he were holding a baby. Curious, James thought while scratching his beard, this friend of only a few hours, as he wandered over to the bench and sat next to Saul, who seemed quite taken with the beat up looking leather case.

"You play?"

"I...tried. I took band when I was thirteen, but up until my college years, my situation was never stable enough to warrant me taking time to really learn how to play. By then it was too late."

"It's never too late, Saul. If you want to play, you can be learning in your nineties."

"I suppose." Saul looked up from the case, profoundly wondering at this dread locked, sax blowing, street person. Such peace, such calm; he was envious as hell. "Prior to this morning, I wasn't even sure I'd make it past my late thirties."

"Nobody's ever sure of that." James leaned back, interlacing his fingers beneath his nappy beard. "Longevity don't mean you accomplished much. And lots of people wind up living short, good lives."

"Boy, don't I know that." Saul recalled Goldie, she of short, but fruitful life, just before impulsively opening the saxophone case. He studied the instrument-brass kind of dull, but well kept and clean-and his looking progressed further to reaching in and handling the saxophone. Suddenly feeling foolish, he looked over at James, who'd adopted an encouraging smile.

"Go ahead, man. Take a lick."

"Huh?"

"Blow. See if you can make some sound with it. Don't worry about germs. I always put a new reed in before I close up."

Saul's lips closed around the mouthpiece of the horn, and his first sound was a melodramatic whisper that turned into a frantic squeal. Catching his breath, Saul tried again, this time producing a flat, clear tone that was stronger than his first attempt, but still fell short of the mark. He took the reed from his lips and breathed heavily, as though he'd just run a marathon. James grinned.

"You'll get it. You should have heard me the first time I played."

"You couldn't have been as bad as my debut, could you?" Saul grinned while putting the saxophone back in the case.

"Saul, the first time I blew my horn, every dog in the neighborhood died, and the music teacher seriously suggested that I be expelled from school, or executed. Course, he also said I'd get better."

Saul laughed, all the while realizing that James had to be right about more than just music. He was determined to find out just how right.

At the heart of Baltimore's red light district on East Baltimore Boulevard, Crazy John's Pizzeria was an oasis of food and beverage for those desiring a respite from the lascivious goings on in the main strip. After the peep shows, strip clubs, and other dens of iniquity, many a haggard soul would check into Crazy John's for a slice of double cheese pizza, or perhaps one of those Philadelphia style cheese steak sandwiches that Maryum chose.

"I'd also like a pitcher of draft beer, please?" Maryum addressed the young woman standing behind the plastic surfaced bar. The girl, probably in her late teens or early twenties, cast curious brown eyes on Maryum and the two men who'd accompanied her to the restaurant as she filled a glass pitcher with dark amber brew. Saul and James were seated at one of the only occupied tables, this being only early afternoon. Maryum took the tray from the girl, who's nearly waist length brown hair, olive skin, and tomato sauce smeared apron, was almost a dim memory by the time she'd walked over to the table to deliver the goods to James and Saul.

"Okay. One salad with Thousand Islands dressing. One hamburger with French Fries." she passed out the items before grabbing her own cheese steak sandwich and taking the pitcher of beer off the tray. She slid one of two mugs over to James while filling her own. "You sure you don't want me to get you a mug, Mr. Ravensword?"

"Certain." Saul sipped orange juice with a straw, seeming a bit out of breath for having retreated to his hotel room and changed into a white dress shirt, a gray double breasted blazer, and neatly pressed black slack before meeting James and Maryum at the restaurant. James wolfed down his burger as though he'd not had a decent meal in months, and Maryum wondered if maybe that weren't the case.

"Your sandwich is going to get cold." James took his eyes away from his quickly vanishing sandwich when Maryum poured him a mug of beer.

"It'll be okay." Maryum responded before sipping from her own mug. "I really haven't been able to hold anything down for the last day or so."

"Indeed. I've been there myself." Saul rattled on while cutting the vegetables in his salad with a knife and fork. "Of course, I've always found an Alka Seltzer to work better than dark lager."

"Oh well." Maryum employed a flip tone, almost forgetting that she was speaking to the best selling author of nightmare, Saul Ravensword. Having read only one of his novels, and finding it too twisted and violent for her tastes, Maryum wasn't sure what to make of this very unthreatening person sitting across from her. "Just out of curiosity, Mr. Ravensword, what brings you to Baltimore?"

"Please, call me Saul. I'm doing research for my next novel."

"What's it about?" Maryum took a bite of her sandwich.

"I haven't the foggiest notion. The only people worried right now are the editors at my publishing house."

"Well...Saul, I guess if I were a best selling author, I wouldn't be too worried either." she continued before finishing her first mug of beer, and pouring a second. Then James reentered the conversation.

"I think Saul might be up for some music lessons before too long. He didn't skip a beat keeping time on the curb while I played this morning."

"Oh?" Maryum took another sip. "So you two met at a jam session, huh?"

"Kind of." Saul was laconic, speaking as slowly as the flow of human traffic in and out of the various adult entertainments that surrounded the restaurant. "I actually spent most of the previous evening drinking mineral water, and somberly contemplating life and death over Edgar Allen Poe's grave."

Maryum set her mug down and looked at Saul, hoping to find a smirk that would betray the joke she knew he had to be telling. But Saul was as serious as an outbreak amongst the unvaccinated, leaving Maryum unsettled.

"So you were taking a hint from the old master?" she took another bite of her sandwich, the flavor of herbs, cheese, peppers, and fried steak biting her back, though not with the impact of Saul's demeanor.

"No. If I went that route, I'd probably be out drinking like a fish and doing opiates. I could still write, I suppose, but that would really mess up my prose."

'As if your current writing isn't twisted and messed up enough.' Maryum thought while munching on her sandwich. She hadn't imagined the ghastly strings attached to James' invitation to lunch, and Saul Ravensword was turning out to be very weird company. She decided to be weirder.

"Such is life, Saul. I just dropped out of school over my sexual involvement with a disabled client. I also reported one of my co-workers for abusing the same patient, and it's turning into a huge legal mess. I'm here in Baltimore trying to figure out just what I'm going to do next with my life. And for the record, I've ended four of the last five days so drunk I couldn't see straight."

"I thought you'd been expelled." James blurted out, his hamburger more than half gone, his mug of been barely touched.

"What does it matter, James?! Here we are, three strangers whose only connection is bad biology, writer's block, and academic distress. I guess that's enough for us to be sharing sandwiches, salad, and beer, huh? Never mind that the three of us weren't even mutual friends before this morning. Now tell me what the hell is wrong with this picture?"

"For starters," Saul asserted. "...you're presuming that I'm probably testing you two to see how you'd work in one of my manuscripts. I assure you that such isn't the case."

"Yeah, right." she refilled her empty mug and donned an incredulous frown while she took another sip, then another, then another, until the mug was more than half past gone. "A year from now, you'll be talking about us on 'Oprah', and declaring how we inspired your next best seller."

"Maryum, there's no need for this." James innocently offered.

"Shut up, James! It's a little late for you to start pulling the 'Father' scene."

"Ms. Dupaul, I meant what I just said." Saul noticed a trickle of new customers, as well as a police officer, entering Crazy John's, telling him that he needed to get things under control, quickly. "As far as mentioning you in my next manuscript, or using characters loosely based on you in my next novel, I don't rule that out. But I'm not interested in exploiting either of you. Nor is James, or I, deserving of this outburst."

"God... You sound like my Dad's new wife." Maryum sunk down in her seat, briefly closing her eyes before taking another sip from her mug and emptying it. "Am I ever going to run into anyone who doesn't try to smile all their troubles away, or cover every situation with psycho therapy gobbledygook?!"

"I actually think that my 'Gobbledygook' would be a world better than watching you get plastered. Fifteen years ago, I dealt with personal tragedy by turning towards the kind of gruesome, horrid garbage I've been writing ever since. I used goblins, ghouls, and ancient curses to hide from my grief, rather than try to drink my way out of the pain. However, I did make a piss poor choice."

"You think I'm trying to run away?" she hissed.

"I wouldn't know. I'm not you, Maryum." Saul took a long sip from his orange juice, trying to keep track of her eyes as she slipped further into inebriated rage.

"That's right, Saul. You're not." she stood up defiantly. "You wouldn't know about lost love, betrayal, and the other ugly shit that has gone down the last fucking week of my life. You have no idea what I've been through, and you've got a lot of Goddamn nerve to think you can advise me about anything. You don't even know me, Saul."

"No, but maybe I'd like to."

"Oh yeah! I'm sure you would." she snarled. "You'd probably concoct all kinds of sick fantasies for me. No thanks, Saul. Why don't you go home with James and maybe you two can do some wild shit to Jasmine?! Provided she's not asleep, that is." then she turned on her heel and bolted out of the restaurant, leaving James and Saul behind, followed only by their astonished eyes, and the notice of a few other patrons who'd been privy to her outrage.

"I should have warned you." James lamented, taking a long breath and painfully observing the almost empty pitcher that his daughter had drank way too much of, and the sandwich she'd barely touched.

His 'Daughter'.

James couldn't imagine a more fitting payback for having betrayed his brother's marriage bed than this angry young woman who would not be mollified. Here was more wreckage, pain, and tragedy, as he observed his offspring walk a wanton path beyond the sphere of his orbit.

"I'll get over it, James. I'm not exactly the crowning standard of normality, you know."

"Maybe not. But I wish she hadn't brought Jasmine into this."

"Jasmine?" Saul whispered the name as though it were a mantra. James and Saul departed Crazy John's, proceeding down Baltimore's crowded avenues, while continuing their conversation.

"If it's not too personal, James, who is this woman Maryum ranted about?"

"Jasmine is someone I met twenty five years ago." James spoke, his eyes searching the street corner near his neighborhood just as school children returned home in the afternoon. "She came to Baltimore to see her lover's tombstone. Had to break out of a mental hospital in Georgia and steal a doctor's car just to get here."

"Really?" Saul' questioned, briefly noticing two young black girls playing patty cake after they exited the yellow school bus. "Tell me more."

"James, thank you for your kindness." she uttered as he made a couple of mugs of hot tea. Inside the row house he'd purchased a few years ago for almost a song, James was entertaining his first houseguest a little past 2:00am, February 1969. Cold winds blew that mid winter. Frozen tears of ice rained upon them as James and Jasmine lamented the terrible losses of the previous year. And in the brittle chill of a winter's morning where they could find no warmth without, they prayed for warmth within to break the cold holding them sad hostage.

"Ma'am, I was only trying to help. You kind of....scared me, walking up to the diner like you did." he stirred the hot tea he'd just made, setting a steaming mug in front of her. He wondered about this barefoot stranger, adorned in naught but a white cotton bathrobe and a gray blue hospital gown underneath. She might have frozen to death had James not looked up from the shoe leather steak and eggs he'd been wolfing down at the diner, and lifted his sad eyes to behold this pitiful woman walking barefoot on a cold Baltimore night. "Is there anybody I can call? You got any family around here, Miss...?"

"Jasmine. My name is....Jasmine." she focused her sorrowful attention on the mug James had given her. "And no. I have no family here. One who loved me dearer than life is buried in this city. My heart would lie besides him, rather than endure this world that took him away."

"Miss Jasmine, you're not making sense."

"The world makes no sense. Evil men slew my Dorian. Battered his body and hung him on a tree until his life fled from him. They took his....life." she sobbed, a tear rolling down her face as James sat there transfixed. "Yet I was the one they incarcerated. Shut up in the halls of a mental ward somewhere and bound in chains and a straightjacket."

"I'm sorry, Jasmine." he laid his mug on the table. "Is there anything I can do to help?"

"I must....rest."

"James, this is totally incredible. I believe I read about this woman only a few days ago. You're certain her name is Jasmine?"

"Yes. Her name is Jasmine."

"The last thing I counted on was encountering her in some way." Saul was dumbstruck, having lost all track of time as he and James made their way to the neighborhood in East Baltimore.

"I didn't count on it either. I still don't understand it, but I don't know that I'd change it."

"So why didn't you turn her in to the authorities once she was sleeping?"

"I couldn't do her like that, Saul." James' stride became slower as he crossed into familiar territory, where, sadly, he also saw blue lights and a crowd gathering off in the distance, though Saul remained unawares. "With all the hell she'd been through, I thought I could at least let her have an hour of sack on my couch. I didn't know she'd be sleeping so long."

"My God. How does anyone sleep for twenty five years?!" Saul was too engrossed in his question to notice the people passing him by, the shocked looks on so many faces. James saw everything. Stared bleakly at white police cars parked ominously in a crescent, effectively blocking off traffic. He observed the men in blue, silver badges on their chests, frantically cordoning off a small area and urging people to move along.

"You'll have to ask her that yourself. She woke up a few days ago, and we've had some deep conversations since then." James spoke while focusing his attention on the sidewalk adjacent to the police cars. He saw a body there. A long, lean corpse laid face down to the ground at the policemen's feet, as they wearily took note of the city's most recent homicide. A pool of blood slowly encircled the bald head of the victim; blood which had flowed inside living veins, now spilled onto the street, flowing like red wine into the open mouth of the sewer. James sighed. He heard a woman's scream; loud, painful, and more harrowing than the ambulance siren in the distance that grew louder as it neared the crime scene.

"Ahhhhhhhrrrrgh! Street!! Stree.....eeet!!!"

She was darker than the uniform worn by the tall white police officer who tried to escort her from the scene. Despite being larger than the frail woman with frizzy, bleach blond shag cut hair, the policeman's struggle with her resembled that of rocks on the sea shore, vainly standing against the crashing waves.

"You shoulda' stayed inside, Street!! No, no, no! Why you had to run out here and die, Street?!?"

Before long, another officer, this one black, stocky, and shorter than his colleague, joined in to help restrain the distraught sister, whose wail and cry roused Saul out of his introspection.

"What...?!"

"Looks like another buddy of mine just went to sleep." James lamented, staring balefully as the policemen covered the body with a grim white sheet. "But this one isn't going to wake up."

Saul shuddered, exhaled to force a hideous heartbeat from his chest before it exploded inside of him. Then he breathed, opening his lips wider than the Chesapeake Bay Inlet. "Yut, ye, sam, say.....slowly I turn. Step by step..."

"You alright, man?" James turned to Saul, who by now was squatting, and who's frightened eyes resembled those of an animal caught in a leg trap.

"Sorry,...James. I guess I'm....kind of having.....a flashback." he tried to explain, running a relay between lungs and tongue and raising a cupped hand to his lips to catch a cough. "A good friend of mine.....was murdered spring of my senior year of college. That was the personal tragedy I mentioned .... to Maryum. I've been running from it...every day of my life since then. I've never....even... been to her grave sight. Pretty sad,...huh?!"

"I'm hip." James' voice held more than a hint of sorrow as he stretched out his arm to help Saul up as they departed the scene. "It's always sad, cause' nobody ever knows how they're gonna cope, or even figures they'll have to go there. But we got to carry on. Sometimes...they have to carry us away."

17

Maryum hadn't counted on thinking so much about the internet address of Starbright Institute, though she knew she'd never forget it. Along with the rest of what happened that final week in Connecticut, *'WWW.SBINST. HUMPOT.NET',* stood out in her mind almost like a siren, almost daring her to engage her computer keyboard, to reach the agency where she'd entrusted her life's greatest friend. But she was currently too afraid to try contacting them.

"My husband has suffered a heart attack because of Miss Dupaul. I've spent all night at the hospital, as well as most of the day getting my nephew settled in at the institute." Cornelia McClain angrily addressed Dean Willis two mornings after having discovered Maryum and Dennis together. Maryum said nothing while she sat on the dean's couch, knowing she had no chance of placating the vehement woman railing at she and Dean Willis. "But I'm not so busy as to not still be angry about her behavior."

"Mrs. McClain, what can I possible do...."Dean Willis wearily ran his fingers through his graying hair, eying Maryum with apprehension. He snapped back to Mrs. McClain as she continued ranting.

"The only way I won't sue this college for every penny it's got is that you expel this girl, and make certain that she doesn't ever contact my nephew again."

'Oh, please!' Maryum wanted to shout at Cornelia. 'You're a miserable old crone, and Darris probably checked out to escape your tired ass!'

Maryum also entertained thoughts of pushing Cornelia in front of a moving train; prying her fingers from the ledge of a ten story building; or stabbing the crotchety woman repeatedly with a dull spoon, though she quickly abandoned such fantasies, since they would only make her more bitter about the situation, and more resemble this woman she so loathed.

In the days that followed, Maryum wondered if she'd actually made things worse, what with Darris incapacitated and Dennis at the mercy of Cornelia.

"I don't know how else to describe her, Brax." Maryum spoke to Quentin as they shared lunch consisting of a couple of boxes of fast food fried chicken, while they sat on a park bench not far from his offices at University of Maryland, Baltimore.

"But, Maryum, 'Absolute Waste of Human Flesh' is a harsh description of anyone, regardless of how messed up they are." Quentin fastened his coat's collar button to protect himself from an early spring breeze, though he seemed more chilled by Maryum's angry words about Dennis' aunt. "Certainly you can understand her not being too happy with you, no?"

"Maybe. But you should have seen she and Darris the day I met them." she chewed on a drumstick, her angry feelings being translated into mutilated chicken flesh between her teeth. "Darris wasn't that far from walking death then, and Cornelia was right behind him to push him into his tomb. Quentin, those two were the most co dependent, hopeless, given up on life, people that I'd ever laid eyes on. Watching them was like seeing a sneak preview to a funeral service. And I have grave reservations about Dennis being in their custody."

"That may be, Maryum." he spoke guardedly while observing the first return of students from spring break. "But you're in no position to do anything about the situation."

"But that means I'd be abandoning Dennis, and I just can't do that. Dennis' mother died giving birth to him. He lived with a wonderful foster family for eight years before the state decided that they couldn't provide proper support for him and forced them to give him up. Then he spent the next thirteen years being shuttled between various agencies and schools, being warehoused by people who didn't care to help him reach his full potential prior to my entrance into his life. I can't be the latest in a long line of people who abandoned him."

"Maryum, again I have to ask. Who are you trying to save here? If you're trying to help Dennis..."

"Yes, Quentin. I'm trying to help Dennis."

"Then you already have." he emphasized while rubbing some French fries in catsup. "I don't know this woman, Cornelia, but I don't think she'd be stupid enough to yank Dennis from Starbright because of your..."

"Total lack of discernment in my relationship with a patient?"

"Well put." Quentin gently laughed. "Mrs. McClain has to deal with her sick husband. She's most likely not minded to also try coping with a severely disabled nephew she's adopted by marriage. Unless she's a total fool, I doubt that she'll pull Dennis out of Starbright."

Maryum prayed that Quentin was right, but she didn't like uncertainty regarding the people she loved.

'Love.', she remembered the word popping up on the screen to Dennis' computer at Starbright. Love was more than she'd anticipated of their relationship. Helping *him find a voice was all that Maryum had been concerned with in the beginning. To Hebert, Jane, Sarah, and maybe even Tina, Dennis McClain would probably never be more than another face, another disabled body to be stored away in their human warehouse. Maryum knew better than that, and would pay a dear price for that knowledge.*

'I'd heard the word all my life, Maryum, but except for a few blessed days, I'd never experienced it. The only love I knew prior to you were the kind ones who tried to keep me from being wrenched away when I was very young.

'There was love inside myself, for I didn't wish to die and be cast into a mindless world of nothingness, so I remembered all the songs sung, words spoken, wisdom and knowledge and understanding granted me by one who's face I'd never seen. I held fast to those things in the hope that some day, I would share them with another. You are the one, Maryum.'

The words would never leave Maryum's thoughts, blazing a trail into heartland that no one else save maybe Rodney, had ever accessed. Maryum pondered the coincidence for a long time; the two men she'd loved the most in this life, both having suffered severed disabilities and both now out of her reach. Rodney was forever gone, but Dennis....

"Maryum, I have access to the Internet on my office computer." Quentin spoke with a hint of reluctance. "You told me that Starbright Institute was on some computer network. Conceivably, you could contact Dennis by email, yes?"

"Quentin, I can't do that. Cornelia will have my head if I even come close to trying to contact Dennis." her soda pop stopped mid straw as Maryum observed Quentin reservedly. "Besides, aren't you the one who told me I had to divorce myself from my feelings about my clients?"

"Yes, I did. But I'm not so clinical that I don't know the human side of the therapist. Dennis was, is, very special to you, and the circumstances of your separation left you with seriously painful issues that need to be dealt with. The only way to resolve these matters is for you to find some way to contact Dennis without Cornelia learning of it." he was serious, though Maryum could see the beginnings of a mischievous smile through his demeanor. "Besides, the last thing this world needs is another psychiatrist with unresolved issues getting in the way."

So it was, Maryum thought, while later walking along the sidewalks of East Baltimore, Quentin unofficially blessing her to seek after Dennis again, at least through email. Were Dennis to have space on the net, she reasoned, she might be able to converse with him without Cornelia ever knowing. Sure, she thought she was sneaky and knowledgeable enough to pull it off, but Maryum was leery of any actions she felt she had to hide. Then again, she'd hidden from James and Jasmine for the last few days, if not most of this trip.

Her thoughts drifted to that duo as she continued to walk, just as she considered the addition of Saul, who she didn't even want to think about understanding. She remembered reading the book 'Loverman' the summer she turned thirteen, and her immediate reaction upon finishing the ghastly tome in one four hour sitting.

"Uggh!! How can anybody write anything this.... sick?!!"

Maryum pondered this not quite gentle, but unthreatening man who'd written about the rape of a three year old girl by a murderous demon. She never read another word by Saul Ravensword, and her brief meeting with him didn't help her connect the dots that would have explained this person who seemed to be far more wounded than his calm demeanor let on.

"Where...am I walking? Why am I walking so fast? Where the hell... am I going?!" she questioned as her steps became more mysteriously intent. She'd showered and left her hotel room nearly two hours before, departing towards town in fresh blue jeans, and a gray turtleneck shirt, while contemplating a trip to a hair stylist some months down the line, provided she chose to grow some more hair. Maybe permit it to grow into dreads like James'.

"Ha. I'm sure mom might call me 'Medusa' were I to come home with a head full of snakes." she laughed while passing a familiar row of houses. She remembered these houses, as well as the faces of the snotty nosed youngsters, black and brown, playing stick ball in the middle of the street. Maryum cast not too cheerful eyes at them as she walked past, feeling more than a little perturbed that someone's parents weren't around to either look after those kids, or snatch them back inside. It was late afternoon, looking towards the bad side of five thirty. Before too long, it would get dark and cool, which made Maryum wonder why these kids were still outside, though not as much as she wondered what she was doing, or where she was going

"Twelve zero, zero, eight. Twelve ten. Twelve...."midway through noticing the street addresses of the houses, Maryum realized where she was. The brownstone three doors down retold the whole strange story before the curtains were parted in the second floor window just above the door.

"Awww..., shit." she whispered like someone about to begin a sad, sweet dream. Jasmine was awake.

"I...don't know where to begin." Maryum admitted shortly after sitting down on the dingy brown couch. The living room of the brownstone hadn't changed any, save the lithe figure who stood in the center of it, dispensing hot Chamomile tea into one of the mugs on the unpolished coffee table. Maryum looked into Jasmine's brown eyes and had trouble understanding this tall woman, who's caramel complexion had no hint of blemish, and who possessed only a hint of gray in her coif-'Wasn't there more salt and pepper when I saw her while she slept?'-and few circled lines on her face to betray the passage of time. Jasmine wore a long gray body dress that covered her slender torso like a smock on wet clay. Her bare feet skipped along the floor like someone who'd danced for a living, rather than one who'd spent the last quarter of a century sleeping.

"Names are always a good beginning. Mine's Jasmine." she smiled as though she were speaking to a lifelong friend, exhibiting not a hint of discomfort at Maryum's bewildered, cautious demeanor. "James spoke of you briefly over breakfast this morning, Maryum."

"Then I guess you know all the gory details." she almost whispered. The steaming gray teacup in her hands registered a small tremor as she beheld Jasmine's face.

"Only what he volunteered." Jasmine sat down besides Maryum, comfortably pulling her legs under her and leaving the younger woman alarmed at this unexpected closeness. Had Jasmine sat any nearer, the two of them would be occupying the same physical space. "It was only the third conversation we'd ever had, and we didn't speak for long before he left to go gig."

"Maybe he's embarrassed to talk about his past." Maryum volunteered.

"We are who we are. Where we've been is part of what makes us, molds us, and gives us the content of our character. I imagine that James has a fascinating story."

"Well, I'm part of that story." Maryum sat up, leaning forward to make space between herself and Jasmine. She desperately needed some distance. "James is.... my father. Or to be exact, he was my mother's lover for awhile. I was conceived because of their....affair. I didn't learn the truth about it until last week."

"Some things are best learned late, if they must be learned at all." Jasmine was refined between sips, seeming to savor the words she shared with Maryum as much as the tea. "Learning this when you were younger might have lead to more pain, caused more sorrow for everyone concerned."

Maryum returned the tea cup to the table, just as she remembered the sight of Jasmine and Dennis dancing together under the pagan moonlight, getting more than a good urge to throw the cup of tea into Jasmine's face.

'Get a grip!' Maryum quickly crossed her arms and chose to ask stupid questions, rather than grabbing her cup and fulfilling her last horrid thought. God knows, she couldn't think of anything more rational to do.

"Jasmine, I'm not sure I should even be talking about any of this to you. I don't know who you are, or any thing about you. According to James, you've been asleep for twenty five years. I mean, I've heard of catnaps, but this is..."

"Ridiculous? Hard to believe? Yes it is, but James knows the truth. He watched over me every day, and played me wonderful music with his saxophone. Opened the door to his sleeping mind and bid me welcome. As did Dennis."

"Wait..... a minute." Maryum felt a chill when Jasmine spoke his name. "How do you know about him? Who said anything about Dennis?"

"I know that he is special to you. This morning, your father told me how the pain of having abandoned you and your mother caught up to him after he learned about the woman in Virginia who died bearing his other daughter. He told me all about his drinking and doing drugs, but he needn't have. I already knew. He couldn't deny these things when he slept. Neither could you. Or Dennis." Jasmine remained calm, though Maryum didn't.

"Lady, who the hell do you think you think you are?! You get an ounce of my life story from ...from James, and then you make up this elaborate lullaby to try convincing me that you're some kind of dream weaver, or something. You got real stones, Jasmine."

Maryum quickly rose from her seat and walked aggressively to the other side of the small room. She'd wanted to walk out, lift her jacket from off the spoke in the wall and bolt out of the door. She stopped at the window and momentarily thought of jumping through it, rather than spending another second in the room with this madwoman. Anything, she thought, would be preferable to hearing Jasmine prattle on about things she couldn't possibly know. Things that she'd not even said to James.

"Oh.....shit." she whispered tearfully while pressing her face to the window pane. A tear rose to mingle with the residue between Maryum and the glass plate. Raising tentative fingers besides her face, Maryum's clenched fingers scraped the glass, and she drew a small screech, disturbing the silence of the room before she sobbed weakly. "How...did you know about Dennis? How could you....possibly...know?"

"You told me. You built a wall to hide him from everyone but yourself."

"I did no such thing!" Maryum turned around to face Jasmine again. The room light was fading fast, and a lone candle, white wax with wick inside a mason jar, gave an ethereal glow to the older woman as she sat on the couch behind the coffee table. "I tried to help Dennis when he was being abused and neglected. I helped him get into the Starbright program. How do you fix your lips to say I hid him?!"

"You did, Maryum. You were too afraid for anyone to share your world with Dennis. You worried that another would try to hurt him. I won't speak for anyone else, but I meant Dennis, nor you any harm."

"Jasmine...., none of this makes an ounce of sense. You hid from all the turmoil and madness of the world instead of fighting it. How do you presume to tell me what I've done wrong?"

"I don't." Jasmine remained non confrontational. "I only know that you feel guilty for having left Dennis behind. You had no choice, Maryum, Neither did Dennis. And you're mistaken for thinking that I've hidden from the evil of this world. I know it far more than you might imagine."

Nine hundred miles of highway were behind her, and one hundred and thirty five remained. It was daylight, but night was soon to fall darker and deeper than a Georgia midnight like the one she hauntingly remembered, the night they took Dorian's beautiful body and battered it bloody before hanging him from a tree.

"I'm coming, Dorian." she whispered, her voice the only sound inside the vehicle, the sound of four wheels against highway the predominant noise without. Four wheels, white car, Georgia

license plate. She wondered why some state trooper hadn't stopped her yet. Perhaps Dorian's spirit hovered above the two lane black top, guided her fugitive journey along the southern back roads that led to where she was headed. Ragged white Ford, weary from the roar of high speed and merciless maneuvering en route to Baltimore so that Jasmine could see where they'd buried her beloved Dorian.

A knock in the engine, the dimming of lights, the transfer of the gas tank needle from 'F' to 'E', and she knew that the time was nearing it's close. With but a final stolen dollar and the last letter from home in her cotton robe, Jasmine drove on, until the lights of the city grew closer to her waiting eyes. She drove on, until the little white Ford finally graced the entrance of Woodlawn Cemetery, leaving her to walk the remainder of the way, at a pace she'd never done before, on a cold February night in Northern Maryland.

She walked and walked, and walked, and walked, until the cotton slippers she'd worn gave away to leave her barefoot and bleeding as she knelt before his grave sight.

"And James just took you in when you passed by the diner that night?" Maryum questioned as she sat on the couch, staring at her cold cup of tea.

"Yes, he did." Jasmine was now standing in front of the window, looking outside to the street. "I've yet to ask, but I suspect that James may be trying to make up for some past transgression. Much of the music I've heard him play has sounded so... sad. He's suffered a lot of grief, but he didn't let it bury his compassion. He was there when I needed him. If not me, James would have found another in need."

Somewhere between sorrow, pity, and outright bewilderment, Maryum fumbled through her thoughts for a question, a word, anything, to rationalize this odd moment in time, as Jasmine turned around and walked back towards her. Their eyes met again as if for the first time, when Maryum found her curious, almost reluctant voice.

"And what did Dennis tell you...about me?"

"Nothing you can't learn by asking him yourself." Jasmine spoke while sitting back down beside Maryum. "He waits, Maryum. He would love nothing more than to hear your voice, or receive some word from you."

"I....can't." Maryum exhaled, wearily covering her face with her hands. "His aunt has instructed the staff of Starbright to notify her if I send Dennis a letter, or note by email."

"But there is a way to find him again. He wouldn't have told me this if there were not. He needs you, Maryum. He waits for you to find your way there."

"Jasmine, I'm not like you." she leaned back into the brown cushion of the couch, as her arms fell listlessly to her thighs. "I don't know how to walk into people's dreams, or talk to them while they're sleeping. I wish you'd tell me how, so I can dream to Dennis."

"I never figured it out, Maryum." Jasmine laughed gently while touching Maryum on the shoulder. "When I went to sleep that night in 1969, I was a nineteen year old girl who'd seen the man she loved get murdered in the most hideous way. When my eyes opened several mornings ago, I didn't expect to find that I'd grown older, or even to remember the flowing images that I'd thought were but a long night's dream.

"Every name, every face, everything that I saw during my long night has returned to me, and there are so many places I must go. Dennis' whispering to me about you is something I'll never forget. Find him, Maryum. Dream."

'Dream', Jasmine whispered, reminding Maryum of the signature on the post card that James had sent her dad so very long ago. With all her heart, Maryum wanted to believe that she could find Dennis again, but it would take more than a five letter ambiguity, and a middle aged 'Dreamer' to convince her that she could make her way back to the one she was so woefully forced to leave behind.

18

From his hotel suite overlooking the inlet of the Chesapeake Bay, Saul waited for the automatic operator on the other end of the phone line to finally kick off and give him a real, live person. He mildly cursed under his breath while listening to the elevator music that serenaded him in the interim between man and machine.

Fresh from an early evening shower, Saul ran his fingers through his still wet hair and scalp. Decked out in a brown cotton bathrobe and anticipating another sleepless night, he nevertheless yawned while reading the brochure he'd picked up in the hotel lobby earlier that evening.

'Erlichman's Catering' it read, featuring a variety of culinary delights and delicacies that could be had for a pretty penny. A penny seemed pretty much all that James could spare two afternoons ago when he and Saul had shared lunch with Maryum at Crazy John's pizzeria. Saul had picked up the check for this outing, later asking James, "What do you do for lunch if I'm not around, or it's been a real slow day with the masses?"

"Whatever I can scrape up with the change I got, or go looking for roots and other plants I find along the way. You can eat real good if you know what to look for." James had responded, leaving Saul to wonder if James didn't care about a more balanced diet, or if it just hadn't occurred to him over the years. In any event, he had a real treat for James and....

'What was her name, again?'

Saul regretted having not gone to East Baltimore two days prior, following his lunch with James and Maryum, but having barely survived the murder scene and it's attendant chaos, he thought it better to return to the hotel, where he'd remained for the rest of the afternoon, and also the following day, taking advantage of the hotel's restaurant, spa, and gym, as well as subjecting himself to the lamentations left on his answering machine in New York City. Most annoying was the memory of Leonard's frantic call the day before.

"Saul, talk to me, brother! You got us hanging here at ARP, and I hope you're not dead or something, okay?!"

Saul conveniently dismissed all thoughts of Leonard, before catching sight of Chesapeake Bay from his hotel room window. He remembered sixteen years ago when he'd caught a ferry out to the middle of the bay with a sight seeing tour, and he'd barely resisted the temptation to shuck his clothing and swim back to the shore. Goldie would have loved that, and it would have been nice to see her waiting on shore, applauding his effort.

Lo these many years later, Saul could still see Goldie smiling at him, the thought beautiful, but jarring, in that he knew it would remain a wishful memory. That was when the phone line clicked on.

"Erlichman's Catering. This is Julie. How may I help you?" a perky female voice came over the line, replacing the monotonous elevator music in time to save Saul's sanity.

"Good evening. My name is Saul Ravensword, and I'd like to order a fruit basket and bagel special sent to this address in east Baltimore tomorrow morning."

After relaying the pertinent information and giving the operator his credit card number, Saul hung up the phone before yawning again.

"Jesus, this is getting to be a habit." Saul muttered, deciding to later take a trip to the address James had given him the previous day, and perhaps meet Jasmine, who's name he suddenly remembered, and who'd become the object of his curiosity with Maryum's angry mention of her.

"Right." he yawned again, before surrendering his body to the king sized bed and laying his arms across his chest. "How....can you be curious about a woman you've never even met? Do I even....believe... that story...James... told...me?"

And soon, it was dark.

Saul's last memory of the evening was cutting off the radio near his bed when he'd heard that high voiced squealer from the musical group Affectation burst into song.

'Close your eyes, so you can ride my night dream to the morning star. / Close your eyes, tonight I know I'll love you, no matter where you are....'

"I don't think so." Saul muttered while shutting off the radio and setting the alarm for eleven AM. He questioned what in God's name had possessed Marceleen to make Affectation her one exception to her favored classics, even as he remembered the night in March of seventy nine when she'd played him the group's most recent album while they were studying together. She'd gone to a concert of classical music in New York City with her cousin earlier that year, and Affectation had opened for classical harpist who would play later. Goldie had truly enjoyed the group's sublime mixture of folk, rock, and classical music, augmented by a rhythm section featuring both a classical nylon string guitar and six string steel acoustic, piano and synthesizer, as well as conga drums and flute.

"These guys are going to make it big!" she declared, leaving Saul agonizingly certain that his friend just had to be wrong about this one.

'Close your eyes, so you can ride my night dream...'

He closed his eyes, it was dark inside. Or maybe it was outside? There wasn't a hint, or a clue as to his whereabouts, just a deep, dark landscape surrounding him.

"Hello?! Anybody home?" dumb question, he thought while turning his head around to survey the alien landscape. It was darker than dark. Saul had no idea what he was doing there, just as he heard the music again.

'Close your eyes...'

Saul opened them instead, finding himself on the green of Boston University's Charles River campus again. It was spring, the grass was green, and the flowers blossomed before his bedazzled eyes. She was walking away from him again.

"Goldie?"

She was Tall and beautiful, as he'd remembered her. Her flaxen tresses fell well below her shoulders. Tee shirt, loose black vest, cut off shorts betraying long, lovely legs that carried her away from him.

"Goldie, come back!" Saul ran, his bathrobe not fully covering him as he bolted full speed across the green. He didn't care. He would run naked through hell, high water, and worse, to stop her from getting into the red convertible he saw driving through the main roadway intersection approaching the campus green.

"Goldie, stop! Don't go!!"

She didn't, or couldn't hear him. Her slow gait carried her closer to the car. Run though he did until his heart nearly burst, Saul knew he would not stop until he kept her from entering that car. He knew he'd do anything, even grasp the car keys and throw them into the nearby river, rather then let them drive on.

"Marceleen?! Goldberg?!!" his impassioned cry echoed louder even than the two sounds that shattered the air as Saul reached Marceleen and placed his hands on her shoulders. He also saw the face of the convertible's driver, her ebony skin almost flawlessly translucent, and knew her not to be Gina. But he thought nothing of the driver's identity upon hearing the two loud bangs again, this time fiercer than the first.

What, he wearily wondered, had that noise been. Perhaps thunder, lightning, the blowout of someone's exhaust pipe, or perhaps the death chant of two tires giving their last life's blood of air when the pressure finally burst through. He wouldn't know until he turned Marceleen around.

"Goldie?!" he whispered in shock, his exhaustion turning to sheer terror at the sight of her once beautiful face, now gone. Two blue eyes that he'd grown to love looking in, were now red craters set on the sides of her nose. Where blue eyes full of love had previously looked on him, hideous punctures now resided. And proceeding from those holes was a flow of blood, like the tears which Saul had long denied to the detriment of his very soul. "No, no,......no."

He closed his eyes and looked no more. He cried instead. He cried, not knowing where the dream ended and the morning began. Eleven AM found him awake and unable to stop crying. He only paused when the radio alarm clock intruded on the scene with the sobering sound of someone singing something incredibly close to what was happening.

'I cried when I woke up./ Seeing you not there./ And I wondered was it worth it to reach out and try to touch you, and maybe end my despair....'

Saul sat up and pressed the spare pillow to his face, astonished by the tears rolling from behind the dam of his long denied eyes, as well as the irritation in the tear ducts.

'Sleep? In my eyes?!'

Rubbing his eyes, Saul dislodged the wet, crusty offenders that he'd become used to not feeling. Glancing over to the clock radio on the bed stand next to him, his disbelief grew deeper as the singer continued.

'....and I froze when my fingers could only grasp the air. Knowing now I need your face to answer my pained prayer. My prayer.'

"Quit praying, dude." Saul quickly hit the off button, the hour of eleven AM fairly shouting at him. He'd expected to have lain quietly awake in bed and greeted this late morning hour totally conscious, rather than stumbling out of slumber. The last lucid thoughts he recalled were of his current disdain for Leonard, James' ruminations on not starving to death, Goldie's fascination with what he thought was the lamest musical group in the western world, and the alarm clock registering eight PM following his call to the caterers. Despite being able to remember every moment of the last fifteen years he'd spent awake, Saul could recall nothing of the last fifteen hours, save the sudden vision of Marceleen's death face that culminated his nocturnal vision.

"Woah." he muttered while wiping away the last traces of tears. He'd dreamed. It came and went with frightening commission, though he'd not expected to see Marceleen in his dreams, or even to sleep again, for that matter. Nor could he deny feeling refreshed, relieved of muscle aches, joint pain, numbness, and overload of mind that had vanished far quicker than the years they'd taken to accumulate. Rising out of bed and looking through the window to see the gray Baltimore morning, Saul finally accepted that he'd aged sixteen years since that last day with Marceleen on the green at Boston University. Marceleen Goldberg had been dead all this time, and he'd never truly mourned her loss, or even had a good nights sleep since then.

These things he remembered before the tears returned, and he raised his hands to catch them, like the rain falling outside.

19

They'd sat for nearly an hour on a hill overlooking Woodrow Cemetery, Jasmine and James, watching the sun begin it's progression from late afternoon to early evening, all the while experiencing the glories, joys, and finally, the sorrows of this day. James was halfway through another song on his saxophone, when he noticed Jasmine's eyes wet with tears. It was only the second time he'd seen her cry, though he imagined her sorrow to be far deeper than he'd previously witnessed.

"Jasmine, are you ready to go back home?"

She was silent for a long moment, staring at the tombstones in the flat land beneath the hill they sat on, before sobbing again.

"Home? Where do I really call home, James? Just where do I belong?"

He touched her on the shoulder and she grasped his hand in appreciation, though neither of them knew where this was going. Like the desire to re-live some of his own ignoble past, James almost wished that he and Jasmine could return to the joyous breakfast they'd shared together earlier in the A.M. The morning had been light, full of fun, and definitely not a prelude to the day's more somber ending.

"Your daughter seems a nice girl. Somewhat angry given all that's happened to her, but she seems more sad than angry." Jasmine spread cream cheese on her third bagel as she looked up at James. "She also looks like you."

"I really think she's much better looking." James glanced out the window, beholding the morning sun that flooded their humble kitchen with light. Jasmine noticed his dark facial features illuminated in the golden sunlight, fully appreciating this dreadlocked, bearded savior of hers.

"You're too modest, James. Not only are you good looking, but you've got a beautiful heart to match." she spoke almost triumphantly. Being awake and alive again felt more wonderful than she'd imagined, though it surprised her that her slumber had lasted so long. It felt like only an overnight. A look at her caretaker proved that it had been a long quarter century.

"Jasmine, before the morning I met you, I'd been a drug dealer, and occasionally, a criminal enforcer." he turned to face her somberly. "I'd used drugs, cheated, lied, and done everything in my power to get over, regardless of who I hurt. And I haven't told you the whole horror story about my 'Fatherhood'. I've never even seen my other daughter. Not that I'd deserve to, given that her mom died giving birth nine months after my night to howl. It wasn't until I ran into you that I actually ever tried to help somebody. That's my 'Beautiful' heart."

"And it's only grown more so as time has passed." she smiled, even while sensing his unease at her not beings asleep anymore.

"I don't know." James admitted. "Sometimes, I wonder if I've just been wasting time, making up for my past bad by watching after you. I can't change the fact that I caused a lot of pain before that."

"No, James, you can't change the past, but you can learn from it. You learned responsibility and caring. You helped me out when it would have been so easy to just turn me over to another. You wouldn't do that. Thank you for being there for me."

"You're welcome." he smiled, reaching over to the stove and grabbing the mahogany tea pot. "I only hope that you won't be the last person I help."

"I won't be." she affirmed. "Your daughter needs you as well, even though she doesn't know it yet. She wants to do right for someone she loves very much, and she'll need your counsel."

"Oh, please." he stumbled, almost spitting out the tea he'd just made for himself. "She doesn't need to follow after me. I messed over her momma in the worst way. I'm probably eighty five percent of the reason she's so pissed off. If anything, I'd tell her not to leave town just cause' the cake starts to rise."

Jasmine laughed as the morning sun painted her soft brunette hair with a sepia tone, making her look beauteously out of place in the common, bland kitchen she and James sat in. James also noticed that her hair seemed less gray than he remembered in time past, though he hadn't purchased any hair coloring with the one thousand dollars that Saul had dropped in his saxophone case two mornings ago. Saul would unexpectedly become the next subject of Jasmine's curiosity.

"Not only do you have a good sense of humor, James, but your friends have good taste in catered food. Tell me again who ordered this breakfast?"

"His name is Saul Ravensword. He's a writer from New York. He seems an okay dude, but he's a little strange." James uttered, almost wanting to take those words back after questioning if he really had the right to call anyone strange. "I met him two days ago, when he sat on the street corner listening to me play over by Camden Yards. The night before, he'd sat at Edgar Allan Poe's grave. He also bought Maryum and me lunch day before yesterday. It.... wasn't a pleasant experience."

"Oh?" Jasmine inquired while biting into a fresh strawberry.

"Maryum and Saul got into it. She kind of talked about you bad, and I'm surprised that you two got along so well after what she said at lunch."

"I like Maryum. I'd also like to meet this Mr. Ravensword. He sounds interesting."

"He's kind of scary." James admitted while sipping his tea and looking at the clock on the kitchen wall. It was almost eleven A.M. "Saul kind of....had a breakdown the other day when he saw Street's murder scene, and caught a taxi back to his hotel. He told me that he was going to try and come by here yesterday, but he obviously didn't make it. I'm glad he sent breakfast this morning, but I'm surprised he hasn't gotten here yet. Maybe I should go down to the corner store and give him a ring."

"No, James. He'll be here in time. Besides, I remember someone hanging out at a graveyard. Only this one was in broad daylight and involved a Dove. Wasn't Poe's bird a Raven?"

The morning passed, and became mid afternoon in time for James to escort Jasmine all around the town. He wasn't certain if she had the stamina to do so, but her firm post breakfast grasp of his hands along with her determined words-"I've slept long enough. I want to rediscover the world."-was enough to convince him to take her out there. He'd dipped into his emergency cash three days ago, prior to Saul's gift, and had purchased her a gray long dress- which she'd worn every day since- a blue knee length dress, and some black flat shoes, from a thrift store. The blue dress sported yellow sunflowers within a stripped pattern that matched the sunny mood of the woman wearing it.

Catching a bus in East Baltimore, they took a trip downtown. Their first stop was at a newspaper stand near the red light district, where Jasmine convinced James to purchase fifty dollars worth of magazines- 'Essence', 'Time', 'Newsweek', 'Ebony', 'Cosmopolitan', 'Money', among them-all of which, amazingly, she read within fifty minutes.

"I've always been a fast reader. I'm itching to get back in a library."

James was flabbergasted, though Jasmine reassured him that she was totally human. That became obvious during the bus ride, as a young family of oriental descent sat across the bus isle from James and Jasmine, prompting her to look up from her magazines.

"Beautiful child." Jasmine warmly asserted, observing the couple and their young toddler. The couple-he short, slight, with shocking black hair, and opal dark eyes; she slightly taller, and somewhat heavier with her thick black hair pulled straight behind her and collected in a blue barrette, conversed in Cantonese and broken English. The father held the little girl, dressed in a purple plaid outfit, and smiled appreciatively as the child cooed, gurgled, and slobbered all over his dress blue shirt and gray tie. Jasmine adored the sight. "There's always a second chance, so long as a new life enters the world."

Not long thereafter, the young family left the bus, and Jasmine read an article in one of the news magazines, gluing her eyes to the urgent caption above a picture of a thriving agricultural community.

'Civil Rights Era Farm Project Commemorates Quarter Century Amid Controversy and Conservative Opposition.'

"Smyrna County." she mumbled.

"Excuse me?" James could discern her sudden disturbance, or perhaps anger, and wondered at it.

"I remember Smyrna County, Georgia. I recall hateful folks saying things that sounded like what this congressman said on the floor of the house of representatives." her downcast eyes angrily expressed her contempt for 'The Distinguished Gentleman' from Georgia. "Back then, people opposing the federal government's forcing them to change their ways, wore hoods and burned crosses. The more things change, the harder some folks fight to hold on to their hatred."

She read the rest of the article pertaining to a bill in congress aimed at preserving a farm community in Southeast Georgia, and the vigorous opposition raised by several conservative southern congressmen. She remembered fighting this same battle as a young woman, and was pained that the war hadn't been won as yet. James had been amazed at her optimism, though mindful that she was looking at the world through eyes tinted by the last year she'd been awake. Today was a long way from February 1969, and he could tell she was not enjoying this knowledge.

The day finally ended with the twosome making their way to Woodrow Cemetery, a few miles northwest of the downtown area. They'd found a tree on a hill adjacent to the cemetery. James wore an orange and green pullover cap on top of his dreadlocks, but he'd removed it before placing the saxophone to his lips and playing a tune he'd played her frequently during the years she'd slumbered. Today, as she looked out over the grave stones and monuments in the distance, the sorrow overtook her. Her weeping began gently, but became fervent enough to more than concern him.

"Jasmine?" he stopped playing.

"It's alright.....James." she mumbled, her eyes still closed. "Please play."

He willingly obliged, filling the surrounding countryside with the slow, melodious sound of his saxophone, even as she covered her eyes. She couldn't control her tears and sobs, and not until James had halted his music for a good number of minutes, did Jasmine dry her eyes and hauntingly speak again.

"Dorian is buried out there, somewhere. On the night.... you found me, I'd found his headstone. I left the car I stole in Georgia at the front gate before walking all over the cemetery to find his grave site. But now, I can't remember where it is. Dorian is....lost."

"Do you remember him?"

"Of course. I would never forget him. How could I?"

"Then he's not lost." James solemnized, placing his saxophone on his lap before touching her on the shoulder. "So long as he stays in your heart and thoughts, he's not lost. Everybody I'd been involved with has stayed in the back of my mind these last twenty five years. Maybe I hadn't seen them, or dealt with them, but I remembered every ounce of pain I inflicted on the folks. And I suffered for it.

"It took your words for me to finally put the demons to rest. You're the first person in life to ever call me 'Beautiful'. You helped me to see that the whole point of living is learning how to deal with the things that happen to us, or to learn how to right the wrongs we've done. I guess I was coming to that conclusion all along, but you helped me get there. Big time."

"Thank you, James." the wind blew softly in response to her gratitude. "You're more beautiful than you even know. And you're so right. Even though I encouraged Maryum to seek after Dennis, I remained locked behind my past sorrow. We're here in this cemetery because I thought to be near Dorian. But my not remembering where he's buried was perhaps the way it should be. No matter how much I may remember him, or want to honor his memory, he is dead. Long gone. But I am not. Neither are you. It is time I began...living again."

Then she rose, looked forlornly at the tombstones, one of which belonged to Dorian, before realizing that this was the last time she would come here.

"We should go." she whispered to James before starting to walk away. He'd wanted to stay at the hillside a bit longer, but he'd been at her side too long to let her go without him. And as they made their way back towards the public highway, where they'd catch the bus, James vaguely wondered where Maryum was.

20

"Dennis misses you. He waits to hear from you."

Jasmine's voice still echoed in Maryum's mind as she drove her rental car to the campus of The University of Maryland, Baltimore. Quentin had given her the spare key to his office in the psychology building, as well as the password to his computer. The only thing lacking on her part, was nerve to follow through on what Jasmine had spoken the previous day.

"Dennis misses you. He waits to hear from you."

'How?', Maryum questioned. How would she find Dennis again, without Cornelia learning about it. She wondered how she'd explain her absence to Dennis, or what she might possibly say to atone for the trauma of her sudden departure. These, and other questions, plagued her as she entered the building and encountered the security guard at the entrance lobby. After checking his log and seeing that Professor Braxley had given her access, the thin young man with a buzz cut on his blond head and a stiff gray uniform on his body, permitted her to pass his desk, though not before looking in her purse and her backpack. Maryum walked to Quentin's office, having little idea what she'd say once she patched on to the Internet via the Pentium II computer in the opposite corner of the room from Quentin's desk.

Maryum took a deep breath before sitting at the oversized mahogany desk the computer sat atop, seemingly a world away from the desk where she'd sat with Quentin and wept several days ago, rather than just on the other side of the room. Quentin had taken the weekend off, gone to visit his 'Soulmate', who had a bungalow on Maryland's eastern shore. Remembering Quentin as most ambiguous and secretive about his sexuality and love life, Maryum wondered whether his significant other was male, female, or some other exotic twist on the human family tree. Whoever, whatever, Maryum could tell it was going to be good given the lascivious smile Quentin wore when he'd informed her of his plans. She quickly forgot those concerns after patching onto the internet server's home page, and typing the institute's address, 'WWW.SBINST.HUMPOT.NET ,on the computer's keyboard.

"Got you!" she exclaimed when the screen filled with an image of a bright white star across a blue field, which dissolved into the word 'Starbright'. The screen vanished into a show of bright light before reappearing with a directory of extensions, numbers, services and questions. Scanning the screen carefully, Maryum saw the numerous directories for staff, instructors, and management, but grew disappointed at what she didn't see. "What?! No way to contact clients?"

She scanned further, seeing nothing to indicate that the patients and clients of the institute could be contacted through the web site.

"Damn." she muttered before striking the escape key, immediately taking herself away from Starbright's web page. She looked at the screen again while wondering what on earth she was doing. It would have been a quick trip out the door and on her way back to Philadelphia had she not noticed the small circle on the side of the computer screen. The earth globe bearing the red arrow atop the word 'GROUPWISE' was familiar to her; she remembered Tracey using this computer email system to keep in touch with Jeff whenever his duties took him overseas. She lit a cigarette while inwardly musing 'No guts, no glory', as she clicked her mouse on the 'GROUPWISE' icon, before opening an envelope through the 'New Mail' function, then typing

'DREAM@SBINST.HUMPOT.NET' , in the 'To' bracket of the envelope, then typing 'Dennis McClain?' in the 'Subject' bracket. Then she prayed, she whispered, she hoped, before clicking on the 'Send' icon. She left the 'From' bracket blank, in fear possibly of some court official appointed by Cornelia McClain's lawyer, coming in to bodily haul her away in handcuffs. When that didn't happen, she continued to puff her cigarette while awaiting a response. Two minutes after sending her initial message, an envelope appeared on screen, and she immediately opened it. The envelope read, *'DREAM@SBINST.HUMPOT.NET'* and bore the words, 'Re: Dennis McClain?'. Upon opening it, Maryum got her answer.

'Yes. Maryum?'

She wanted to say yes so badly. She desired to scream out who she was, even as she remained unsure about revealing herself. Then she threw caution to the wind before finding time to be rational again.

'Hello, Dennis. I promised myself that I'd find you again. I am concerned that Cornelia might learn of this and I was afraid to take the chance.'

'You shouldn't worry, my friend. Cornelia is too concerned about my uncle's health to worry about whom I speak with on the Internet. Besides, I saw to it that my hard drive had special entry codes, so she has no chance of entering in and learning of whom I talk to. Over the last week or so, the institute had become very interested in training me to do computer work for them, considering what I've shown them so far. If you ever call while Cornelia's in the room, I'll either send you elsewhere, or re-code your signature so that your name doesn't come up.'

'Clever. I like.' she regretted that he couldn't see her laughter across the computer screen. 'How is Uncle Darris?'

'Uncle Darris....'a hint of sadness permeated the brief pause. 'was not well before the morning we were discovered. I fear he's not much longer for this world.'

'Dennis, I am so sorry.' she took another drag on her cigarette, knocking the ashes into the nearby glass ashtray. 'So much of what happened is my fault, and I was afraid that maybe you hated me for leaving you like I did.'

'No, Maryum. I don't hate you. How could I? Your love and friendship was the most wonderful thing to ever happen to me in this life. My aunt and uncle simply didn't,- or couldn't- understand what was between us. You could not help the reaction that tore us apart. You don't need to smoke, either.'

'Dennis, how do you know I'm smoking?' Maryum stopped in mid puff, pulling the half smoked cigarette from her lips in disbelief. 'Did you switch on your screen, or something?'

'No, I didn't. Cigarette smoke affects the electrons relaying your message, causing the letters to appear smaller, or distorted, on my screen, and thus more difficult to read. I can always tell who's smoking when we talk on the net, and it saddens me to know that they choose to dig an early grave. I'd like to see you live a long, wonderful life. Smoking would only shorten it, and I love you too much to see you die early.'

Maryum quickly crushed out her cigarette, stunned at his ability to detect something like this on his computer, but also curious as to what else Dennis was harboring in that intellect few people realized he possessed.

'Dennis, I love you too. I wish to God I had said it to you before...'a tear got in the way. Maryum wiped her eyes before continuing further. 'I had to go. I didn't want to leave you. I would never leave you alone.'

'I know, Maryum. I knew it the morning Cornelia discovered us. I could not tell her then how much you meant to me. She and Uncle Darris still haven't accepted my word on it, either. Of course, it may all be moot, should he die.'

'If he does,' she cautioned. '...then you need to know that you have certain rights that Cornelia can't take away. You're an adult. No one has the right to treat you like a child again.'

'I know this.' he asserted, before reassuring her. 'I thank you for standing up for me like you did. For helping me find this program. For....touching me, as you did.'

She couldn't see his face, though she imagined his brown eyes were just as bright and wide and beautiful as she'd remembered them being. 'I love you.' he said, '...too much,' he'd added, though Maryum knew he'd spoken of cigarettes and death. She wondered if maybe she hadn't loved him too much. Hadn't abandoned her common sense in submitting to the affection she'd felt.

'No!' she reminded herself, snapping out of the mournful reverie. Now wasn't the time to indulge in self indulgent introspection.

'What now, Dennis? I don't know what to do next.' she confessed. 'I miss you fiercely. I dream about you almost every night. I go through every day of my life silently praying that I'll find my way back to you.'

'You have, Maryum.'

'No, Dennis. I want to hold you close to me again. I want to hear your breathing. Feel your heartbeat when I lay my hand on your chest. I want to see you smile again.'

'And I you.' he responded. 'But I don't know when and how we shall touch again. Even Starbright will not violate Cornelia's wishes.'

"Damn her!!" Maryum blurted out angrily, as tears filled her suddenly closed eyes.

"Maryum?"

This time she heard a voice, sweetly soft and low, pleasant and engaging that emanated from the speaker box, which she hadn't cut on.

'Dennis?! How are you speaking to me? I hadn't even turned on my speakers.', She hadn't wanted his words reduced to electronic clap trap, so she'd intentionally not turned them on. She'd recalled his previous, unsuccessful attempts at speech, and was amazed at the sounds she'd just heard. 'How in the world did you hear what I'd said?'

"It would take a lot of time to explain. Computers are unique in what you can accomplish with them, and in time, I'll explain everything. But please, Maryum, do not fall into the same bitterness and sorrow that my aunt has succumbed to. It doesn't become you."

'Dennis, I don't know what to do.' she typed in, exhaling deeply and wondering if she wanted to just speak instead of type. She was also tempted to light up another cigarette, but she wouldn't ever do anything to cause him pain again. 'Every step I take leads me back to you. Starting my life over isn't so easy knowing how very much it hurts us both being apart. And worse...'

She trailed off, he eagerly inquired.

"Yes?"

'I'm...jealous.'

"Really?" Maryum eyed his response on screen, but marveled even more at the smooth, romantic voice coming from the speaker. "Let me guess. It's Jasmine."

'Yes. I saw her holding you in my dreams, and it was difficult seeing her do that when I wasn't able to do so myself. But it's more than just her.'

she felt juvenile expressing her jealously, even as she quickly revealed what else troubled her. 'I was also selfish in thinking that I was the only person who cared enough to help you when you needed it. I wasn't totally ready to surrender you to anyone else. Even though I've cursed your aunt every time I've thought of her in the last few weeks, I realize that in her own way, she's trying to do her best for you. Strangely enough, I'm grateful for that. I have to stop being afraid of sharing you with other people, Dennis.'

"And I will forever be grateful for all you've done for me, Maryum. The best any of us can do is to be true to those we love, and be the very best we can hope to be. You're a bit more forgiving about my aunt than am I, but I understand as well. In time, I'll see you again, so that we can speak of these things face to face. I look forward to that, Maryum."

Somewhere between Maryum's response and the arrival of late afternoon, a green rental car made it's way back to the eastside environs where awaited it's passenger for the drive to Pensauken, New Jersey. Maryum was behind the wheel, maneuvering the narrow streets in spite of the tears that rolled down her face. She couldn't stop crying yet, though most of the pain was gone. Dennis had been right; she couldn't submit herself to the bitterness that so marred the lives of Darris and Cornelia, and led them to so much sorrow and premature aging.

It was raining, wet, miserable, and cool enough for the frumpy denim jacket she wore, and the clouds overhead added more gloom to the afternoon, but Maryum was determined not to let the light inside of her go out and leave her sobbing in the darkness. She'd forgotten how long she'd stayed online with Dennis,-two hours, three; maybe more-but thought only of how much it meant to hear his voice. He loved her, this she knew, and it more than warmed her heart to hear him say it. The electronic voice that she'd dreaded for so long came through with more reassurance and hope than she'd dared dream possible.

By the time she finally approached James' neighborhood, the rainfall had faded into thin mist and drizzle. Drying her eyes while watching the sidewalk in front of the brownstone townhouse, Maryum saw James standing alone, Saxophone case in one hand, black flight bag she'd purchased him, in the other.

"James. What's going on?" she'd parked her car near the sidewalk where he stood, her eyes radiating quiet alarm as she exited the vehicle.

"Nothing's going on. I'm here. We ready to go?"

"What about Jasmine? I thought she was going with us."

"She's long gone. I took a quick nap after we got back from the cemetery and when I woke up, she was gone. She left me a note."

He held a small sheet of blue paper in front of him, his hands grasping the note as though he were afraid to drop it. Maryum gently took it from him to examine.

'Were I to say thank you a million times, it would scarcely be enough. James, you've truly been a friend. I owe you my life, and I don't know how to repay you except to free you to live again. Live with all the love and generosity that you've shown me. Whatever time we're both blessed with should be a wonderful adventure like we've shared in our time awake and asleep. I knew that I would one day arise and leave you, and my fear that I wouldn't find another so giving and special vanished with the presence of your daughter. Maryum is special, James. She carries a seed within her that may one day sprout and fill the surrounding world with more love than it's ever known before.

'I'm going back to Georgia. People I left behind long ago still wait there. I've a home in land that I was forced to forsake. Hearts still remain hard and closed to love, but I'm ready to face that again. So are you and Maryum.

'Be blessed, my friends. Dream.

'P.S. Oh. I borrowed three hundred bucks from the stash that Saul left you. Leave a change of address card so I can repay you.'

Maryum nearly laughed aloud about the money, even as her face showed the extent of her confusion. .

"Maryum?"

"I'm... alright." she exhaled. "I don't understand. Where is she going?"

"Well, she said something about Georgia, but she didn't say whether it was Atlanta or Macon." James moved towards the car's trunk as he wistfully reflected. 'My Daughter.', he thought, a pinprick of pride rising up inside despite the previous recriminations. Though he thought himself undeserving of such pride, James didn't deprive himself from feeling it. Denial and remorse could wait a day, he supposed. "She didn't tell me anything before she left. I didn't ask."

"I didn't get to say goodbye." she muttered while searching for the keys and opening the trunk for James. He laid his horn and the flight bag next to Maryum's own blue bag before looking back at her.

"No need for goodbyes. No such thing, I've learned. Somewhere, someplace in time, Jasmine and I will meet up again. So will you. Maybe she'll tap you on your shoulder while you're sleeping."

"Maybe." she uttered a wishful whisper. "Then again, I didn't think I'd ever hear Dennis speak to me, either."

"Dennis?" he puzzled.

"I'll tell you about him." she walked around to the driver's side and opened the car door. "We've got a hundred and twenty miles ahead of us, and lots of catching up to do."

He raised his eyebrows at her comment, eagerly entering the passenger side of the front seat. They drove off, leaving the brownstone empty for the first time in more than a quarter century. James looked back one last time, almost as though he expected to hear the sound of soft breathing from the upstairs bedroom window.

21

Saul saw her from a distance in the terminal of the Baltimore Greyhound bus station, wondering why she'd enter his world just as he prepared to leave the city he'd haunted for the last week.

The station, near a crowded street leading from the center of town, was a small rectangular building with a loading dock in the back that lead to a dead end alley. Such, Saul might have considered this trip, had not fifteen hours of slumber interrupted his vacation in addition to the other interesting sidelights that kept him interested and invigorated.

It had been an interesting seven days in Baltimore; seeking inspiration, scaring the hell out of dancing girls, sojourning at the grave of Edgar Allen Poe. He grinned, while recalling the facial expression of the old woman at the bus station's cashier's desk, when he'd exited from a limousine. He figured she'd maybe questioned why he'd settled for a Greyhound bus when he looked as though he could have afforded a Lear Jet.

Dressed in simple gray cotton slacks, and a light brown wool sweater, Saul hadn't intended to stand out amongst the less well dressed crowd. Surrounded by fellow passengers adorned in dingy blue jeans, consignment and second hand store reject, sneakers and other shoes worn beyond belief, Saul simply tried to ignore the undue attention he'd attracted.

"I probably should have walked." he mumbled, regretting among other things, having accepted the hotel's free limo service. A perk of wealth and power, but one he might just as well have done without today. He looked forward to finding the back seat of the bus and falling dead asleep, like he used to do during his college years. Sleeping again was wonderful, and he had a lot more slumber to catch up on.

He also considered James' account of how he met Jasmine-how frequently did one encounter half mad, barefooted women wandering in the freezing cold at two a.m. in the morning?- but lamented the likelihood that he'd learn nothing more about her.

An hour before his arrival at the bus station, Saul had directed the driver of the limo to the address in southeast Baltimore that James had given him. The journey had been fruitless, Saul finding nothing but an empty row house, a locked door, and no hint that anyone had ever lived there. The almost empty street gave no clue concerning the house's owners, but when Saul noticed an open trash can on a nearby curb with a large brown bag saying 'Ehrlichman's Catering' inside, he knew that he'd not fantasized at all. He knew that Maryum and James were real, so it stood to reason that Jasmine was real as well, for all the good that knowledge did him while he waited for the bus that would take him back to New York City.

He looked at his silver plated Timex watch, glumly seeing three fifteen p.m. before noticing the Greyhound that loaded eighty five yards away in dock seven. Miami, the glass plate above the bus windshield read, and Saul wondered if maybe that shouldn't be his destination for vacation next year. Then the station's intercom interrupted his train of thought.

"Your attention, please; Greyhound bus number Three Sixteen, to Miami and points south is now loading in dock number Seven. Destinations include, Bowie, Fort Washington, Washington D.C......."

Saul was barely listening, since he wasn't headed to Miami. New York, Leonard, and American Reader's Press, awaited him, but he remained baffled as to what he'd do next. He didn't have a new novel. He also anticipated difficulty with Leonard and the editors at ARP, since he remained totally unwilling to churn our further horror for mass consumption. Nor could he resist looking down towards dock number Seven in a vain attempt to draw a story out of the assorted humanity that boarded the bus for the trip down south. In particular, he couldn't take his eyes off of the tall woman with the sepia toned complexion and bright brown eyes.

"Who?" he asked while observing her, ordinarily decked out in a colorless gray dress and conversing with a darker woman, weighted down with a handbag and three hundred pound girth surrounded by a dark blue dress. Saul observed the two women as they talked and moved along in the line. Something about the younger woman fairly shouted to him. Her caramel skin, long black hair with mild highlights of gray, weren't particularly eye catching, but Saul couldn't pry his attention away from her.

"Okay. Maybe we were lovers in another life." he muttered. "Maybe I dreamed about her ..."

He stopped, recalling his recent dream of early spring, of a dearly beloved friend walking away from him into the face of forever, to find room in the back seat of a red convertible. "No. It can't be. It...can't."

He took a step in that direction, only to see the woman boarding the bus. Passengers had moved along, tickets were taken, the bus driver-a tall white man with hair whiter than he was-had taken the last ticket and was shutting the bus door before starting his engine. The bus then began backing out of the dock, and Saul continued his trek. He wanted a glimpse of her face.

"What ....am I doing?" he asked himself some feet short of his goal. He scanned the dark windows, seeking a moment's connection, hoping maybe she'd look in his direction and grant him a gram of inspiration, or at least let him see her face. But no, the bus was rapidly moving out of the terminal, far from his powers of observation, leaving him clueless and even more baffled.

'Why....couldn't I see her?' he thought while staring blankly at the space the Greyhound bus rapidly moved away from, even as he wondered why he couldn't have saved Marceleen, or even better, why he couldn't have spared himself the agony of the last decade and a half by simply accepting that he hadn't been able to rescue her from her fate. A perplexing thought, but in the moment he conceived it, he remembered that Marceleen was dead, and that all the questions, mysteries, and unfathomable queries he could concoct wouldn't bring her back. Saul Ravensword beheld the scene no more upon that realization. Someone who should never have left, returned to remind the man that New York City, and all the life he'd sought to escape, awaited his return.

But not before he took a detour through Reading, Pennsylvania.

EPILOGUE

I recently completed my first musical composition on saxophone, and sent a recorded copy to my friend, James Spencer, in Pensauken, New Jersey. James answered with a diplomatically encouraging letter. "Very good. Continue on." were his exact words, though I honestly expected him to trash my fledgling efforts. That he didn't only proves that there's room for growth and change in the sometimes evil world we live in.

The tune, which I entitled 'Goldie', was written for a deceased friend who'd inspired me to believe in hope and love, rather than hate and fear. The alternative to hope and love, I'd learn in a sad, horrible fashion, was death. No, I didn't suffer the heart stopping, flat line, brain dead, clinical type stuff. My own 'Death' was a conscious attempt at avoiding the emotions arising from Goldie's untimely demise. Rather than mourn, like I should have, I chose a fifteen year odyssey of anger, pain, and cynicism, which I emerged from only in the last year.

Seventeen years ago, Marceleen Goldberg and I were classmates at Boston University. She was the healthy, athletic, life loving, and impossibly optimistic offspring of semi rural Reading, Pennsylvania. She'd been nurtured by three generations of intact, loving family, and was studying to become a physical therapist, as well as preparing for the 1980 Olympic Swim team trials. I was a child of New York City's Greenwich Village, who's parents were separated, divorced, and bitter enemies by the time I was nine years old. My world had been one of dope, drink, self delusion, and hopeless cynicism about the world into which I'd been so woefully born.

In the fall of 1978, Marceleen and I encountered each other, and by the spring of the following year, we were determined to make a wonderful new world of our own. However, unkind fate deemed differently. Marceleen was murdered under horrible circumstances that I won't relate for this article, and my response to her death only compounded the tragedy, further hastening the living demise that she'd nearly helped me escape from.

Death and tragedy are intrinsic to our human existence, but many of us deal with them either through denial, or burying them with other stimuli. My own response was kind of a combination of the two. For fifteen years, I tried to blot out the sorrow of Marceleen's loss by churning out page after page of possibly the most graphically horrifying prose fiction ever written. I delighted millions of readers with every stroke of my pen, and became filthy rich doing so. Upon reading my first novel, my good friend Stephen King reportedly said, "Damn! This guy is sick!" Sadly, no one, save myself, could appreciate the truth of Steven's observation.

Despite having all the trappings of 'Success'-multimillion dollar bank accounts, houses on both east and west coasts, a luxurious apartment in Manhattan, among other things-I was miserable. My life was an endless parade of book deadlines, fawning fans, readings, signings, and other activities which only increased my loneliness. I was married for nearly four years, though I think it would have been better had my wife and I walked away from each other, rather than marched together down the aisle. Worst of all, I suffered chronic insomnia from the time I learned of Marceleen's murder, until my visit to Baltimore, Maryland a year ago. While there, I met a man who'd also suffered horrible tragedy, and sought escape from the pain in dope and drink. But long before I did, he found refuge in the power of love, and rescue from his self inflicted despair.

James Spencer is a musician. Probably the best saxophonist I ever remember hearing. Twenty six years ago, he and his musical group, Axis, had signed with a major record label, when he learned of the death of a woman he'd shared a one night stand with. The knowledge caused him to walk away from the fame and fortune that might have been his, and he expressed his thoughts in these words.

"My screwing around got a woman killed. You don't know how much that's going to hurt, unless you find yourself there. Learning about what happened to that lady in Virginia got me started digging my own grave. I felt like I had no business crying, since she died giving birth to my child, so I spent the next six months getting trashed to keep from feeling the pain.

"I just thank God that somebody else found me, who needed me a lot more than I needed to kill myself. Jasmine told me that I saved her, but more likely, she saved me from myself.

'Jasmine', whom James spoke so fondly of, remains a mystery to me, save what James related regarding her, and what I could glean from several newspaper clips concerning her own traumatic circumstances. James became the caretaker for this person after encountering her on a cold February morning in Baltimore that surely would have been her death had it not been for his compassion. Besides accepting someone else's hour of need, James found the courage to face the tragic reality of his own life, and to live with love, compassion, and reality as the basis of his day to day existence. Something I myself had not learned.

Sadly, the world does too often seem hollow, full of peril, trouble, and gross evil. And yet, there is always the bright light of love to let us know that all is not darkness and despair. That we need not abandon hope when faced with heartbreak we think beyond our ability to heal. I learned that lesson, as well as got my first decent nights sleep in fifteen years, during my sojourn in Maryland last year. In time, the truth will set us all free, but only if we are willing to face it, and accept it for what it is.

David Green, Editor in Chief
Horizon Magazine

Baltimore, MD

Maryum was impressed. Moving the long dread locks which now adorned her head from in front of her eyes, she marveled at this cryptic individual she'd met in Baltimore a year ago. She was surprised to find him the publisher and executive editor of Horizon Magazine, which if it continued in the vein established by the debut issue, would be a truly unique publication. She wasn't disappointed, though she also wasn't ready to be a 'Contributing Correspondent', as David had requested of her in a letter he'd sent her a few months ago.

"Well, I see why you changed your name back then." she mused humorously, reading the premier issue's editorial page while sitting near a beige wall in the Paley Library at Temple University in Philadelphia. Tapping her fingernails on the polished pine table she'd placed her text books on, Maryum wondered if her testing professor would be in a good mood today.

It was slightly after 2:00pm. Maryum's exam was in two hours, but she'd spent the last three days studying her textbook, and reviewing all of her previous tests from the semester. What she really looked forward to, was the concert at Mindful this evening. James would to be in top form, playing his most recent compositions on saxophone, harmonica, and piano, while being accompanied by Raymond on guitar, sitar, cello, and bass violin. She laughed out loud at the notion of Brianne joining them on congas, and drew the attention of several fellow students.

"Sorry. I was just thinking of my dad's wife beating on some conga drums." she explained, even as everyone quietly returned to whatever they'd been reading before her interruption of the library's peace and quiet. Maryum smiled, thinking that for fun she might go up to the meeting hall stage, give Brianne a big hug, plant a kiss on her forehead and say something exuberant like 'You did great, 'Ma'! Keep practicing.'

She even considered inviting Rosalie to the concert, wondering if her mother would ever admit to still loving James,- after all these years- and overcome her revulsion of Gerald and 'Those Heathens' in Mindful, to face her long term affection.

Maryum also pondered whether Cornelia McClain would ever understand the depth of love that Dennis and she shared, despite the physical separation made bleaker by the death of Darris McClain six month's prior, and Cornelia's overwhelming sorrow. Maryum winced while recalling her most recent communications with Dennis.

"She cries not, Maryum, nor weeps. Rather, my aunt digs a slow grave by consuming parts of what heart she has left, and choosing to bury the pain she pretends not to feel. She has ceased living, my friend. Inwardly, that is. Yes, her heart still beats, the lungs breath air, all appearances say to others that she 'Lives', yet she lacks but a stone atop a grim turn of earth to signify what is all too apparent to me."

Maryum wasn't surprised at Cornelia's circumstance, thinking of what David said in his editorial, as well as lamenting Dennis having to witness this sorrow and loss. She sighed, but smiled again as she thought of his final words from the previous morning, and the image he sent to her computer screen.

"If nothing else, Maryum, I can see your face when I close my eyes in slumber. There, no one can tell me not to love you."

The words, accompanied by the computer image of the star illuminated patio above she and Dennis as they danced together, soothed her in a way almost supernatural. She swooned, reaching out to touch the screen as she heard the music and saw the image. For there, as well as in her heart and mind, she danced. Holding Dennis close to her as they danced and whirled in the dreamscape, Maryum knew that regardless of how much physical distance separated the two of them, she'd never truly be far from him again in this life.